Toll for the Dead (Large Print)

An Oxford Murder Mystery

Bridget Hart Book 7

M S Morris

Acknowledgements

With heartfelt thanks to Nicola and John for showing us around their beautiful manor house. Huge thanks are also due to Josie Morris for her help in proofreading this book and the rest of the books in the Bridget Hart series.

CHAPTER 1

The pews of St Michael and All Angels were already filling up. It was going to be a good turnout for the funeral.

From her vantage point in the ringing chamber of the church tower, Amy Bagot peered through the interior latticed window into the nave below. It looked as if the whole village had come to pay their respects to Mr Henry Burton, the *old squire*, as he was fondly known to the residents of Hambledon-on Thames. The old man, who had been ill for some time, had died peacefully the previous week, at home in Hambledon Manor, having been cared for by his loyal housekeeper and, latterly, a nurse from a private agency. Amy knew all this because her parents, Robert and Sue Bagot, ran the Eight Bells pub in the village and were therefore privy to all the gossip and goings-on in this close-knit community.

A keen bellringer from a young age, Amy was delighted to have been asked to join the band of eight ringers to ring a quarter peal at the end of the service. It would be a fitting tribute to Henry Burton, who had contributed generously towards the restoration of the bells in the year 2000 as part of the village's millennium celebrations. The previous evening she had accompanied Bill Harris, the tower captain and the man who had taught her everything she knew about change ringing, into the bell chamber, two floors above where the ringers now waited, to fit leather muffles to each of the eight bell clappers. As a mark of respect, the bells would be rung half-muffled, creating an eerie echo effect that never failed to send shivers down Amy's spine.

She checked her watch. Ten to twelve. The funeral was due to start at midday, to be followed by a wake at the Eight Bells pub, the traditional venue for all village celebrations and memorials. Amy had persuaded her boyfriend, Jake Derwent, to take the day off work and meet her in the pub after the bellringing. Once they'd had something to eat, she thought they might go for a walk along the Thames Path.

She'd been dating the detective sergeant for precisely two months, three weeks and five days. She had met him through an online dating app, although her early attempts at finding love that way had not gone well, and she'd almost given up hope. But then Jake had popped up, and she'd taken an instant liking to the ginger-haired and bearded Yorkshireman. *He looks like a decent sort of guy*, she'd thought. And she hadn't been wrong. At six foot five inches tall, he definitely stood out in a crowd. He was funny and kind, and didn't think she was a nerd for being so passionate about bellringing. And she was fascinated by his work. She'd always loved reading murder mysteries, and here was her very own detective who solved crimes and caught real-life killers. She'd never been happier.

'Five minutes to go,' said Bill Harris in his soft Oxfordshire burr. Amy didn't know how old Bill was, but he must be seventy-five if he was a day. Tall and white-haired, with overgrown eyebrows, a lifetime of climbing belltowers and ringing the tenor bell had kept him lean and fit. Amy admired that sort of dedication in a person. She hoped she'd still be ringing bells when she was his age.

She peered again through the latticed window. Down below, Harriet Stevenson, the churchwarden, was handing out orders of service and directing the last stragglers to the few remaining spaces in the packed pews. Bossy and officious, Harriet was clearly in her element as organiser-in-chief. Amy tried to spot people she knew. Her dad, Robert, was sitting on the edge of a pew close to the north door so that he could slip out during the last hymn. Her mum had stayed behind at the pub to prepare the food for the wake, and her dad had promised to join her before the end of the funeral to help. But he wanted to pay his respects, as the old squire had owned the pub and had always been a fair and generous landlord, never stinting on repairs to the half-timbered building that dated back to the seventeenth century.

Harriet Stevenson was directing a small group of three women and a man to one of the reserved pews closer to the front. These were the people from the manor house, and heads turned to watch as they took their places. Lindsey Symonds, an imperious woman in a striking black hat, had been Henry Burton's estate manager. Amy only knew her by sight because Lindsey rarely came into the pub or got involved in village activities. Behind her was the diminutive figure of Josephine Daniels, the old squire's devoted housekeeper. Amy and Bill had run into Josephine the previous evening when she'd been in the church doing the flowers for the funeral. In her capacity as the church flower arranger, she had done her old employer proud, adorning the church with exquisite displays of white roses and irises, grown, as she had told them, in the gardens of the manor house. Her son, Shaun, who was the gardener at the house, came next. Amy had never seen him wearing a suit and tie before, and he tugged self-consciously at the collar of his shirt as he shuffled forward. Bringing up the rear of the party was a short, plump woman with a kindly face. Amy didn't recognise her, but wondered if she might be the nurse who'd cared for the old man in his dying days.

On the other side of the aisle, Amy recognised the blonde head of her old schoolfriend Kayleigh Simpson, now the local primary school teacher and fiancée of Jamie Reade, one of the eight bellringers. Their forthcoming wedding at the weekend would be another, more joyous, occasion for ringing the bells, and one that Amy was especially looking forward to. Maybe one day she and Jake would get married in this church and a quarter peal would be rung in celebration. She imagined herself in a simple, ivory gown, nothing too fancy, just...

'It's time,' said Bill, getting to his feet and taking hold of the sally of the tenor bell. Amy's attention switched immediately from thoughts of matrimony, back to the funeral. With a firm, practised stroke, Bill pulled down on the sally and, two floors above in the bell chamber, the heaviest and lowest pitched of the eight bells rang out its solemn toll.

The toll for the dead.

At the sound of the half-muffled bell, a few heads in the nave turned towards the north door in anticipation of the arrival of the coffin. The members of the church choir, seated in the stalls near the altar, rose to their feet in readiness. At a nod from the conductor, the organist began to play the opening bars of Mozart's *Ave Verum Corpus*. Then, following their instructions in the order of service, the congregation also stood. The funeral was about to begin.

As the single bell continued to toll and the choir sang, the coffin, adorned with a simple bouquet of white lilies, was borne into the church on the shoulders of six black-clad pall bearers supplied by the funeral directors in Oxford. The

5

Reverend Martin Armistead, a youngish man who had been appointed vicar of St Michael and All Angels twelve months earlier when the last incumbent had died after a record-breaking stint of thirty-seven years, led the small procession. Behind the coffin, the deceased's immediate family followed.

The old squire's son looked to be in his mid-forties or thereabouts, with a thick head of hair, greying only slightly at the temples. Amy supposed that this man, Tobias Burton, who held himself so ramrod straight, was the squire now. But if she knew anything about the villagers of Hambledon-on-Thames, it was his father who would always be known as *the squire*. The villagers were a loyal bunch, but their loyalty had to be earned.

Next to Tobias, her hand looped in the crook of her husband's elbow, walked his wife, slim and elegant in a black dress, fitted jacket and high heels. Their two children, a boy and a girl aged about twelve and ten, followed dutifully behind their parents. Amy's heart went out to them, having to walk behind their grandfather's coffin at such a young age. Couldn't they have sat with a relative or friend of the family? But maybe they didn't know anyone here. The family didn't actually live in the village. That in itself was a matter for gossip and speculation in the pub and village shop. Apparently the son was "something big in the City" although actual facts were rather thin on the ground. Some said he'd made a fortune in the property business. Others said it was the stock market, or overseas investments of dubious propriety. Whatever the case, the talk of the village was what he would do with the manor house now that his father had passed away. Amy hadn't paid that much attention to the gossip – she'd been far too distracted with Jake – but she understood that feelings were running high in some quarters. There was even talk of a schism in the village. Things could turn nasty.

The coffin was placed on a bier at the front of the nave, just below the pulpit, and the tenor bell came finally to a halt. The family took their places in the empty front pew. The vicar, always slightly nervous and ill-at-ease in Amy's opinion, spoke some words of welcome and the service began.

In his eulogy, the vicar spoke warmly of the dead man. It sounded as if the vicar and his wife had personally appreciated the welcome extended to them by the old squire. Particular mention was made of Henry Burton's generosity towards village life, how he'd contributed towards the upkeep of the church, how he wasn't above enjoying a pint in the pub, and how he had opened up the gardens of the manor house every year for the annual summer fête. Heads nodded in agreement and handkerchiefs dabbed at eyes as people remembered the old man. The village hadn't just lost its lord of the manor. It had lost a dear friend.

As the organ struck up the opening chords of

the final hymn – *And did those feet in ancient time, Walk upon England's mountains green* – the pall bearers hoisted the coffin onto their shoulders once again, and the eight ringers took their positions, facing each other in a circle, ready to ring the quarter peal. Amy now had her back to the latticed window, but even if she'd been facing it, she would have paid no attention to what was happening down below. The focus of the ringers was now entirely on each other. The quarter peal would last for around forty-five minutes, during which time Henry Burton would be laid to rest in the family plot in the churchyard. As the ringer of the treble bell, it was Amy's job to begin the round. Opposite her, on bell number five, Jamie Reade gave her a reassuring smile. She clutched the sally in both hands and, at a nod from Bill, said the words that heralded the start of the ringing.

'Look to, treble's going.' She pulled down firmly on the rope. 'Treble's gone.'

★

Harriet Stevenson walked diligently up and down the rows of pews, putting hymn books back in their place the right way round, straightening the kneelers and seat cushions, and gathering various items of lost property. Really, it was quite astonishing how careless people could be with their belongings. She'd already found a pair of reading glasses, a mobile phone, and two folded umbrellas whose owners had sensibly come prepared for the vagaries of an English summer. Small mercies that the rain had held off, since the missing lead from the church roof still hadn't been replaced and the roof had a tendency to leak on the third pew from the front, south side of the aisle. She would have to speak to the vicar – again – about getting it fixed. He'd been in the job for a year now and it was high time he dealt with the issues that she raised, repeatedly, at their monthly meetings.

Harriet took her job as churchwarden very seriously. She was pleased with how well the funeral had gone, thanks in no small part to her organisational skills. It was she who had arranged for the printing of the orders of service and spoken to Josephine Daniels about the appropriate choice of flowers. She had even selected all the music and the hymns. The squire's son had left these matters to the vicar and he, in turn, had delegated them to her. Well, that was only right and proper. Harriet had known Henry Burton for many years and believed she knew exactly what sort of music he would have liked. She felt that *Jerusalem* as the final hymn had been an inspired choice – moving and uplifting in equal measure. If only the bells hadn't started their ringing at the same time as the organ was playing. What a din! Harriet was all for tradition, but those bellringers were a law unto themselves, and you could hardly hear the organ once they started ringing, even if the bells were half-muffled. They were still going now. Would they never stop?

She placed the items she'd found in a neat pile on the front pew on the north side of the church and then began her inspection of the south side. This was where the squire's family had sat during the service: the children fidgeting, their mother dry-eyed and coldly indifferent to the whole proceedings, as if the funeral were nothing more than an inconvenience to her. Henry's son, Tobias Burton, had never once bowed his head, even during the prayers.

What would poor Henry have made of such a display from his own family?

She was going to have a battle on her hands in the coming weeks and months over the son's plans for the manor house. Tobias Burton had made no secret of his intention to turn the house into a luxury hotel and spa and clearly couldn't wait to get his hands on his inheritance. He had even begun scoping out the site while his poor father lay dying, insensible to the world. Harriet didn't believe for one minute that Henry Burton would have sanctioned his son's mercenary plans. The manor house was a cornerstone of village life, and the lord of the manor's place was in the house, not living away in London.

Harriet relished the prospect of taking on Tobias Burton and his greedy scheme to redevelop the manor house and its grounds. Her long and distinguished career as an Oxford academic hadn't been achieved by taking the easy route in life, and she had no intention of spending her retirement tending her roses and baking cakes. In addition to her duties as churchwarden, she was also chairperson of Hambledon parish council. Nothing happened in Hambledon-on-Thames without Harriet's knowledge, and rarely without her say-so.

She was a great believer in the values of continuity and tradition, and if continuity and tradition were to be trampled into the mud and thrown to the winds in a small village in south Oxfordshire, then there really was no hope for the future. No, as long as Harriet Stevenson had blood in her veins and air in her lungs, she would fight tooth and nail for what she believed in. And she certainly did not believe that a Tudor manor house whose foundations dated back to before the Wars of the Roses should be turned into a hotel.

As if she didn't already have enough on her plate, what with the threatened closure of the village school. That was another battle she intended to win, for the sake of the children, as well as for the teachers, especially that nice Kayleigh Simpson. The school had stood for a hundred and fifty years, and if Harriet had her way, it would continue to serve the community for a hundred and fifty more.

From the pews on the south side, she retrieved a second pair of reading glasses and no fewer than six carelessly-dropped orders of service. She gathered all of the lost property into a single pile

11

which she would display at the back of the church later for people to collect. Then, with the weighty ideas of history and tradition still on her mind, she stepped into the north transept for a moment of contemplation at the tomb of Henry Burton's distinguished ancestors, Lord Edmund and Lady Ellen Burton. Edmund, who had been a wealthy merchant in Tudor times, had been granted the manor house as a favour by Henry VIII after the king seized it during the dissolution of Abingdon Abbey in 1538. The husband, who had died in 1577 during the reign of Elizabeth I, and his wife who had passed away a year earlier, were now immortalised for all eternity, their limestone effigies lying in peaceful repose atop the elaborate marble tomb that dominated the north transept. Here was tradition for you, but also a powerful *Memento Mori*. Remember that you will die.

As Harriet stood in quiet contemplation, the bells continuing their incessant ringing – how they irritated her! – she sensed, rather than heard, a movement behind her. It was probably one of the owners of the reading glasses come back to reclaim their lost property. She hoped they would be suitably grateful to her for having taken the trouble to gather all of the lost items together. She turned to see who it was, but in that moment a heavy object came crashing down on top of her head. Her knees buckled under her and she collapsed onto the cold flagstones.

If Harriet Stevenson had been capable of

thought in that moment, she would no doubt have deplored the mess that her blood was making as it spilled over the floor. But all thoughts – whether of lost property, the future of the manor house, the weight of tradition or the leaky church roof – were beyond her now. The bells continued to ring, but she had ceased to hear them. They would never bother her again.

CHAPTER 2

'Have you got your calculator?'

'Yes, Mum.'

'What about your protractor?'

'Yes, Mum, stop fussing.'

'A Ruler? Spare pencils?'

'Mum, you're making me nervous.'

'Sorry. It's just that I had a dream last night. I was about to do a maths exam and when I turned over the paper, I realised I'd forgotten my pencil case and wouldn't be able to answer any of the questions.' Bridget put the car in gear and headed out of Wolvercote.

Chloe laughed. 'Honestly, Mum. Anyone would think that you're the one sitting your GCSEs.'

'Trust me,' said Bridget, 'this is ten times worse.'

Chloe was in the middle of her GCSE exams at school and Bridget had never felt more stressed, even when she'd been sitting her History finals at Oxford. Her daughter had been at home on so-called "study leave" since Easter but Bridget constantly fretted over how much actual studying was being done. Too often she would pop into Chloe's room with a cup of tea and find her on a video call with her best friend Olivia, or more often, her boyfriend Alfie.

'Olivia and I were just testing each other on chemistry,' Chloe explained on one such occasion. Bridget wasn't sure she entirely believed her. She didn't recall chemistry eliciting such gales of laughter when she'd been a schoolgirl. Maybe it was taught in a more engaging and creative way nowadays, but there was only so much fun you could get out of the periodic table of the elements.

On top of Chloe's exams, Bridget's sister Vanessa was giving her a hard time over her latest project – to persuade their ageing parents to sell their house in Lyme Regis and move to a retirement home, preferably closer to Oxford. It was a good idea in principle. Their mother's health had been poor in recent years, and their father was finding it increasingly difficult to cope, despite all protestations to the contrary.

'A nice retirement home would be ideal for them,' Vanessa had insisted. 'So much easier and more comfortable.'

But their mum and dad didn't see it that way, and despite Bridget's half-hearted encouragement, had refused to move.

'Perhaps they'd be happy if we just let them stay where they are,' Bridget had told Vanessa last time they'd discussed the matter.

But Vanessa was impossible once she'd made

up her mind about something. 'You're only saying that because you hardly ever go to see them. I do all the work, driving up and down to Dorset to sort things out.'

The accusation was unfair, as Bridget couldn't easily get away from work, but Vanessa was right about her parents needing more support. A retirement home might well be the best solution, but her mum and dad were as stubborn as Vanessa, and an impasse had been reached, with neither side willing to budge, and Bridget caught in between.

As if her parents' living arrangements and Chloe's exams weren't enough to worry about, there was the upcoming wedding of Bridget's ex-husband, Ben, to his fiancée, Tamsin. Bridget was dreading the event, and still hadn't bought an outfit for the occasion. Chloe, meanwhile, would be chief bridesmaid and was supposed to attend yet another dress fitting in London this weekend, but Bridget had put her foot down and insisted that the dress fitting would have to wait until the exams were over. That didn't leave much time before the wedding, but for once Bridget had got her way and had savoured every moment of this small victory.

Right now, Chloe was in the thick of the exams, which entailed her sometimes going into school in the mornings and sometimes in the afternoons, depending on the exam timetable. Whenever she could, Bridget gave her a lift to make sure she got there on time. That was another of her recurring nightmares – arriving late for an exam and finding the doors locked and bolted against her. Just one more week of this and she'd be able to relax.

Today's paper was Pure Mathematics, the thought of which was enough to make Bridget break out into a cold sweat. She couldn't for the life of her remember the first thing about simultaneous equations or trigonometry.

She turned onto the Woodstock Road, praying that there wouldn't be any traffic hold-ups. It would be just like Oxford City Council to embark on major roadworks in the middle of the exam season. But for once, her prayers were answered and she dropped Chloe off at the school gates twenty minutes ahead of schedule.

'Good luck,' she called as Chloe got out of the car.

'Thanks, Mum.' Chloe waved and walked away.

I forgot to ask her if she's got a pencil sharpener, thought Bridget. But it was too late now. Chloe had disappeared.

She was about to drive away – a mound of paperwork awaited her on her desk in Kidlington – when her phone rang. Bridget checked the caller display. It was the duty sergeant. He wouldn't be calling her unless it was something important.

'Detective Inspector Bridget Hart speaking.'

'Ma'am, there's been an incident at the church in Hambledon-on-Thames.'

Bridget recalled the pretty little village where she and Jonathan had once enjoyed a pub lunch after an invigorating, if muddy, walk along the Thames Path. She listened to what the duty sergeant was telling her – a woman brutally murdered; uniform at the scene – and immediately all concerns about exams and weddings were pushed firmly from her mind.

'I can be there in half an hour,' she said.

She slid the car into gear and drove off in the direction of the Oxford ring road. A murder investigation. Just what she needed to cure her of exam anxiety.

CHAPTER 3

The church of St Michael and All Angels enjoyed a picturesque location at the heart of the village of Hambledon, directly opposite the war memorial and next to the old manor house. It was hard to imagine a more tranquil setting. And yet, as Detective Sergeant Jake Derwent examined the body lying in the north transept of the church, it was apparent that an act of savage violence had been committed here. The amount of blood that had spread across the flagstone floor indicated a vicious attack involving a heavy object, although he hadn't yet been able to locate the murder weapon.

Just half an hour earlier, he'd been relaxing with a lunchtime pint in the Eight Bells, chatting to Amy's mum and dad as they laid out food for the wake.

'The church is packed,' Robert Bagot had reported after returning from the funeral. 'It's nice to see people making a real effort to send off the old squire.'

'He'll be missed in the village, that's for sure,' said Sue. 'What a fine gentleman he was.'

Jake had grown to like Robert and Sue Bagot very much. Meeting your girlfriend's parents could be a daunting experience, but in the case of Amy's parents, Jake had hit it off with them straightaway. They were relaxed, easy-going and chatty – an ideal couple to be running a village pub – and seemed delighted that he was dating their daughter. 'A policeman?' Sue had said approvingly, on hearing what he did for a living, quickly followed by, 'And aren't you tall?'

Jake was more than happy to wait in the pub with them while Amy finished ringing the quarter peal, or whatever it was called. She had tried to explain the principles of change ringing to him, but he had quickly become bewildered by all the jargon, and unable to grasp the difference between Grandsire Triples and Kent Treble Bob Major. He was quite content to leave the world of bellringing to her.

He and Amy had been going out for a couple of months now, and he was surprised at how quickly she had become such a big part of his life. He never imagined that he would get on so well with someone who worked at the Bodleian Library, and whose idea of a good evening out was climbing an old church tower to ring bells. And yet he felt completely relaxed in her company. She was such an easy person to hang out with. And the fact that her parents ran a pub, and that Amy herself was a keen beer drinker, could only be a bonus.

People had started arriving at the pub just after

a quarter to one. They had helped themselves from the lavish spread of food that was laid out, and then spilled out into the pub garden which sloped down to the riverbank, making the most of the warm June sunshine. Jake had overheard snippets of conversation – *weren't the flowers lovely* and *hadn't the choir sung beautifully* and *didn't the vicar give a fitting eulogy*. People seemed to have enjoyed the funeral, if that was the right way of looking at it. The bells had continued ringing while the coffin was being interred in the family burial plot, the sound carrying easily on the summer's air.

And then shortly after one thirty, Amy had rushed into the pub, red-faced, with the shocking news that the bellringers had discovered the body of an elderly lady in the church, and could Jake come with her at once to take charge of the situation.

'I'll come and take a look,' he'd told her, setting down his half-finished drink on the bar. 'But there won't be much for me to do. The paramedics will deal with everything when they arrive. Someone has called for an ambulance, haven't they?'

'You don't understand,' said Amy breathlessly, grabbing his hand and pulling him off the bar stool. 'She's been murdered.'

He had accompanied her to the church where Bill Harris, the senior bellringer, had met them at the door. 'This way, Sergeant,' he said gravely. 'It's a bad business. A very bad business.'

The six other bellringers were standing guard inside the church. Jake recognised Jamie Reade, who was the same age as him and due to get married at the weekend to Amy's best friend, Kayleigh Simpson. The four of them had enjoyed a drink in the pub only the other week.

'I called the police as soon as we discovered the body,' said Jamie. 'A car is on its way from Abingdon.'

'You did the right thing, mate,' said Jake. 'Now, show me where the body is.'

It had indeed been a brutal attack. The victim was an elderly woman, smartly dressed in a tweed skirt and jacket, but that jacket was now splattered with blood. More blood had spread out in a large arc around her head. It was smudged at the edge, as if someone had caught it with the toe of their shoe.

'Did one of you accidentally step in the blood?' Jake asked.

The bellringers all shook their heads.

'No,' said Bill, 'we were careful not to disturb anything.'

Jake nodded. The bellringers may have been careful, but someone had left bloody footprints on the flagstone floor. To Jake's untrained eye they were just smears, but it was possible that the scene of crime officers would be able to glean something from the marks. He kneeled next to the body to examine the victim more closely.

'It's Harriet Stevenson,' volunteered one of the women bellringers in answer to Jake's unasked question. 'She's the churchwarden here, or she was. I expect she'll have been tidying up after the funeral when she was attacked. I'm trained in first aid, so I checked for a pulse and signs of breathing, but there was nothing. And then when I saw the head wound...' The woman trailed off.

Jake would have to wait for an official pronouncement from the police medical examiner to be certain of death, but the first-aider looked competent and Jake was sure she was right. The badly-fractured skull of the victim, and the amount of blood that had leaked from the head wound left no doubt in his mind that the victim was far beyond saving. Now the most important task was to secure the crime scene and to preserve any evidence.

'I'm going to have to ask you all to leave the church now,' he said, standing up again. 'This is a crime scene and I need to protect it from contamination.'

So much for his day off. It looked like the riverside walk he'd hoped to take with Amy that afternoon wasn't going to happen. Neither was lunch at the Eight Bells. He wished he'd grabbed a bite to eat from the buffet while he'd had the chance.

He waited while the eight bellringers, including Amy, filed out of the church, then followed them outside into the bright sunlight. 'I'd like you all to stay here, if you don't mind,' he told them. 'You'll be free to go once you've given a statement to one of my colleagues.'

'Of course,' said Bill Harris. 'But I can tell you now that none of us witnessed the attack. It must have happened when we were up in the tower, ringing the bells. By the time we came down the stairs at the end of the quarter peal, Miss Stevenson was already dead.'

'All eight of you were in the tower the whole time?'

'We were,' said Bill. 'That's what makes this even more dreadful, to think that we were up there in the ringing chamber' – he indicated the solid, square shape of the church tower – 'while this was going on down below.'

'Did you hear anything?' asked Jake.

Bill shook his head. 'What you have to understand, Sergeant, is that while we're ringing, we're concentrating so hard on getting the changes right that we're completely oblivious to anything else. Besides, as I'm sure you know, when the bells are being rung, they can be quite loud. So I'm afraid we didn't hear a dicky bird.'

Jake nodded. The bells had been loud enough even from the pub on the other side of the village. In the belltower itself, they must have been deafening.

'Maybe one of you saw something?' he suggested.

'Not a thing,' said Bill. 'We were standing in a circle facing each other. And in any case, although you can see into the nave from the ringing chamber if you peer through the lattice, you can't see clearly into the transepts because of

24

the angle.' The poor man looked quite distraught. Amy threw an arm around his shaking shoulders to comfort him.

While Jake waited for assistance to arrive, he drew Jamie Reade to one side. He'd liked Jamie when he'd met him the other week, and found the young engineer who worked at the nearby science park to be level-headed and straight-talking. 'Any idea who might do something like this?'

'I really don't know,' said Jamie in an undertone. 'But between you and me, Harriet Stevenson wasn't the most popular person in the village.'

'Oh?'

'I didn't have much to do with her, but she was a bit of an interfering busybody by all accounts. Not to speak ill of the dead or anything, but there'll be a few people around here who won't be sorry to see the back of her.'

The approaching blues and twos – flashing blue lights and two-tone siren – announced the welcome arrival of a police car and an ambulance. Jake breathed a sigh of relief. Now he would be able to secure the scene properly and get the investigation under way.

CHAPTER 4

Bridget made good progress as she left the Oxford ring road and headed south, passing through the pretty villages of Nuneham Courtenay and Clifton Hampden, but she slowed down when she reached the sign that read, 'Welcome to Hambledon-on-Thames. Please drive carefully. Thank you.'

She drove into the village along the old Toll Bridge Road, passing a half-timbered pub with a brightly-coloured display of hanging baskets. From there, she followed the High Street past a row of quaint brick cottages, a small Church of England primary school and the grounds of the manor house where expertly trimmed displays of topiary were visible through the wrought iron gates. Whitewashed houses with thatched roofs and abundant cottage gardens gave the place an idyllic charm. She found the church at the heart of the village, just opposite the green, and close to the post office and corner shop.

She parked her red Mini behind a police car and ambulance, then walked through the lychgate, the old wooden entrance that led into the churchyard, and up the uneven path towards the church door. Old and crumbling headstones filled the graveyard, and there was evidence of a fresh burial in one of the larger plots. The duty sergeant had said something about the lord of the manor's funeral taking place that day.

A small crowd was gathered near the north door of the church. Eight in total, presumably people from the village. Bridget showed her warrant card to the uniformed officer standing guard and went inside.

It was a large church for such a small place. Bridget had already noticed its tall, square belltower with castle-like battlements on her way through the churchyard. Now she took in the lofty nave rising to a timbered roof, the stained-glass windows depicting Biblical scenes, and an intricately carved rood screen separating the nave from the chancel. An extraordinary floral display was arranged in front of the altar – cream and ivory wreaths of roses, freesias and peonies. As she walked up the north aisle, the age-old smell of wood polish and dusty hymn books transported her back to her childhood. She had grown up attending Church of England services at St Mary Magdalene in Woodstock. But the murder of her younger sister, Abigail, at the age of sixteen when Bridget was a student at Merton College, had shaken her faith to its core. Now she was no longer sure what she believed in, except catching criminals and obtaining justice for victims. Forgiveness no longer occupied such a prominent position in her belief system.

She was surprised, but pleased, to see the familiar figure of her sergeant, Jake Derwent on the scene. She spotted him at once, towering above everyone else around him. Bridget, measuring just five foot two, had a bit of a complex about her height, especially in situations when she wanted people to know she was in charge. She wondered what it might be like to gaze down on people from such a lofty height, instead of constantly tilting her chin upwards, hoping to be noticed.

He strode over to her, covering the length of the aisle in a few easy steps. 'Ma'am.'

'Sergeant.' She noted his casual dress of jeans and trainers. 'Wasn't this supposed to be your day off?'

'It was,' said Jake. 'I was in the pub, waiting for my girlfriend, Amy, when she rushed in with the news about the murder. She's one of the bellringers. They were ringing after the funeral, and when she came down from the tower, she found the body lying here.'

So that explained the crowd outside. Eight bellringers for eight bells. Bridget recalled that one of them had been a freckle-faced redhead about the same age as Jake.

'Did they disturb the scene?'

'I don't think so, ma'am. They seem like a sensible bunch. One of them did check the body for signs of life, but as soon as I got here, I asked them all to wait outside.'

'I'll speak to them in a moment,' said Bridget, 'but first...'

She followed Jake over to the body of the victim. Dr Sarah Walker, the forensic medical examiner, was getting to her feet as they approached. 'Ah, Bridget,' she said. 'I thought you might be taking charge here, after I saw your sergeant.'

'It was just coincidence Jake being here. He's not supposed to be on duty today. He just happened to be nearby.'

'Lucky for him,' said Sarah dryly.

Bridget turned her attention to the victim. A woman, aged around seventy. She was lying spreadeagled on her back, her arms splayed out. The fracture to her skull was very visible. She looked like the kind of churchgoing woman Bridget had seen so many times in places like this, turned out immaculately in her Sunday best of tweed skirt and dark jacket over a pale blouse. A stalwart of the community no doubt, and a very unlikely person to have been killed in such a brutal manner. Her hair was grey and cut short. Her earrings were simple bands of gold, and she wore a string of pearls around her neck, but no wedding ring adorned her finger. A divorcee, perhaps, or a spinster. She might have been beautiful once, and even in old age her features bore a haughty and refined appearance. Other than that, there was nothing remarkable about her, other than the fact that she had been viciously bludgeoned to death in a village church in the aftermath of a funeral.

'First thoughts?' asked Bridget.

'Blunt force trauma to the head with a heavy object,' said Sarah briskly. 'I'm sure that Roy will come to the same conclusion once he's had a chance to give her a good poke.'

'No doubt.' Bridget still hadn't got to the bottom of the ongoing relationship between the taciturn medical examiner and the lugubrious pathologist, Dr Roy Andrews. Was romance blossoming over the dissection tables of the morgue? It was hard to picture, but then it was hard for Bridget to imagine what drove someone to choose a career spent in such close proximity to corpses in the first place. Every time she'd been obliged to attend a post-mortem herself, she'd been very relieved to get back out into the sun and leave the cold interior of the morgue far behind. She was just about to ask Sarah whether she'd seen Roy recently, when another voice cut short her nosey interest.

'This village is far too pretty for a murder.'

She turned to see Vikram Vijayaraghavan, the head of SOCO, approaching with his team of white-clad scene-of-crime officers.

'Vik,' said Bridget, pleased to see the friendly investigator.

'Bridget.' Vik paused to take in the sight of the murdered woman. A frown passed across his face. 'Not exactly what you expect to find in a place like this.'

'Quite,' said Bridget. 'But hopefully you'll be

able to shed some light for us.'

'We'll do our best.' His keen eyes roamed around the dim interior of the church. 'How many people have had access to the crime scene?'

'Apart from the police?' said Jake. 'Eight bellringers, all told. And pretty much the entire village was here for the funeral service immediately beforehand.'

'Terrific,' said Vik with his characteristic good humour. 'I do enjoy a challenge. Best get to work, then.'

'I'll get out of your way so you can do your job,' Bridget told him. 'Come on,' she said to Jake. 'Let's go outside and you can introduce me to your girlfriend.'

★

The June afternoon seemed very bright after the subdued lighting inside the church. Bridget emerged from the cool stone interior of the building to warmth, fresh air and birdsong. Outside, she took a moment to take in her surroundings. The church was tucked away at the southern end of the churchyard, close to a low stone wall that separated it from the grounds of the manor house. It was well tended, with neatly-clipped grass around the gravestones, and broad, dark yews dotted around the edge. Several onlookers had gathered on the village green, but were being kept away from the church by uniformed officers.

Jake led her over to the group of bellringers waiting outside the north entrance to the church. 'This is Amy Bagot,' he said, introducing the petite redhead who Bridget had noticed on her arrival. 'Amy was the one who first saw the body.' A flush was spreading up the back of Jake's neck. He clearly felt awkward about introducing his boss to his girlfriend.

Amy, however, seemed to feel no such embarrassment. She reached out a warm hand to grasp Bridget's. 'Pleased to meet you,' she said with a beaming smile. 'Jake's told me so much about you. He always says you're a great boss.'

'Does he, indeed?' Bridget glanced sideways at her sergeant, whose colour was quickly blossoming into a fuchsia pink. 'I hear that you're a bellringer.'

Amy nodded with enthusiasm. 'We were ringing a quarter peal after the funeral service. That must have been when the murder took place. We'd finished ringing, and I'd just gone down the stairs to return the key of the belltower to the vestry when I saw the body in the north transept and raised the alarm. Jamie phoned for the police and I dashed over to the pub to fetch Jake.' She gazed proudly up at Jake's face. 'I knew that he'd know exactly what to do.'

Bridget was pleased to see that Jake had met someone so refreshingly down-to-earth and who so quite clearly adored him. For a while, he had dated Detective Constable Ffion Hughes, but that relationship hadn't ended well, resulting in several months of tension in the team. But now the two of them seemed to have moved on – Jake with a new girlfriend, and Ffion by throwing herself into studying for her detective sergeant's exams. It was good to see the two members of her team getting on with their lives again.

'So, can you tell me what you saw?' Bridget asked.

'Not much, to be honest,' said Amy. 'Harriet was just lying there, with blood everywhere. I raised the alarm, and then went to fetch Jake.'

'Is there a possibility that you might have stepped in the blood when you first discovered the body?' asked Bridget. She had noticed a smear of blood, and a few faint footsteps on the stone floor near the body.

Amy shook her head. 'Definitely not. I didn't even go near.'

'You said that the victim's name was Harriet?'

'Yes,' said Amy. 'Harriet Stevenson. She was the churchwarden. Everyone in the village knew her.'

'I see. And what can you tell me about Harriet Stevenson?'

A man's voice came from behind. 'Perhaps I can help you with that, Inspector?'

Bridget turned to find a good-looking young man in a dog collar striding down the path that led from the road. He was aged around thirty perhaps, but had a slightly careworn air about him. He looked tired, and his forehead was crinkled with lines of worry, as if he bore all the concerns of the parish on his own shoulders.

'Martin Armistead,' he said, extending a hand. 'I'm the vicar here at St Michael and All Angels. This really is such a terrible shock to us.' His hand was cool and clammy to the touch, and he held on to Bridget's hand as if he had forgotten to release it. His face looked very pale in the summer sun, and Bridget worried that he might be about to faint at any minute.

'You knew the victim well?' she asked.

The vicar released her hand at last. 'Yes... yes. Of course. Harriet and I worked together very closely, as you can imagine.' He raised his hand to his brow. 'I can't believe that she's dead. People are saying that it's murder. Can that really be true?'

'Perhaps I could speak to you in private, and you could tell me everything you know.'

'I ...' The vicar nodded. 'Of course, yes. Somewhere private. Would the vicarage do?'

'I'm sure that would do very nicely.'

Bridget drew Jake to one side. 'I know it's supposed to be your day off, but do you think you could take statements from the bellringers, and then go over to the pub and start organising the investigation? Get a list of everyone who was at the funeral today, and find out if anyone noticed anything unusual, like a stranger hanging around or something.'

Jake grinned. 'No problem, ma'am. I'd already figured that my day off was ruined.'

'Sorry about that,' said Bridget. 'Although to

be fair' – she nodded in Amy's direction – 'your girlfriend seems to think that this is the most exciting thing that could have happened.' She winked at her sergeant. 'In the meantime, I'll see what the good Reverend has to say about his churchwarden.'

CHAPTER 5

The vicarage, a double-fronted Georgian property with well-proportioned sash windows, stood next to the Church of England primary school and overlooked the village green. A curving gravel path led up to its front door, which was decorated with stone pilasters. Pink and yellow roses rampaged through the beds to either side of the entrance, and an out-of-control ivy scrambled across the brickwork, threatening to obscure the upstairs windows.

'What a charming house,' said Bridget.

'It needs quite a bit of work inside,' said the vicar apologetically, ushering her into an entrance hall covered in peeling Anaglypta wallpaper painted a rather dingy shade of brown. 'The Church of England isn't made of money… but' – he brightened – 'you know, we were very lucky to be offered this parish. You mustn't think that we're ungrateful.'

'We?' enquired Bridget.

Martin Armistead touched his fingers to his wedding ring, twisting it nervously back and forth. 'Come through to the kitchen. I'll introduce you to my wife, Emma.'

Bridget followed him through to the large kitchen at the back of the property. Although the room was bright and cheerful, it looked as if it hadn't been updated for at least thirty years. A young woman wrapped in a pale linen dress stood before the sink, absent-mindedly staring out of the window. She was very slender, perhaps a little too thin, and had a wraithlike quality to her, as if she were a trick of the light and might disappear at any moment.

'Darling?' prompted the vicar. 'This is the police officer who's investigating the, um, murder.'

Emma Armistead turned slowly and greeted Bridget with a sad smile, her features half-hidden behind a long strand of fine, blonde hair that fell carelessly across one eye. She brushed it aside, revealing a face devoid of make-up, but which held a haunting beauty. She wasn't at all Bridget's idea of a vicar's wife. In her experience, vicars' wives were usually robust, cheery characters, always busy running the Sunday School or organising jumble sales to raise money for Africa. Emma Armistead seemed altogether too fragile for such a role.

'Shall I make tea?' she asked in a quiet voice.

'Yes, that would be wonderful,' said her husband, clapping his hands together. 'Tea always makes everything so much easier to bear, doesn't it?'

Emma filled an electric kettle with water and

drifted over to a cupboard to retrieve a mis-matched selection of mugs. She dropped a tea bag into each, and turned again to face the window.

'So, how long have you been in this parish?' asked Bridget while they waited for the kettle to boil. The vicar didn't look old enough to be long out of the seminary.

'About a year,' he said. 'We moved here from Birmingham.'

'Birmingham? That's quite a change of scene. From the big city to a little Oxfordshire village.'

'It suits us well enough,' he said. 'I mean, we're very happy here.'

'Good.'

The kettle boiled and Emma splashed hot water into the mugs.

'Milk and sugar?' enquired the vicar.

'Please,' said Bridget. She waited while he fussed with the drinks, passing her one of the mugs.

'Let's take the tea through to my study,' he said. 'We'll be more comfortable in there.'

Bridget followed him through to a small room off the hallway, furnished with a desk and an assortment of chairs, and cluttered from floor to ceiling with books and papers. The study overlooked the rear garden, a modest rectangle enclosed by a tall brick wall, with grass that had been allowed to grow too long, bordered by crowded flower beds bursting with roses, peonies, foxgloves and clusters of red and pink poppies, looking like jewels. There was also, Bridget noted, a good collection of stinging nettles, dandelions, goosegrass and ragworts. It reminded her very much of her own sadly-neglected garden.

She waited while the vicar cleared a pile of papers from a sagging armchair, and then made herself comfortable as he took a seat behind his desk.

'So, Reverend –'

'Please, do call me Martin.'

'Martin, what can you tell me about Harriet Stevenson? First of all, did she have any living relatives?'

He shook his head. 'I don't believe so. She was unmarried, and as far as I know she had no brothers or sisters. Her parents passed away some years ago.'

'She lived alone?'

'Yes, in a house in the village. She was retired. A former academic, I believe.'

'At Oxford?'

'That's right.'

'And she held the post of churchwarden at St Michael and All Angels?'

'Yes, for some years now. I have to say that she always performed her duties with the utmost dedication. She was tireless. Indefatigable.'

'You must have worked quite closely with her.'

'I did, yes. We held weekly meetings, and I saw her at various parish meetings too.'

'How did you get on with her?' asked Bridget.

'Well, as I said, she was very conscientious. I certainly had nothing to complain about. In fact, Harriet was what you might call a pillar of the community.'

'In what way?'

'Well, she wasn't only the churchwarden. She was also the chair of the parish council;' – he began to tick off Harriet's duties on his fingers – 'chair of governors at the local primary school; she ran the Women's Institute and organised the cake and produce competitions at the summer fête; she campaigned for traffic calming measures to be installed in the village. I mean, I could go on but I'm sure you get the picture. She practically ran Hambledon-on-Thames.'

'A strong character, then,' said Bridget. 'Was she well-liked? Did people appreciate the efforts she was making on their behalf?'

The vicar steepled his hands, tapping his fingertips together. 'I don't think it's my place to try and guess what other people might have thought about her. And I certainly wouldn't want to repeat any malicious gossip or tittle-tattle.'

'I'd appreciate it if you would, Martin,' said Bridget. She added, when he still looked uncertain, 'After all, it would appear that someone murdered her, and it's my task to find out who and why. I can't do that if I'm not privy to all the relevant information.'

'Yes, I see that. I do want to help.'

'So, was Harriet a popular person in

Hambledon?'

He continued slowly, clearly choosing his words with care. 'If I'm being completely frank with you, I would say that she was quite unpopular. Although she was hardworking and tried to do her best, she did tend to treat the village as if it was her own private fiefdom.'

'She had a domineering personality,' suggested Bridget.

The vicar gave a rueful smile. 'I couldn't have put it better myself.'

Bridget nodded. She had met the type before, on many occasions. A headstrong woman who, having followed a high-flying career, had now in retirement diverted her considerable energies and abilities into serving the community in which she lived. Her own sister, Vanessa, was a good example. She already bossed Bridget around, and once her children had grown up and flown the nest, Bridget could easily imagine Vanessa taking on the role of general busybody. There had been several occasions when Bridget had briefly felt the urge to bash her sister over the head with a heavy object.

Yet in the case of Harriet Stevenson, someone had gone way beyond mere frustration or anger, and had carried out a brutal assault leading to her death.

'I suppose that a person like that,' said Bridget, 'with her finger in every pie, might rub people up the wrong way, even if she had the best of intentions.'

The vicar gave her a grateful look, as if she had expressed his thoughts precisely without him having to speak ill of the dead.

'Did Harriet make any enemies in the course of her tireless organising and campaigning?' asked Bridget.

'Enemies?' echoed the vicar. The word seemed to frighten him. 'I wouldn't say "enemies" exactly.'

'Opponents then. People who didn't see eye to eye with her.'

He turned his head to gaze out of the window. His wife, Emma, had entered the garden and was wandering barefoot through the long grass, bending down to smell the roses. The vicar turned his attention back to Bridget. 'It would be fair to say that not everyone agreed with Harriet all the time,' he conceded.

'Who, precisely, didn't agree with her?'

He shuffled around in his chair, lifted a pen off his desk, and then replaced it. 'One specific matter does come to mind.'

'Yes?'

'Harriet had just embarked on a campaign to prevent the manor house from being redeveloped. The old lord of the manor, Henry Burton, died last week. It was his funeral that took place today. His son, Tobias, has returned to the village and is apparently making plans to turn the house into a private hotel.'

'And Harriet Stevenson objected to this?'

'She did. In the strongest possible terms. And

as chair of the parish council, she was in a position to do something about it.'

'You're suggesting that Tobias Burton may have had a motive to murder her.'

The vicar looked alarmed. 'I'm not suggesting any such thing. Please don't put words into my mouth. I'm just telling you that Harriet was intent on putting a stop to Tobias's plans. I don't know any more than that.'

Outside, Emma was now idly deadheading some of the roses, clipping the spent flowers with a pair of secateurs and tossing them into a wicker basket. Her dress had caught on the sharp thorns, but she seemed not to have noticed.

Bridget wasn't entirely sure she believed that the vicar knew no more about the feud between Harriet and the new lord of the manor, but decided to move on to the details of the day's events.

'As churchwarden, did Harriet have a role to play in the funeral?'

The vicar looked relieved to be back on safer ground. He nodded. 'Yes. Harriet helped to plan the funeral arrangements. She would have been in the church early, making sure that everything was ready. She greeted people as they arrived and handed out the orders of service. During the funeral she sat at the back of the church and kept a close eye on everyone because she was also the church's appointed first aider.'

'What about after the funeral service?'

'She'd have been tidying up. On Sundays she

always made a point of checking the pews for lost property. She had a bit of a bee in her bonnet about people leaving things behind. If she'd had her way, everyone who wore reading glasses would have been forced to stick name labels inside their glasses cases.' He laughed. 'And on their umbrellas and phones too. She could be rather schoolmarmish at times.'

'How many mourners attended the funeral?'

'I don't have numbers, but the church was full. In fact there were far more people there than on a regular Sunday service. I wasn't surprised at that. The old squire – that's what people around here called the lord of the manor – was very popular. He'd lived in the village all his life and was a very decent sort of man. Very generous.'

'What time did the funeral start and how long did it last?'

Martin rummaged through the papers strewn about his desk and pulled out an order of service. He handed it over to Bridget. 'The service started at midday and lasted about forty-five minutes. People don't like these things to go on too long. By a quarter to one we were heading outside for the burial.'

'I noticed a freshly dug grave in the churchyard.'

'Yes. Most funerals these days take place at the nearby crematorium, but the Burtons have a family plot. They've been buried at Hambledon for generations. Henry's wife is buried there.'

'Who attended at the graveside?'

'Just a small group of people. The old man's son, his wife and their two young children. Then there was his estate manager, his housekeeper and the nurse who cared for him at the end of his life. The sexton was there too, of course. Everyone else went to the pub for the wake.'

'Apart from the bellringers,' said Bridget.

'Ah, yes, we're very proud of our bells at St Michael and All Angels. We have an excellent band of ringers, and Henry Burton donated a considerable sum of money towards the maintenance of the bells. Everyone thought it would be a fitting tribute to ring a quarter peal in his honour. Everyone except Harriet, that is.'

'She wasn't a fan of bellringing?'

'She didn't like noise of any kind. She used to say that the bells drowned everything else out. She had a bit of a row about it with Bill Harris, the tower captain.'

'I see.' The list of people that Harriet had disliked or offended seemed to be growing by the minute. 'How long did the burial take?'

'No more than twenty minutes, I should say. It was over by ten past one.'

'And how long did the bells ring?'

'I think that a quarter peal lasts about forty-five minutes. Bill Harris would be able to tell you precisely. They started at the end of the service, while the coffin was being taken outside and carried on until after the burial was finished.'

In her head, Bridget was assembling a timeline for the murder. It couldn't have happened during the service itself when the church was full of people. Allowing five or ten minutes for everyone to leave the church and make their way to the pub, then the earliest time the murder could have occurred was just before one o'clock. The body had been discovered by the bellringers when they came down from the tower at half past one. Therefore, the murder must have taken place while the burial was in progress, or during the following twenty minutes.

'What happened to the mourners at the graveside? Do you know where they went after the burial?'

'Sorry, no. I expect they went to the pub for the wake, but I can't confirm that. You'll need to ask them.'

'We will,' said Bridget. 'And what about you? Did you return to the church after the burial?'

The reverend looked her straight in the eye. 'No. Actually, I came back here straight after the burial. I wanted to check on Emma.'

Bridget turned to look out of the window once more, but the vicar's wife had disappeared. 'Wasn't she at the funeral?'

The question seemed to take him by surprise. 'Emma? No, why would she be?'

'I got the impression that the whole village had turned out for the occasion.'

'Yes, but Emma didn't know Henry Burton all that well. And besides, she finds funerals... unsettling. It wouldn't have done her any good.'

It was a puzzling response, but perhaps a

vicar's wife wasn't expected to attend every service that her husband led. 'So why did you want to check on her?' Bridget asked. 'Is she unwell?'

'Not at all. I just wanted to see how she was.' Martin glanced nervously at his desk, shuffling papers around. 'The truth of the matter is that I didn't feel like going back to the church after the funeral. I knew that Harriet would be there tidying up and I didn't want to get in her way.'

'It sounds as if you were trying to avoid her.'

'What can I say?' He gave a helpless shrug. 'Maybe I was.'

'For any particular reason?'

'As I've indicated, Harriet could sometimes be difficult. Perhaps it would be more accurate to say that she was often difficult. She was always nagging about something or other. The leaky roof, the arrangements for Sunday School, the choice of hymns. The fact is that I found our weekly meetings quite sufficient and didn't want to give her any further opportunities to harass me.'

'"Harass" – that's quite a strong word, if you don't mind me saying.'

He looked abashed. 'Well, bother me, if you prefer.'

'I see.' It was apparent that Harriet Stevenson had displayed something of a talent for harassing people during her life. But she wouldn't be bothering anyone again. Bridget stood up. 'Well thank you for your time, Martin. One of my officers will be here to take a written statement from you later.' She handed him her card. 'Do call me if anything else comes to mind.'

★

When Bridget arrived at the Eight Bells, she found Jake in the pub garden chatting to a group of locals. It was a very scenic place to enjoy a drink, with the garden giving directly onto the bank of the River Thames, a short distance upstream from Hambledon Lock.

'How have you been getting on?' Bridget asked.

'Everyone's shocked at what happened,' said Jake, 'but no one I've spoken to so far noticed anything suspicious. They all left the church immediately after the service and came to the pub for some food and drink. Everyone's been saying how much Miss Stevenson did for the village, although reading between the lines I'm starting to get the impression that she wasn't all that popular.'

'She exerted too much power?'

'Certainly that. One person called her a bossy boots.'

A bossy boots. An image of Bridget's sister sprang unbidden to her mind, and Bridget pushed it firmly away. It was bad enough to have Vanessa hassle her in person, without allowing her spectre to intrude when she wasn't even present.

'Let's go and check out the victim's home,' she told Jake.

Harriet Stevenson had owned a detached, nineteenth-century house located near to the primary school. Situated in a large, well-tended garden with mature trees and shrubs, it was one of the biggest houses in the village, apart from the manor house, and struck Bridget as a large property for a single person. Its size and central location, facing the village green, reinforced the impression that Harriet had occupied a prominent position in village life. Bridget unlocked the door, and stepped into the hallway.

The house was certainly in better condition than the rather dilapidated vicarage. A mosaic-tiled floor led to a stairway with a runner fixed with brass rods. The white walls were adorned with prints of Lady Margaret Hall, one of the first women's colleges, a reminder of Harriet's days as an academic at the university just a few miles up the road.

The lounge had the feel of a gentleman's club – dark brown leather Chesterfield sofa and matching armchairs, Turkish rug over a wooden floor, a carafe of whisky and set of crystal tumblers on a side table. Oak bookcases were stacked with hardbacks, mainly British history – the Wars of the Roses, the Tudors, the Jacobeans, the English Civil War. The subject matter immediately transported Bridget back to her own university days. A framed degree certificate on the wall confirmed that Harriet had been awarded a first-class degree in History.

It was a fine room, but what it lacked was anything to soften it. It was devoid of feminine touches – flowers, ornaments, personal photographs. Perhaps its owner hadn't required any soft touches.

A room overlooking the rear garden had been used as a study. Bridget could well imagine Harriet sitting behind the large mahogany desk, carrying out her various duties and running her campaigns to improve the life of the village.

She picked up a leather desk diary that lay next to a laptop, and thumbed through it. 'She was a busy lady,' she said, scanning the weeks leading up to the present date. 'Look at this. Last week she had a school governors' meeting on Monday, the village fête planning sub-committee on Wednesday, and a meeting with the vicar on Friday. This week she was scheduled to attend a parish council meeting on Thursday, and she had arranged another meeting for Friday to discuss the proposed plans to redevelop the manor house into a hotel.'

'When did she relax?' said Jake.

'Perhaps she didn't,' said Bridget. 'Some people like to keep themselves busy.' As an Oxford academic, no doubt Harriet had been used to hard work and had simply carried the habit of a lifetime into her retirement. It was possible that her relentless timetable of committee meetings had been a substitute for friends and a social life. An unmarried woman living alone in such a huge house might well have felt lonely.

It was getting late and there was little more they could do that day. 'Go and enjoy what's left of your day off,' she told Jake. 'I'll see you at the station first thing tomorrow.'

CHAPTER 6

'So, do you have any idea who did it?' For the first time that day Amy had Jake all to herself and she was bursting with questions.

They were walking hand-in-hand along the Thames Path, the evening sun glinting on the torpid water and casting long shadows over the fields. It was almost midsummer, Amy's favourite time of the year, when the meadows surrounding Hambledon were green and lush and studded with wildflowers, and the garden at the Eight Bells rang with voices and laughter late into the night.

'Not yet,' said Jake. 'The investigation has barely got off the ground. We'll have to wait for the results from SOCO and forensics, and there'll be a post-mortem on the body. There'll be lots of questioning and sifting through witness statements, and examining the victim's laptop and mobile phone records. We have to build up a detailed picture of her life and try to work out who might have wanted to kill her, assuming it wasn't just a random attack. Gathering evidence can be quite tedious at times.'

'It doesn't sound tedious to me,' said Amy. 'It sounds fascinating.'

She supposed she ought to be feeling revulsion at the murder, but the fact was, this was the most exciting event to have taken place in the village since a peal of Stedman Triples lasting over three hours had been rung to mark the 450th anniversary of the founding of the bells. Harriet Stevenson had objected to the "noise" resulting from the bells being rung for such a long time, but at a public meeting to discuss the matter, Henry Burton had politely but firmly overruled her. The old squire had been a keen ringer in his younger days, and fully supported such a massive feat of bellringing. A wooden plaque with the names of the bellringers in gold lettering now hung in the ringing chamber to commemorate the occasion. Amy had rung the treble, Jamie Reade had rung number five, and Bill Harris, as usual, had taken the tenor.

'How are you feeling, anyway?' asked Jake, interrupting her thoughts.

'Fine. Why?'

'It's just that discovering a dead body can be a shock, especially one that has been bludgeoned to death. If you want to talk to someone about it, I can arrange –'

'The only person I want to talk to is you,' said Amy, giving his arm a squeeze.

'You know I won't be able to share any details of the investigation.'

'Of course not. I wouldn't expect you to

behave unprofessionally.' But she was already thinking about how she might be able to help Jake solve the case. She knew everyone in the village, and people might talk more freely to her than to the police. The pub was always a good source of local gossip, not to mention the other bellringers. She kept her thoughts to herself, but her mind was already racing ahead, coming up with ideas.

'You look happy,' said Jake.

'I am.'

She loved dating a detective.

★

It was late when Robert Bagot finally climbed, exhausted, into bed beside his wife, Sue. What a day it had been! It would have been quite busy enough with the funeral and the wake, but with the churchwarden's murder on top, well, he could barely get his mind around it. The sight of police cars all over the village green with their flashing blue lights was like something off the telly. That sort of thing just didn't happen in Hambledon-on-Thames.

There had only been one topic of conversation in the pub that afternoon and evening. A great variety of opinions had been expressed about the murder, but as publican, Robert had kept his thoughts to himself and had refused to be drawn into the debate. He couldn't afford to take sides if he wanted to keep all his customers happy.

'Everything all right?' asked Sue, laying aside the book she'd been reading – an Agatha Christie of all things – and snuggling up beside him.

'All fine. But I must say, I was glad to see the back of everyone.' When he'd rung the bell behind the bar for last orders, the snug had still been packed with folk from the village. They'd shown no willingness to leave, and it had been a real job to get rid of the final stragglers, especially Shaun Daniels, the gardener from the big house, who could get quite rowdy after a few pints. And he'd drunk more than a few today.

'Any news from the police?' Sue asked.

'Nothing more,' he said. 'I expect it will take them a good while to gather all the evidence and work out what happened. I'll tell you one thing, though, love – they won't be short of people willing to give their opinion. I've heard just about every theory under the sun today about who killed Harriet Stevenson and why.'

Sue dropped her voice even though it was just the two of them. 'I don't like to speak ill of the dead, but I can't help feeling she had it coming to her.'

He sighed. 'I know what you mean.' In the five years since Harriet Stevenson had retired from her job and returned to the village, she'd stuck her nose into everyone's business and had managed to put quite a few backs up in the process. Robert and Sue had even had a few run-ins with her themselves over the noise in the pub garden on summer evenings.

'What a good thing Jake was on hand,' said Sue. 'Amy's so lucky to have found him.'

'Jake's a good bloke,' said Robert. He knew that his wife was hoping that the relationship would stay the course. She liked the idea of having Jake for a son-in-law, and Robert would be very happy if things went that way. But he would never dream of saying anything to his daughter. It was up to Amy what she chose to do with her life.

'Do you think Tobias will still go ahead with his plans for the manor house?' asked Sue, suddenly changing the topic.

'Let's hope not,' said Robert.

His opposition to the rumoured plans to convert the manor house into a hotel was one of the few things he and Harriet Stevenson had seen eye to eye on. It was no secret in the village that Henry Burton's son and heir had been scoping out the site, and meeting with contractors to discuss work. If a new hotel opened up in the village, it might not be good for business at the pub. Robert had hoped that the plans would come to nothing. But now the person who had been leading the opposition to them was dead. It was certainly food for the rumour mill. But he was far too tired to talk about that now.

He kissed his wife on the cheek and switched out the light.

CHAPTER 7

Chloe's next exam wasn't until the end of the week, so Bridget was able to go into work the next day without any fresh exam worries hanging over her.

The stress she'd already endured was quite enough. When asked how the maths paper had gone the previous day, Chloe had shrugged and said, 'Good.' But when Bridget pressed for more detail, Chloe eventually admitted that she'd run out of time on the final question and left it unfinished.

'Not good, then,' Bridget concluded.

'But Mum, it was an impossible question. Only one person in the whole class managed to answer it.'

'So not impossible. Just difficult.'

'You're not helping me, Mum.'

Bridget took a deep breath. 'Never mind,' she said in what she hoped was a more encouraging voice. 'If everyone found it hard, I'm sure the examiners will take that into account in the marking. Put it behind you and focus on the next one.'

'I already am, Mum.'

Bridget refrained from reminding Chloe not to waste her revision time chatting with Alfie and Olivia. She had already reminded her a hundred times. Now it was time for her to take her own advice and focus on the job in hand. A woman had been brutally murdered in a peaceful village on what should have been a day of mourning and reflection. It was a tragedy for the woman concerned, but for Bridget a renewed sense of purpose. The start of a new investigation always reinvigorated her sense of justice, reminding her why she had wanted to become a police detective in the first place – to put right the wrongs of the world. She drove to work feeling remarkably free of anxiety.

She strode into the incident room at Kidlington at a quarter to eight, keen to get things started, and was pleased to find Jake already at his desk.

'Morning, ma'am. I thought you'd want to make an early start.'

'I do,' she said. 'Team meeting as soon as everyone's here.'

It was perhaps no surprise to find that Jake was the first to appear. He had a personal connection with the case given that his girlfriend had been the one to discover the body. Bridget wondered whether it was appropriate to allow him to work on the investigation, but on reflection decided that it shouldn't be a problem. She could certainly make good use of his common sense and empathetic nature, a quality that not all members of her team excelled at.

Detective Constable Ffion Hughes was the next to arrive, clad as usual in her green biker's leathers. *A case in point*, thought Bridget. Ffion's ability with computers, and her sharp, analytical mind were unrivalled, but her "people" skills needed some work. After the breakthrough Ffion had made in the previous case involving the death of a writer at the Oxford Literary Festival, Bridget had recommended her for promotion to detective sergeant, and she was now spending every spare minute of her time studying for her exams – far more than Bridget had ever seen Chloe do. If the young constable's skill at handling personal interactions could be brought up to scratch, she would make a fine detective sergeant. Bridget had sent her on a course recently, and was hoping to see some improvement.

'Got your message, ma'am,' said Ffion. 'I'll just grab some tea. Can I get you one?'

Bridget decided to take this offer as a promising sign. 'Coffee, please. Milk and two sugars.'

She had texted all the members of her team the previous night to let them know that she'd be holding a briefing at eight o'clock sharp. It remained to be seen whether they would all make it on time.

The approaching banter of male voices in the corridor outside heralded the arrival of DS Ryan

Hooper, DS Andy Cartwright and DC Harry Johns. Bridget checked her watch. Two minutes to eight. They were cutting it fine, but at least they'd made it. Now they could get started. Or at least, they would be able to as soon as everyone had acquired an appropriate beverage – a herbal tea for Ffion, a builder's tea for Jake, a Starbucks for Ryan, an energy drink for Harry, and an indifferent coffee from the dispensing machine for herself and Andy.

After a quick sip of her own drink – it hardly merited the name of coffee – she clapped her hands together for silence. 'Right. Let's get started.'

The incident room chatter quickly died away, and Bridget took her place in front of the whiteboard. She had retrieved a photograph of the victim from the church noticeboard under the heading *Our Team at St Michael and All Angels*, and fixed the photo to the whiteboard now. A severe woman with a helmet of lacquered steel-grey hair. Formal blouse and pearls. The face of the dead woman stared back at Bridget, as if judging her.

'Harriet Stevenson: churchwarden at St Michael and All Angels in Hambledon-on-Thames. Yesterday, at twelve o'clock, Harriet began officiating at the funeral of Henry Burton, lord of the manor, and commonly known in Hambledon as the old squire. Harriet's duties that day involved greeting mourners on arrival at the church, handing out the orders of service, and tidying up afterwards. An hour and a half later, her body was discovered by one of the bellringers in the north transept of the church, with a fractured skull after having been struck by a blunt object.

'The window for the time of the attack is between the end of the funeral service at twelve forty-five and when the bellringers finished ringing and descended from the church tower at approximately half past one. If we allow ten minutes or so for all the mourners to leave the church, I think it's most likely that the murder took place after one o'clock and before the end of the bellringing. That narrows the time down to approximately thirty minutes. During that period, the burial was taking place in the churchyard, but finished by ten past one, which means that the attacker could have been anyone who attended the funeral. Any questions so far?'

'You mentioned a blunt object,' said Ryan. 'Do we have a murder weapon?'

'Not yet,' said Bridget. She pinned up a couple of photos of the victim's body that had been taken by the SOCO team *in situ*. 'As you can see, the victim's skull was very badly fractured, but so far the weapon hasn't been recovered.'

'Could this have been an opportunistic attack?' asked Andy. 'A robbery, perhaps?'

'The victim's purse was found on her,' said Bridget, 'and contained cash to the value of around fifty pounds. So unless the attacker was disturbed before being able to take the money,

I'd say that we're looking at a different motive.'

Ffion raised a hand. 'Ma'am, you said that the bellringers were ringing during the time of the attack. Didn't they see or hear anything?'

'I can answer that,' said Jake, speaking up. 'I've been inside the ringing chamber at St Michael and All Angels. You can see into the nave from the ringing chamber if you peer through the slats of the interior window, but you wouldn't have a good view into the transepts. The ringers would have been standing in a circle, facing each other, and concentrating on ringing the bells. Change ringing is quite a complicated business. And as for hearing anything, I can tell you that the noise from the bells is far too loud for that.'

'Thanks for clarifying that,' said Bridget.

Ryan nudged Jake. 'What were you doing inside the bell chamber?'

'My girlfriend, Amy, took me up there once to show me how change ringing is done.'

'Change ringing,' sniggered Ryan. 'Is that what you call it?'

Jake looked away, clearly embarrassed. Ffion, too, turned away from the guys, her face dark.

'Have we interviewed the bellringer who discovered the body?' asked Andy. 'I'd have thought they were an obvious suspect.'

'That was Amy,' said Jake quickly. 'And she's most definitely not a suspect.'

'But if she found the body...'

Jake's temper flared. 'She was with the other bellringers in the tower, all right? They all came down together. Amy just happened to be the one who spotted the body first.'

Bridget began to wonder once again if it was wise to include Jake as part of the investigating team. He would certainly have to demonstrate better detachment than this if she was going to allow him to remain. 'DS Derwent,' she said. 'Please try to keep your emotions in check. Can I remind you that our job here is to gather evidence, not to prejudge the outcome of the investigation.'

He bowed his head, stung by the rebuke. 'Yes, ma'am. Sorry, ma'am.'

'But Jake is correct,' she continued, smoothing over the incident. 'The bellringers were together the whole time in the tower, and came down together. I think that we can safely rule them out as suspects.'

'Can we eliminate anyone else at this stage?' asked Ryan. 'Or do we have to interview the entire village?'

'I spoke to the vicar, the Reverend Martin Armistead,' said Bridget. 'He's a young clergyman, who's only been in the post for a year. I got the impression that he relied on the churchwarden quite a bit regarding the running of the church, although he found her a rather formidable character to deal with. He did hint that there might be some bad blood between her and the heir to the manor house. Jake, did you pick up on this when you were talking to people in the pub?'

'Yes,' said Jake. 'Definitely. Basically, it seems that Henry Burton's son and heir, Tobias Burton, wants to turn the manor house into a hotel and spa. The plan has split opinion within the village. Not everyone is against it, but Harriet Stevenson vehemently opposed the idea and was preparing to lead a campaign to stop it. There's supposed to be a meeting in the village hall this Friday evening to discuss opposition, but I expect it will be cancelled now.'

'A peasants' revolt,' quipped Ryan.

'Except that Harriet Stevenson was no peasant,' said Bridget. 'She was a retired Oxford academic, and from what the vicar said, she wielded a lot of power in the community. As well as being churchwarden, she was chair of the parish council and chair of the school governors at the local primary school. She was also in charge of organising the summer fête. But despite being an authority figure in the village I don't think that many people liked her. Jake?'

'That's right, ma'am. Everyone I spoke to was shocked that she'd been killed, but no one was shedding any tears.'

'Was everyone who attended the funeral a local?' asked Ffion.

'Mostly,' said Jake. 'Except for the immediate family of the deceased. Tobias Burton lives in London with his wife and two children.'

'What about strangers in the village?'

'So far, no one has reported seeing anyone out of place.'

'It sounds as if this Tobias Burton had the most to gain from Harriet Stevenson's death,' said Andy.

'I'll definitely be interviewing him as a top priority,' said Bridget. 'The only reason I didn't speak to him yesterday was out of respect. It would have been rather insensitive on the day of his father's funeral.'

'Anything from SOCO yet?' asked Harry, speaking for the first time. The young constable was a diligent hard worker, but timid, and Bridget wished that he would participate more in team meetings. It was good to hear him ask a question for once.

'Not so far,' she said encouragingly. 'As I said, no murder weapon has been found yet. But there were some marks on the floor near to the body, suggesting that someone may have stepped in the blood.' She consulted the provisional assessment that Vik had emailed her. 'There isn't anything as useful as a full footprint, but Vik believes that the marks come from a shoe with a smooth leather sole, most probably a man's. We'll see what forensics make of it, but in the meantime, we're going to have to do some digging of our own. Jake, Ryan, I'd like you two to go to the village and continue taking formal statements from everyone who was at the funeral.'

'We're on it,' said Ryan who looked happy at the prospect of a day out of the station.

'Andy, Harry, could you do some background research into Tobias Burton? See what you can find out, if anything, about his business interests. What does he do for a living? Is he really planning to turn the manor house into a hotel?'

Andy nodded and made a note in his notebook.

'And Ffion,' said Bridget, 'I'd like you to come with me. It's high time we spoke to Tobias Burton.'

CHAPTER 8

The day after the murder that had rocked the village, Hambledon-on-Thames looked no different than it had the previous day. The sun shone brightly on the village green, and the reassuring babble of children's voices could be heard from the playground of the primary school. It would clearly take more than the death of one person to shake the calm of this tranquil community. Yet, as Bridget drove along the High Street, net curtains twitched in the windows of the thatched cottages to either side, and a young woman emerging from the bakery followed them with her eyes. The murder had thrown suspicion into the hearts of the local residents, and perhaps fuelled passions already simmering beneath the surface.

Bridget turned her Mini at a set of wooden gates leading to the manor house, and leaned out of the car to press a buzzer. The gates opened silently in response, and she entered the grounds of the house, the tyres of her car making a satisfying crunching sound on the gravel path.

The grounds were extensive, enclosed behind

a solid stone wall that bordered the church on the right. To the left, the full extent of the property was obscured by mature trees and shrubs, but a number of outbuildings were visible at the far side of the plot. The entire area must have covered around ten acres. A thickset man in denim dungarees was clipping a huge topiary hedge with a hedge trimmer. As Bridget passed, he stopped what he was doing and turned to stare.

When she and Ffion stepped out of the car a moment later, he was still standing there, halfway up his ladder, watching them with a surly expression on his sun-browned face.

'Do you get the impression we're not welcome?' said Ffion.

Bridget didn't dwell on the unfriendly gardener as she took in the ancient manor house that now stood before her. Somewhat rambling in appearance, but impressively large, the honey-coloured stone building was topped with a row of four gables, above which rose three immensely tall chimneys. The morning sun reflected off the mullioned and leaded windows around which climbed an exuberant wisteria with gnarled roots as large as small tree trunks. The porch leading to the arched front door was flanked by two giant ceramic pots containing further specimens of skilfully pruned topiary. Bridget gave a tug on the old-fashioned bell-pull at the side of the door and somewhere deep inside the house a bell chimed.

The heavy oak door was opened by a woman aged somewhere in her mid to late sixties, wearing a long-sleeved black woollen dress that looked rather too warm for the sunny June day. Her grey hair was tied in a loose knot at the back of her head, from which strands had escaped around her pale features. She regarded Bridget and Ffion with weary eyes.

Bridget produced her warrant card. 'Detective Inspector Bridget Hart from Thames Valley Police. This is my colleague, Detective Constable Ffion Hughes. We were hoping to speak to Mr Tobias Burton. Is he in?'

'I'm sorry,' said the woman, 'but Mr Burton isn't here at the moment. He's gone into Oxford on business and I don't know when he'll be back. Would you like me to give him a message?'

'No need,' said Bridget. 'If you give me his number, I can call him myself.'

The woman looked uncertain, but nodded. 'Would you mind waiting here for a moment?'

'Actually,' said Bridget, 'while we're here, we'd like to speak to you about the murder of Harriet Stevenson.'

'Of course,' said the woman. 'In that case, you'd better come inside.'

She opened the door wider to allow them into the broad, panelled entrance hall that was as large as any room in Bridget's own house. A number of doors opened off the hallway in various directions, and a wide wooden staircase led to an upstairs gallery. A stag's head mounted on a shield gazed down at them with sorrowful eyes from the wall opposite. The house smelled strongly of age and beeswax.

'I'm Josephine Daniels, by the way; the housekeeper here at the manor.' She seemed more assured now that they were inside the house. 'Please, come through to the kitchen.'

They followed her through an open door, along a second narrower passageway and into a large and airy kitchen with a flagstone floor. An array of brightly-polished copper saucepans hung on the wall above an enormous Aga, occupying an alcove where once there might have been a coal-burning stove, or perhaps an open log fire in centuries past. The window above the Belfast sink looked out onto a vegetable garden filled with neatly planted rows of runner beans and tomato plants. A greenhouse was visible in the distance.

Josephine invited them to sit at the large wooden table while she put the kettle on the hotplate. 'I'm not sure I'll be able to tell you much,' she said. 'But I'll do my best to help.'

'Thank you,' said Bridget.

Once the water had boiled, Josephine brought the tea to the table in a large, brown pot, and set out three cups, a bowl of sugar and a small jug of milk.

'Have you been the housekeeper at the manor for long?' asked Bridget.

'All my working life,' said Josephine as she poured the tea. 'Over fifty years. I started here when I was sixteen.'

'That is a long time. You must have known the late squire very well.' Bridget recalled that the vicar had mentioned the housekeeper being one of the few people who had attended the graveside.

'Yes,' said Josephine. 'He was already squire when I entered service at the manor. His father was killed in 1944 leading his men at the Battle of Normandy, so Mr Burton was just a child when he became lord of the manor.' She stirred two sugars into her tea and looked at Bridget with large, blue eyes that looked as if they might overflow at any minute. 'He was a dear man. I shall miss him very much.' She pulled a cotton handkerchief from the sleeve of her dress and dabbed at her nose, sniffing.

'I'm very sorry for your loss,' said Bridget.

'Thank you,' said Josephine, tucking the handkerchief back into her sleeve. Bridget noticed that she wore no wedding ring. 'He'd been ill for some time,' she continued. 'There was talk at one point of moving him to a hospice, but he was determined to die here, in his home. He loved this house. It meant everything to him. In the end, the young Mr Burton arranged for a nurse to come in, so the old squire got his wish.'

Bridget took a sip of her tea before moving on to the real reason for her visit. 'Can I ask how well you knew Harriet Stevenson?'

'Fairly well,' said Josephine. 'In a village this size, you get to know people soon enough,

71

although I wouldn't have described her as a friend. Our paths crossed mostly in the church, what with her being the churchwarden and me doing the flowers.'

'You arrange the flowers for the church?' said Bridget. 'I must say, there was a very fine display at the funeral yesterday.'

'Thank you. The old squire always insisted on providing flowers for the church. He was generous like that. He believed that the lord of the manor had a duty to give back to the community. It's my son, Shaun, who grows them. He's the gardener here.'

Bridget's thoughts darted back to the unfriendly welcome she had received from the man with the hedge trimmer. 'Was that Shaun I saw working outside when I arrived?'

'That's right,' said Josephine. 'He's a good boy, Shaun. You mustn't mind if he comes across as a bit rude, that's just his way. And we've all had such a terrible shock, what with the old squire's passing and then the business with Miss Stevenson yesterday. As you can imagine, we don't know whether we're coming or going at the moment.'

Bridget nodded. 'Can you think of any reason why anyone might have wanted to hurt Miss Stevenson?'

Josephine pursed her lips. 'I wouldn't describe her as a popular woman. She didn't go out of her way to be nice to people. But what you're really asking me is whether I know of someone who wanted her dead. The answer to that is no. Nothing like this has ever happened in the village in living memory. It's just not that kind of place.'

'No,' said Bridget. 'I'd already gathered that impression.'

Ffion's gaze was moving restlessly about the kitchen. 'Do you live here in the manor house?' she asked.

'That's right,' said Josephine. 'I've lived here all my adult life.'

'And your son lives here too?'

'Not in the house. He has a cottage in the grounds.'

'He lives there alone?'

Josephine hesitated for a moment before responding. 'Yes. He's always been unlucky in love.'

Bridget waited to see if Ffion had any further questions, but her DC seemed to have satisfied her curiosity for the time being.

'You attended the graveside for the burial, is that right?' Bridget asked Josephine.

The housekeeper nodded. 'Yes, it was just a small gathering – young Mr Burton and his wife and children, plus myself, Rosemary Carver, the nurse who cared for the old squire at the end, and Ms Symonds, the estate manager. The new vicar said some nice words.'

'What time did the burial finish?'

'I believe it was about ten past one or thereabouts.'

'And what did you do afterwards?'

'I came back here, to the manor house.'

'You didn't go to the pub for the wake?'

'No. I don't really like big crowds. Rosemary tried to persuade me to go, but I told her I wanted to be on my own, and she understood.'

'Where did Rosemary go after the burial? And the estate manager, Ms Symonds?'

'I expect they both went to the wake. But I can't say for sure.'

'What about your son, Shaun?' asked Ffion. 'Didn't he attend the funeral service?'

'Yes, of course he did. Nearly everyone in the village was there.'

'But he wasn't at the burial with the family and the other estate workers?'

'No,' said Josephine, her expression giving nothing away. 'I expect he took himself off to the pub. He doesn't get on well with formal gatherings. He's shy like that.'

'What about Tobias Burton and his family?' asked Bridget. 'Do you know what they did immediately after the burial?'

'I think they were planning to put in an appearance at the pub. They needed to show themselves at the wake for form's sake. Although' – Josephine dropped her voice even though there was no one else present in the room – 'between you and me, I think that Mrs Burton was keen to get the children back to London as quickly as possible. She didn't like them missing school.'

'She's already left the village?'

'Young Mr Burton drove her and the children to the train station later that same afternoon. He's staying on alone to sort out his father's affairs.'

'So,' said Ffion, 'did you see where Tobias Burton went immediately after the burial?'

'No,' said Josephine. 'I didn't see him myself. As I explained, I returned to the house alone.'

'When did you see him next?'

'It was after he returned from the station. That must have been about four o'clock.'

Ffion shot Bridget a meaningful glance across the kitchen table. It was obvious that her suspicions about Tobias Burton had not in any way been appeased by the housekeeper's testimonial.

'So,' said Bridget, 'apart from you and Tobias Burton, is anyone else living in the house at present?' The manor house seemed an enormous building to house just two residents.

'Shaun has his cottage in the grounds, of course. The nurse, Rosemary, has been living in for the past few months, but now that her work is done, she'll be leaving. Ms Symonds, the estate manager owns her own house in the village.'

'So once the nurse has gone and Mr Burton has returned to London, it'll just be you in the house?'

Josephine shook her head. 'No, I only stayed on this long for the sake of the old squire. Now that he's gone, my plan is to retire. I have some savings put aside. So I'll be moving out of the manor house and looking for a small place of my own to rent in the village.' She clasped her hands together. 'I'm not worried about my own future, but I do worry about Shaun.'

'Why is that?'

An anxious look clouded the housekeeper's face as if she wished she hadn't revealed so much. 'The old squire always believed in looking after his staff. Shaun's cottage on the estate came with his job. But if what they say is true, and the young squire is planning to turn this place into a hotel, I don't know what will happen to Shaun...' Her voice trailed away.

'A hotel would still need a gardener,' said Bridget. 'And in any case, I'm sure that there are plenty of people in this part of the world who would pay good money for someone with his skill and experience.' Her own sister, Vanessa, had a young chap who came in once a week to tackle the bigger jobs and there were many people in Oxfordshire with even larger gardens than Vanessa.

'Perhaps,' said Josephine doubtfully. 'But change is always difficult and not necessarily a good thing.'

'Is that what Harriet thought, too?' asked Ffion.

'Oh, yes,' said Josephine. 'Miss Stevenson was a great one for upholding traditions. She certainly didn't like the notion of turning this place into a hotel.'

'Did she ever express her objections to Tobias

Burton?'

'On more than one occasion, I believe,' said Josephine. 'But the young squire wasn't ever going to listen to an interfering old busybody like her. Let me get his number for you.' She rose to her feet and returned with a business card that had been pinned to a noticeboard on the wall. 'Here you are.' She passed the card to Ffion who added Tobias Burton's number to her phone.

Bridget thanked the housekeeper for her time, and followed her back through the two connecting hallways to the front door. This house really was a maze. She was about to leave when she heard heavy footsteps coming down the wooden stairs. A stout, middle-aged woman with a florid complexion was making her way laboriously down, lugging a hefty holdall. It banged against her leg with each step, hindering her progress. When she saw Bridget and Ffion, she stopped on the bottom step, and looked enquiringly at the housekeeper.

'Inspector Hart,' said Josephine Daniels, 'this is Rosemary Carver. She returned to Hambledon for the funeral and stayed here overnight to keep me company. Rosemary, these two ladies are detectives from Thames Valley Police.'

Rosemary's eyes widened at mention of the police. She lowered her bag to the floor and held out a pink hand. 'I expect you're here about that dreadful business with the churchwarden.' She put her other hand to her bosom and shook her head. 'Shocking. I could scarcely believe it. I said to Josephine, you're not safe anywhere these days. And to think that such a terrible thing could happen on the day of the old man's funeral, God rest his soul.'

'I hear that you cared for Henry Burton throughout his final illness,' said Bridget.

'I did,' said Rosemary. 'I was here for the last three weeks of his life, all told. He was in a poor way by then, but he still had his wits about him, at least when he wasn't doped up on painkillers, the poor lamb. We had some nice little chats, the old squire and me. Such a lovely man.'

'Did you look after him all by yourself?'

'That's right. I lived in, so that I was available around the clock if needed. That's the service my agency provides, you see. We give palliative care to people in their own homes at the end of their lives.' Her eyes wandered around the hallway. 'Although, I have to say, most of my patients don't live in such grand houses as this.'

'Were you with him when he died?' The nurse seemed quite chatty and Bridget hoped she might confirm that the old man had died of natural causes without her having to put the question so crudely. One suspicious death was enough to be going on with.

'We both were,' said Rosemary, taking hold of the housekeeper's hand and giving it a friendly squeeze. 'He died very peacefully in his sleep, I'm pleased to say. I always tell people that's the best way to go.'

Bridget tried to phrase her next question

carefully so as not to give offence. 'Do you often attend the funerals of patients who have passed away?'

'No, not usually. It might sound unfeeling, but in my line of work, you can't afford to get too attached to your patients. All of them die, I'm sorry to say. But I must admit that this case was special to me. I grew very fond of the old man, and Josephine and I have become good friends. I can tell you that it's been an absolute pleasure working here. Such a kind old gentleman and such a lovely house.' She gazed with wonder at the wood-panelled walls as if she still couldn't believe her good fortune at being sent here.

'You work for a private agency?' asked Bridget.

'Yes, *Oxford Angels* it's called. I used to work for the NHS, but you can't imagine how stressful it is working on the wards.' Her hand was back on her bosom, as if mention of the NHS was enough to bring on heart palpitations. 'We were always rushed off our feet. In the end, I couldn't stand it anymore so I signed up with *Oxford Angels* and I can honestly say that I never looked back.'

'I understand that you were present at the burial itself,' said Bridget. It seemed that a simple prompt was sufficient to get the nurse talking at length. Bridget wished that all her interviews with witnesses ran so smoothly.

'Yes,' said Rosemary. 'I wasn't sure if I ought to be there, since it was mainly for family and people who'd known the old squire for a long time, but Josephine insisted I should be there.' She glanced affectionately at the housekeeper. 'She said that I'd become as close to old Mr Burton as almost anyone. Although,' she added, 'I'm not sure that young Mr Burton saw things the same way. He didn't say anything, mind you, but I just got the impression he thought I should have minded my own business.'

'What did you do immediately after the burial?'

'Why, I walked back through the churchyard, looking at a few of the headstones – it's such a lovely old church, isn't it? – and then I made my way over to the pub on the other side of the village. The Eight Bells, I think it's called. They'd put on a good spread for the wake, I must say. All nice home-made sandwiches and cakes. I asked the landlady, Sue, for her recipe for the cream buns. I said to her, Sue, these are the nicest cream buns I've ever tasted. And I wasn't exaggerating.'

Before Bridget could ask her next question, Rosemary ploughed on, 'But listen to me rambling on about cream buns! You're here about the churchwarden and you'll be wanting to know if I saw anything suspicious. The answer is, no, I didn't see a thing. I can't imagine who might have committed such a terrible crime. It's such a friendly village. All I can think of is that someone from outside must have come here looking for mischief. That's what I think, anyway.'

'Thank you for that,' said Bridget. She handed Rosemary her card. 'Just in case anything occurs to you, you can call me on that number.'

'Of course.' Rosemary slipped the card into a pocket of her cardigan then turned to Josephine. 'I'll be in touch, I promise. We must get together for a nice cup of tea and a good gossip.' She gave her friend an affectionate hug and a peck on the cheek. 'But now I really must get back to my husband. He's been living on baked beans and toast all the time I've been away, the poor dear.' She picked up her holdall and bustled out of the house.

★

'Shall we take a stroll around the grounds?' said Bridget once they were outside.

'And see if we happen to bump into the friendly gardener?' said Ffion.

'Exactly,' said Bridget. 'Let's find out for ourselves if he's really the shy, misunderstood soul his mother would have us believe.'

'Or the ill-mannered oaf he appears to be,' concluded Ffion.

Shaun Daniels was no longer trimming the topiary at the front of the house, and so they explored further afield, passing deep herbaceous borders, a small circular rose garden, and an ornamental pond covered in water lilies. As they ventured further from the house, the garden became less formal. They crossed a wooded area planted with wildflowers between the trees, and a field where a single track had been cut through the long grass. Down by the river they found a single-storey stone cottage. The window frames were rotting, the paint flaking off, and a length of guttering hung loose, revealing a dark stain where rainwater had seeped deep into the stone wall. The grey, slate roof was covered in moss and missing a few tiles. The windows hadn't been cleaned in a long time. Bridget knocked on the wooden door but there was no answer. There was an old boathouse a short distance away, but the building was locked. Bridget peered through the cobweb-covered window, but there was nobody inside, and little sign that the place had been used for years. Next to the boathouse was a grass tennis court, which had long since been invaded by weeds.

'This place is enormous,' said Bridget. 'And rather neglected.'

'Over there,' said Ffion, pointing towards the far side of the house.

The gardener appeared to rise out of the ground. As they got closer, Bridget realised that he had emerged from an ice house, half buried underground, covered in a grassy mound. He was holding a rake. Maybe he used the old ice house for storing his tools, now that the invention of the fridge-freezer had rendered ice houses obsolete.

'Mr Daniels?' called Bridget.

'Yeah. What is it?' His tone was gruff and

defensive.

'I was wondering if we might have a quick word.'

'I daresay you could. But I might not have much to say to you.' He stood stock still, holding the rake aloft like a trident.

Bridget stopped a short distance away. Shaun Daniels cut a forbidding figure. He was a tall man, with muscular arms and dark unruly hair. His overalls were grubby, his hands and fingers blackened by soil, and he carried a smell of stale sweat. But there was something captivating about him too. A wide and heavy brow concealed sensitive eyes beneath a veil of rugged masculinity. A latter-day Heathcliff? If treated to a hot bath and a fresh set of clothes, he might easily be described as handsome.

'This garden is beautiful,' said Bridget truthfully. Her own plot, which was the size of a postage stamp compared to the grounds of Hambledon Manor, had long ago reverted to a state of wilderness and she had given up all hope of reclaiming it from nature.

Shaun acknowledged the compliment with a shrug of his broad shoulders.

Ffion gave no indication of having been charmed by his male good looks. 'We'd like to speak to you regarding the death of Harriet Stevenson,' she said.

The gardener scowled. 'I already spoke to one of your lot at the pub yesterday. And before you ask, yes, I was at the funeral and no, I didn't notice anything suspicious. I didn't kill Harriet Stevenson, and frankly I couldn't give a damn who did.'

'Well, thank you,' said Bridget. 'That's saved us the bother of asking you a whole lot of questions. But since we've come all this way, we have a few more.'

He grunted. 'Go on, then.'

'Perhaps you could begin by telling us about your work here at the manor house.'

'What's there to tell? I'm the gardener.'

'And what exactly does that entail?'

He sneered. 'I'd say gardening, mainly. I thought you lot were supposed to be detectives.'

'Mr Daniels, we can do this interview here or back at the station. It's up to you.'

He sighed. 'All right, then. I'm responsible for maintaining the grounds of the house. It's far too big a job for one person, as you can probably tell. In the old days, there would have been a head gardener and three or four juniors. Now it's just me. On top of that the old squire wanted me to look after the churchyard, cutting the grass, keeping the gravestones clear. Oh yes – and growing cut flowers for Sunday services too.' He scowled. 'And for all that he paid me a pittance.'

'We understand that you received free accommodation in addition to a salary,' said Ffion.

He tilted his head in the direction of the river. 'A draughty old cottage next to the boathouse, yeah. Cold in the winter; damp all year round. It didn't cost the old squire a penny.'

'You don't sound very grateful,' said Bridget. 'If you felt that way, perhaps you should have looked for another job.'

At that, the gardener fell silent. He turned and started walking round to the front of the house. Bridget hurried to keep up with him.

Suddenly, he stopped and turned around. 'The old squire wasn't bad. He was a gentleman, not like his son. But folk like that… they're so far removed from the likes of me, that there's no common ground.' He gestured towards the house and grounds with the rake. 'How can one person own so much when the rest of us are struggling to make ends meet? It wasn't easy for Mum bringing me up on her own here. We may have had a roof over our heads, and food on our plates, but we never had much money. Do you think I could afford to buy a place of my own around here? Now the new squire wants to turn this place into a posh hotel. Who knows if I'll have a job or even a home this time next week? It's just not right.'

'Have you spoken to Tobias Burton about his plans?'

'He never tells me anything,' said Shaun. 'People like that never do. They don't need to.'

'Can you tell us about your movements on the day of the funeral?' asked Bridget, keen to move on from what appeared to be Shaun Daniels's favourite subject: the haves and have-nots.

'Not much to say. I put my best suit on and

showed my face at the church. Then I spent the rest of the day at the pub.'

'You didn't attend the burial, then?'

He showed Bridget his soiled fingers. 'I see enough dirt every day of the week. I don't need to watch someone being put in the ground.'

'I thought you might have wanted to support your mother, since you obviously care for her a lot. And since she thinks so highly of you.'

He winced, and Bridget guessed that she'd hit home. Shaun Daniels wasn't quite the uncaring oaf he pretended to be. He clearly felt a strong bond of loyalty to his mother, even if he feigned indifference to his former employer.

'Listen,' he said, 'Henry Burton was my landlord as well as my employer. He wasn't a bad one, and I respected the old squire. But he was never my friend. How could you ever be friends with someone like that? So I paid my respects to him in the way I do best... with a pint of ale in my hand.' He brandished the rake tightly in his large fist. 'Now, if you don't mind, I've got work to be getting on with.'

They had arrived back at the topiary at the front of the house, and Shaun started to rake up the hedge trimmings from the lawn. Bridget left him to it and returned to the car.

CHAPTER 9

Deep underground, in the tunnel that connected the Radcliffe Camera to the Old Bodleian Library, Amy Bagot had murder on her mind.

She liked it down here, far away from the hustle and bustle of Oxford's busy streets. The old Underground Bookstore, or "stacks", where once upon a time only library assistants had been granted access, and from which books had been transported up to the reading rooms on a clanking conveyor system dating from the 1930s, had been refurbished in recent years and turned into a modern study space with comfy chairs and Wi-Fi. The tourists ambling around Radcliffe Square, gazing skywards at the dome of the Camera or the spire of St Mary's, had no inkling of the clandestine world hidden beneath the cobblestones.

As she wheeled a trolley of books back to the shelves, she pondered the events of the day before. Had the murder been committed by someone in the village? As far as she knew, no one had seen a stranger hanging around. Most people claimed to have been in the pub at the time the murder had taken place. That left the people at the graveside. Could one of them have done it? It was well known that Henry Burton's son had a good reason for disliking the churchwarden and wanting her out of the way, and this was by far the most popular theory doing the rounds of the Eight Bells. It was frustrating to think that she had been ringing in the church tower just a short distance away from where the attack took place. A murder had been committed almost beneath her feet!

Amy wondered what Jake was doing right now. Was he speaking to people in the village? Had the police made any breakthroughs yet? What about the forensic evidence from the crime scene? She was desperate for news but resisted the urge to text him. He had told her that he wouldn't be able to discuss any details of the investigation with her. No, it was no good speculating. She needed to focus on her work.

She picked up the first book on her trolley, checked the classification details on the spine, and searched for the book's home on the shelf. It was important to be diligent when shelving books. An incorrectly shelved book was as good as missing.

'Amy, there you are.'

She turned to see her colleague, Evan, approaching. A skinny, bookish young man with a pronounced stoop and a pallid complexion, he'd asked her out once and she'd had to let him down gently. She didn't like hurting people, but he really wasn't her type. Now she tended to avoid him. 'What is it?' she asked.

'The Librarian wants to see you.'

'What about?' The Librarian was the most senior administrator at the Bodleian Library, in charge of the Subject librarians, and all the junior staff like Amy herself. She didn't see much of him on a day-to-day basis. She was too far down the pecking order.

'He didn't say. But he was looking pretty pleased about something.'

Amy's interest was piqued. But she couldn't just abandon her trolley of unshelved books.

'I'll put these back for you,' said Evan. 'You go and see what he wants.'

Amy gave him a grateful smile – she really must find a way to be kinder to Evan without giving him false hope that they could ever be anything more than colleagues and friends – and made her way up to the Librarian's office in the Old Bodleian.

'You wanted to see me, sir?' she said when she had knocked and been summoned into the sanctuary of his office.

'Ah, yes, Miss Bagot, do take a seat.'

A genial man in his late fifties, Professor Patrick Danvers had been appointed Bodley's Librarian a few years back. As the man ultimately responsible for the storage and preservation of over twelve million printed items, including maps and documents dating back a millennium or more, he was very highly regarded by his colleagues, and held in awe by Amy herself. She waited for him to explain why he had asked to see her.

He rubbed his long nose and leaned back in his chair. 'You live in Hambledon-on-Thames, is that right?'

'Yes, sir. My parents run the village pub.' She hoped he hadn't asked her here simply to enquire about the quality of the beer, or to make a reservation.

'Excellent. Then I have just the job for you. I think you'll enjoy it, and it will help to develop your skills.'

'Sir?'

'I've been contacted by a firm of solicitors in Oxford handling the estate of the late Henry Burton. I expect that you knew him, coming from the village as you do?'

'Yes!' said Amy. 'I was in the band of bellringers at his funeral.'

Danvers looked impressed. 'A woman of many talents, I see. Well, it appears that Henry Burton has left his entire collection of books to the Library. I don't know exactly what the collection contains, but I understand that there are around a thousand titles, many of them first editions. It seems that Mr Burton wanted the collection to be preserved for posterity. I've arranged for a team to go over to the manor house tomorrow and start packing up and transporting the books back here. Your job will be to supervise the work and then take charge of cataloguing the books.

Do you think that's something you'd enjoy doing?'

'Absolutely,' said Amy, beaming. 'It would be a pleasure.'

'Splendid. In that case, don't bother coming into Oxford tomorrow. Go straight to the manor house and meet the chaps there. I've already spoken to the housekeeper and told her to expect you.'

'Thank you so much.'

Amy returned underground feeling that life couldn't possibly get any more exciting. Not only had the Librarian given her a special assignment, but she would have an opportunity to snoop around inside the manor house and ask a few questions of the people who lived and worked there. There was a real chance she might pick up a clue that could solve the murder.

★

'I think we deserve something to eat after all that hard work,' said Ryan, pushing open the door of the Eight Bells and striding up to the bar. He picked up a copy of the menu and turned straight to the burger section.

Jake wasn't about to argue. After a long morning working their way around the village, talking to as many people as possible, he was ravenous. And he could vouch from personal experience that Robert and Sue Bagot did the best burgers in Oxfordshire.

'I'll have a cheese and bacon burger with chips, no salad, please,' said Ryan. 'And a couple of extra portions of ketchup.'

'Make that two,' said Jake.

'Anything to drink?' asked Robert, making a note of their food order.

'Just a couple of Cokes,' said Jake. The selection of beers at the Eight Bells was extensive, but there was still an entire afternoon of work to be done, and it was important to keep a clear head.

'Right you are.' Robert filled a couple of pint glasses with Coke from the tap. 'Drinks are on the house.'

'Cheers,' said Jake, picking his up and taking a large mouthful. 'Much appreciated.'

'So how are you getting on?' asked the publican. 'Any breakthroughs yet?'

'I'm afraid that we can't really discuss it, Robert,' said Jake, although the fact of the matter was that there was very little to discuss. No one they had spoken to so far had observed anything of note.

Robert nodded understandingly. 'I was at the funeral myself, and I've been over it in my mind a hundred times, but I can honestly say that I didn't notice anything suspicious. No strangers present, or anything like that. Doesn't mean there wasn't someone there, of course. There are plenty of corners in the churchyard where you could hide behind a gravestone or a hedge. But that seems a bit far-fetched.'

'What are the gossips saying in the pub?'

'All manner of things,' said Robert, 'but of course the main subject is the rumour about Tobias Burton wanting to turn the manor house into a hotel.' He leaned his elbows on the bar and dropped his voice. 'It had already caused a schism before the murder. Harriet Stevenson was leading the charge for the opposition, and she had a lot of support on her side. People don't like change. They like things to stay the way they've always been, especially in a place like this. But some of the younger people, and by "younger" I mean those under fifty, think it could be good for the village. More job opportunities. Put us on the map, so to speak.'

'What do you think?' asked Jake.

The publican tapped his nose and leaned conspiratorially across the bar. 'One thing you learn very quickly in this trade is to keep your opinions to yourself. I don't want to alienate half of my customers by taking one side or the other. But between you, me and the gatepost, I'm not all that keen on the idea of a fancy hotel. I was no fan of Harriet Stevenson, but on that issue, she had a point.'

The pub was starting to fill up and Robert needed to serve some more of his customers. 'Sue will bring your food over to your table when it's ready,' he told the two detectives. 'Tell you what, if you want to find out more about life in the village, you should speak to Maurice.' He pointed out a table by the fireplace where an elderly gentleman with a high bald forehead and a mane of feathery white hair was sitting with a pint and the *Times* crossword. The red silk cravat he wore at his craggy neck, teamed with a pristine white shirt and tweed jacket, gave him a dapper, jaunty look. His intelligent, darting eyes behind silver-framed spectacles seemed to belie his years. 'Maurice Fairweather,' explained the publican, 'is our local historian. He's written a book all about the history of the village. There isn't much that's gone on in Hambledon in the past few hundred years that Maurice doesn't know about.'

'I hope that our enquiries won't have to go back quite that far,' said Ryan, but he and Jake took their drinks over to the table where Maurice was sitting. The old man looked up as they approached and studied them through his thick lenses.

'Detective Sergeant Jake Derwent,' said Jake, 'and...'

'DS Ryan Hooper,' said Ryan. 'Mind if we join you, mate?'

'*Enchanté*,' said Maurice, extending a bony hand with long, thin fingers. His smile revealed long, yellowing teeth. 'So you're the great detectives, are you?'

'We're part of the team,' said Jake, not sure if the old man was making fun of them.

'Hmm, let's see what you're made of.' He ran a manicured fingernail down the list of crossword clues. 'Ah yes, try this one. Likelihood of person catching criminal? Eight, six.'

Jake scratched his head. He'd never been any good at crosswords. If Maurice expected them to get this right before he was willing to share any information with them, then there was no hope.

'Sporting chance,' said Ryan. Jake looked at him in astonishment.

'Very good, young man,' said Maurice with an approving nod. He folded his newspaper away so that there was space for them to put their drinks down.

Sue arrived then with their food before Jake could ask Ryan how he'd worked out the crossword clue. It was probably for the best – he didn't want to look stupid in front of Maurice. His stomach rumbled at the sight and smell of the thick juicy burgers topped with cheese and bacon and a generous side portion of hand-cut chips. It seemed a bit rude to be eating their food at Maurice Fairweather's table, but Ryan was already chomping away and the old man didn't seem to mind. In fact, he looked as if he relished the opportunity for a chat.

'Of course,' said Maurice, 'this isn't the first murder to have taken place in St Michael and All Angels.'

Jake's ears pricked up at the news. Why hadn't he heard about this? Maybe it had happened before he'd moved to Oxford. He looked to Ryan, who shook his head, equally baffled.

Maurice's eyes twinkled with amusement. 'It was in 1555. I take it you know what happened in Oxford that year?'

Jake wished that Maurice Fairweather would stop testing them with his cryptic clues and knowledge of history. But Ryan seemed willing to play along.

'Let's see,' he said between mouthfuls of burger and chips, '1555… that would be the time of the Tudors. Am I right in thinking that Bloody Mary was on the throne?'

'Go on,' said Maurice, clearly enjoying himself.

'And Mary, as the daughter of Catherine of Aragon, was a staunch Catholic. So, was 1555 the year that the Oxford martyrs were burnt at the stake?'

'Very good.' Maurice Fairweather held up his pint in a toast. '"*Be of good comfort Master Ridley, and play the man. We shall this day light such a candle by God's grace in England, as I trust shall never be put out.*"

Jake stared at him, mystified. Between Ryan and Maurice, he was beginning to feel like a complete dunce.

'Those were the last words of Hugh Latimer to Nicholas Ridley before they were burned as heretics outside Balliol College,' explained the amateur historian. He pointed to Ryan, and said, 'That one's smarter than he looks.'

'I know,' said Jake miserably. He had long held suspicions that Ryan's outwardly blokeish demeanour was just a front. Maybe he spent his evenings secretly reading history books.

'Hugh Latimer, Bishop of Worcester, and Nicholas Ridley, Bishop of London, were martyred in 1555 for their Protestant teachings,' explained Maurice. 'The following year, Thomas Cranmer, the Archbishop of Canterbury, suffered the same fate. Cranmer tried to wriggle out of it by recanting his beliefs, but he'd already cooked his own goose by helping Henry VIII obtain an annulment from Mary's mother, Catherine of Aragon. So in the end he withdrew his recantations and died a martyr to Anglicanism.'

'And what does all this have to do with Hambledon-on-Thames?' asked Jake.

'I'm coming to that,' said Maurice, pausing to take a sip of his pint. He clearly didn't like to rush his stories. 'Now, the lord of Hambledon Manor at that time was a man called Edmund Burton. No doubt you'll have noticed the effigies of him and his wife, Ellen, in the north transept of the church.'

'Er, yes,' said Jake who had a vague recollection of a tomb with figures lying on top, although to be fair he'd been more focused on the flesh-and-blood corpse lying on the ground than on stone effigies hundreds of years old.

'Edmund Burton was a supporter of the English Reformation. A dangerous position to hold when Protestants were being burnt at the stake just up the road in Oxford. Then one dark night in November 1555, just a month after Latimer and Ridley had gone up in flames, the priest of Hambledon-on-Thames was found battered to death in almost exactly the same spot as the churchwarden was killed yesterday. History always repeats itself.'

'But these two deaths aren't in any way connected,' protested Jake. 'They're hundreds of years apart, and religious persecution is a thing of the past.'

'Is it?' said Maurice giving him a sharp look. 'I'm not so sure. Don't you think the location of the two murders may be more than a coincidence?'

Jake remained silent, not willing to rise to the bait, but Ryan appeared genuinely interested in Maurice's story. 'So, this Edmund Burton must have been quite a big cheese if he's got his own effigy in the church?'

'He was precisely that, as you so aptly put it,' said Maurice with a throaty chuckle. 'And fortunately, he was clever enough to avoid religious persecution and lived on to a ripe old age. In fact, it was Edmund who paid for the construction of the church tower, and oversaw the installation of the bells there in the year 1570.'

'My girlfriend is one of the bellringers,' said Jake, relieved to be able to make a pertinent contribution to the conversation.

'Young Amy Bagot,' said Maurice, making Jake wonder just how much the canny old man knew about his personal life. 'Change ringing is a long-standing tradition in the village, and has always been supported by the Burton family.'

'What is this mysterious change ringing I keep hearing about?' asked Ryan, making Jake pleased to discover that Ryan didn't know everything.

'It's a peculiarly English tradition,' said Maurice, 'although it also takes place in Wales, and to a much lesser extent in other English-speaking parts of the world. You see, unlike the bells that are found in churches in other European countries, English bells swing full-circle, or mouth-up to mouth-up. This means that the timing of the bells can be controlled with a high degree of accuracy, so they can be rung in order. In change ringing, the bells are sounded in successive rows in which every bell strikes once, and the order of the bells changes between consecutive rows, according to the method employed.'

'The methods have names like Plain Hunt or Oxford Bob Triples,' said Jake, doing his best to recall what Amy had told him.

'That's right,' said Maurice approvingly, 'although modern methods can be far more complicated, like Spliced Surprise Major or Stedman Sextuples. The earliest books on change ringing were published in the seventeenth century, most famously Duckworth's *Tintinnalogia* in 1668, and Stedman's *Campanalogia* in 1677. Henry Burton's grandfather, Francis, was a keen ringer and a collector of books on the subject. He also paid for the replacement of the church organ in 1909.

And of course it was the late Henry Burton himself who paid for the bells to be refurbished in 2000. It's a family tradition.'

Jake decided to use this mention of Henry Burton to try and steer the conversation back to the present day. 'I take it that you were at the funeral yesterday?'

'Naturally.' Maurice gave him a sharp look. 'Are you about to ask me to provide you with an alibi for the time of the murder?'

'We're asking everyone in the village where they were at that time,' said Ryan.

'Yes,' said Maurice, nodding. 'Of course you are. Well, I was at the funeral along with everyone else. I wouldn't want to miss an occasion like that. In fact, as funerals go, it was one of the best I've been to. I just hope that when it's my turn the organist doesn't drag the hymns so badly.'

It occurred to Jake that Maurice Fairweather was likely to have observed everything that went on at the funeral service. If anything unusual had happened, he would surely have noticed. 'Did you notice anything out of the ordinary at the funeral, sir?'

'Let me see,' said Maurice. 'Harriet Stevenson was bossing everyone around, so nothing remotely unusual there. I recall her telling Shaun Daniels, Henry's gardener, to turn his phone off. I noticed the publican slipping away early during the last hymn hoping that no one would notice. As for Tobias Burton, well I don't think he looked too upset that his old man was dead. And then, of course, a quarter peal was rung to mark the end of the service. That was most unusual. I don't suppose it's likely to be repeated when I pass on.'

Jake glared at the old man in annoyance. Far from providing insight into the murder, it seemed that Maurice was intent simply on amusing himself at Jake's expense.

'Oh, come now,' said Maurice when he caught Jake's expression. 'Did you expect me to reveal that I'd seen a masked man lurking outside the church, or overheard a whispered conversation between Harriet Stevenson and her attacker? You're going to have to work harder to solve the case than that.'

'Is there anything useful you can tell us, sir?' asked Jake. 'What about the schism in the village between those for and against the proposed plans for the manor house?'

'Rumoured plans, you mean? Well, I think that's an obvious line of enquiry. Personally, I hope that Tobias gets his way. Who needs a manor house in this day and age? A luxury hotel would be far more beneficial for the future of the village.'

'Really?' said Jake, surprised by Maurice's declaration. 'I'd have thought that you'd be more wedded to the past.'

'On the contrary,' said Maurice. 'History is fascinating, but it's change that makes it so interesting. Woe betide the man, or woman for

CHAPTER 10

Bridget's interviews with Josephine Daniels, her son, Shaun, and the nurse Rosemary Carver, had given her some valuable insight into the inner workings of the manor house and the various tensions at play there, but she still hadn't managed to speak to the man at the very heart of the matter – Tobias Burton, the young squire. After leaving the grounds of the manor house, she dialled the number that the housekeeper had given her.

The voice that answered was deep and resonant, and managed to convey a strong note of irritation in just two words. 'Yes, hello?'

'Mr Tobias Burton?'

'Speaking. Who is this?'

'Detective Inspector Bridget Hart from Thames Valley Police. I was given your number by Josephine Daniels. I'd like to speak to you about the death of Harriet Stevenson.'

'Look,' said Tobias, 'I'm rather busy right now. I'm in a meeting with my architect and then I have an important appointment with my solicitor.'

'Mr Burton, I'm heading an investigation into a murder, and I need to speak to you as a matter of urgency. I'm currently at the manor house, but I'm willing to come to you if that will help.'

A short silence followed. Then, 'Yes, all right. I'll be at Quod on the High Street in forty minutes. Do you know it?'

'I know it,' said Bridget. 'That will be perfect.'

Ffion gave her a wry smile as she ended the call. 'He seemed reluctant to speak to you.'

'I can't imagine why,' said Bridget. 'Lunch at Quod sounds like a lovely way to pass the time. Are you hungry?'

They drove into central Oxford and Bridget managed to squeeze the Mini into a parking space on St Giles' not far from Martyrs' Memorial, the stone monument dedicated to the memory of Latimer, Ridley and Cranmer. She glanced up at the forbidding Gothic spire as she passed, and shuddered briefly at the thought that people had been consumed by flames close to this very spot.

From there it was only a short walk to the stylish restaurant situated on the ground floor of the Old Bank Hotel. There was no one of Tobias Burton's description present when they arrived so Bridget selected a table with a good view of the door and ordered sparkling mineral water for herself and Ffion.

Ten minutes later the door opened and a tall, dark-haired man in a business suit strode in and looked around expectantly. He was accompanied by a woman with outsized sunglasses perched on the top of her head. The man caught Bridget's eye and came over.

'Detective Inspector Hart?'

Bridget stood and shook his hand. 'Thank you for making time to see me, Mr Burton. This is my colleague Detective Constable Ffion Hughes.'

'And this is Lindsey Symonds, my estate manager.'

The woman, who was dressed in a white silk blouse and smart trousers with a Dior handbag over her shoulder, offered Bridget a cool handshake. 'Pleased to meet you, Inspector.'

'Can I buy you lunch?' asked Tobias, snapping his fingers to summon a waiter to the table. 'It'll have to be quick, I'm afraid. As I explained, I have a meeting with my solicitor.'

'That would be very nice.' After perusing the menu and placing her order – a light dish of cod fillet with roast fennel – Bridget enquired after the meeting with the architect.

'Excellent meeting,' said Tobias. 'Things are really starting to move forwards, at last.'

'You're referring to your plans to redevelop Hambledon Manor into a hotel?'

'You've heard about that?' Tobias gave her an approving nod. 'It's what the place needs. What else would I do with a house that size? I already have a place in London. My wife doesn't want to move out to the sticks and, quite frankly, neither do I. I'm investing a lot of money into this project. All the rooms will be individually furnished to the highest specification and there will be a spa facility in the grounds. A hotel of that quality will provide a real boost to such a sleepy little village.' As he spoke, Tobias fixed her with his deep-set eyes. He had a natural charisma, and a charm that Bridget found compelling. It was easy to be persuaded that his plans were just what Hambledon needed.

'Maybe some people enjoy living in a sleepy little village,' said Ffion, drumming her green-painted fingernails on the tabletop. 'Does everyone in the village support your plans?'

Tobias looked irritated at the interruption. 'I haven't made my plans public yet, so I couldn't possibly comment.'

'Is it true that Harriet Stevenson had called a meeting to gather opposition to the proposed hotel?' persisted Ffion.

'As I have already stressed,' said Tobias, 'no hotel has yet been proposed.'

'And yet a meeting in the village hall was called to discuss the matter. If Harriet Stevenson hadn't been killed, that meeting would have gone ahead tomorrow evening.'

Now the estate manager spoke up. 'Harriet Stevenson didn't know when to leave well alone. What business was it of hers to interfere in the plans of the estate?'

'As chair of the parish council,' said Bridget, 'I expect she thought that she had a duty to act in the best interests of the village.'

Tobias waved away the suggestion with a hand. 'As I have repeatedly said, no plans have been published yet. When they're finalised, we'll submit an application through the relevant planning process. Everything will be above board. I don't believe in taking shortcuts.'

The food arrived, and Tobias began to attack his plate of wild salmon and asparagus. He squeezed lemon over the fish and set to work, a scowl on his face.

Bridget allowed him to eat for a while before continuing with her questions. 'Perhaps I could ask about your dealings with Miss Stevenson?'

'I didn't have any,' said Tobias flatly, a morsel of pink salmon impaled on his fork. 'She only moved to Hambledon about five years ago, by which time I'd long been in London. I've certainly not had any "dealings" with her, as you so coyly phrased it. In fact, I barely ever met the woman.'

'When did you last meet her?'

'I spoke to her very briefly after the funeral service in the church. She offered me her condolences, which I accepted.'

'I see,' said Bridget. 'Now, if you don't mind, I have some questions for Ms Symonds.'

Lindsey Symonds gave Bridget an appraising look. 'Of course. Anything I can do to assist the investigation.'

'Can you tell me how long you've been the estate manager at Hambledon Manor?'

'I started working for Mr Burton senior just

over ten years ago.'

'You must have come to know him very well over that period.'

'Yes, we had a close working relationship.'

'And what exactly are your responsibilities as estate manager?'

'I supervise the staff, manage the tenant farmer, oversee maintenance of the property, whatever is required. It's a very varied role, and that's what attracted me to it.'

'You live in the village?'

'Yes. I have a house there.'

'You live alone?'

'I'm unmarried, so yes.'

'Did you ever come into contact with Harriet Stevenson through your work?'

The estate manager forced her lips into a thin smile. 'I had dealings with her from time to time in her role as chair of the parish council.'

'And how would you characterise your relationship?'

'We were civil to each other.'

'But you didn't particularly like her?'

'It wasn't my job to like her. My duty is to represent the interests of the estate.'

'And those interests didn't always align with those of Miss Stevenson?'

'I didn't say that.'

'What would you say, then?'

'I'd say that we maintained a professional distance, and that there was no acrimony in our dealings.'

'Thank you very much for your assistance, Ms Symonds.' Bridget turned her attention back to Tobias, who was still munching away at his salmon. 'Now, if you don't mind, Mr Burton, I'd like to ask you some questions about the events of yesterday. Firstly, let me say how sorry I am for your loss.'

He gave her a curt nod. 'Thank you.'

'Could you tell me about your movements during and after the burial service?'

He set down his knife and fork and took a sip of mineral water. 'Once the church service ended, my family and I accompanied the vicar out to the churchyard. The Burtons have a family plot there. A few other mourners also came to see my father buried.'

'Did that include you, Ms Symonds?' Bridget asked the estate manager.

'Yes,' she replied. 'As well as Josephine Daniels, Mr Burton's housekeeper, and also the nurse who cared for old Mr Burton at the end of his life.'

'Rosemary Carver?'

'Yes.'

'Thank you. Do go on, Mr Burton.'

'The vicar's new to the village,' said Tobias. 'A young man – well-meaning of course – but he didn't really know my father. I told him what to say during the service. He officiated at the burial, and then handed over to the sexton.'

'At what time did the burial finish?'

'It didn't take very long. I'd say it was done by

ten past one.'

'And then what happened?'

'What do you mean?' asked Tobias. 'There was nothing more.'

'I mean,' said Bridget, 'what did you do immediately after the burial?'

For the first time during the conversation, a dangerous glint appeared in Tobias Burton's eye, and Bridget caught a glimpse of the powerful man who had built a large and successful business, and who was clearly used to getting his own way. 'You're asking me to account for my movements at the time of the murder?' he asked.

'We haven't yet pinned down precisely when the attack on Miss Stevenson took place,' said Bridget calmly. 'I would simply like to establish what you did after leaving the graveside.'

Tobias stabbed a spear of asparagus with his fork and popped it into his mouth, chewing it thoughtfully. 'My father and I didn't enjoy a very close relationship,' he said at last. 'No doubt everyone that you speak to will tell you that he was a fine old gentleman, and of course that's true. He was a man of great dignity, and highly respected within the community. But you should understand that a man of his generation and of his social class was constrained by a great weight of convention. He didn't find it easy to express affection or love, especially not to those closest to him. As a child, he was a distant figure to me, and then when my mother died...'

He paused for a moment, as if lost in memories, his gaze distant. 'In recent years, we didn't see a lot of each other. I believe that we both found it easier that way. And in his final days and weeks, he was insensible much of the time. We didn't get a chance to say goodbye. And so that's what I did after the burial. I lingered at the graveside, and bade my farewells.'

His eyes refocused on Bridget, and he seemed to snap back to the present. 'Is that what you wanted to know?'

'Thank you very much,' said Bridget. 'I know that this must be difficult for you.'

Ffion leaned forward. 'Where did you go after you'd finished bidding farewell to your father?'

Now his eyes flashed with undisguised anger. 'Really, Constable, I'm finding your questions rather hostile. If you must know, I took a stroll around the churchyard to clear my head.'

'Did you go back inside the church?'

'No.'

'Can anyone confirm that?'

'How should I know?' he demanded. 'It's your job to find out who saw what.'

'Actually,' said Lindsey Symonds, 'I can confirm that what Mr Burton has told you is true. I was standing under the lychgate at the time, taking a call on my phone. I saw Tobias walking around the churchyard. He looked as if he wanted to be left alone, and so I kept my distance. After I'd finished my call, he joined me at the gate and we walked together to the pub

111

where his wife and children were waiting for him.'

'Thank you, Ms Symonds,' said Bridget. 'That's very helpful.'

'Good,' said Tobias. 'Excellent.' He snapped his fingers once more to attract the attention of the waiter. 'If we're finished here, I'll get the bill and we can move on.'

'Thank you for lunch,' said Bridget. 'But before we go, could I just ask about your plans for the next few days?'

'I'll be rather busy, actually. I have a lot to do, settling my father's will, making arrangements for the house, and so on.'

'So you'll be staying in the manor house?
'Yes.'

Bridget smiled and rose from her seat. 'Thank you, Mr Burton. If you do decide to leave, please could you let me know? Just in case we need to speak to you again.'

★

'I'm home, love.' Rosemary Carver pushed open the front door of her pebble-dash semi in Cowley, sweeping aside a pile of letters and fliers that Simon hadn't got round to picking up. She dumped her holdall on the floor and scooped up the mail. It was the usual junk: fliers from pizza delivery companies; a window cleaner touting for business; something from the council about rubbish collections. And the inevitable demand for money – this time from the electricity company. Her sister, Maureen, had told her you were supposed to switch suppliers to keep your costs down, but Rosemary never had time for things like that and wouldn't have known where to start. They were probably paying over the odds for their electricity and no doubt their gas, too. No wonder they never had enough cash to make ends meet.

She could hear the sound of the telly coming from the sitting room. That was all Simon did these days. Watch telly, and eat and drink.

She usually felt happy to be back home, but this time the walls of the small house seemed to close in around her. She supposed it was only natural, after the enormousness of Hambledon Manor.

For the first few days in the manor house, she hadn't been able to get over the vastness of the rooms, the sweeping staircase and the wide first-floor landing. She'd been tickled pink with the "olde world" charm of the place – all those exposed oak beams, the Flemish stained glass and fancy wood panelling – "linenfold panelling" Josephine, the housekeeper, had told her it was called – and in her quieter moments she had imagined herself in one of those period dramas on the telly, all dressed up in silk and lace. But then she'd grown accustomed to her new surroundings, and the manor house had started to feel like home.

She'd been kidding herself, of course. The

likes of Rosemary Carver didn't belong in such a grand place. Sooner or later, she'd known she'd have to return home, to a dilapidated house, and a useless husband.

Josephine had always made her welcome in the kitchen, setting the kettle to boil on the enormous Aga and chatting to her over a cup of tea and a slice of homemade cake. And as Rosemary had grown used to the manor house, she had started to explore. Once, out of sheer curiosity, she'd opened a panelled door and almost fallen down a hidden spiral staircase. Her imagination had gone into overdrive. Maybe one of Henry Burton's ancestors had kept a secret mistress? She imagined the scarlet woman creeping up and down the stairs in the middle of the night. Next to the hidden staircase, behind another door disguised as panelling, was a secret cubby hole. She wondered what had been kept in there? Jewels, perhaps. Or gold? But Josephine had explained to her that the secret cupboard had been a priest hole – a place where the priest from the nearby church could hide from persecution in days gone by – and that the staircase had been a way for the lord of the manor to escape if soldiers came to arrest him. Rosemary didn't care much for that story. She preferred her own, more romantic, theories involving secret lovers and clandestine assignations. She wondered what Henry Burton had been like in his younger days. She could see from the old photographs dotted around the house that he had been a good-looking man. But as a nurse it was her fate to tend to people when they were old and dying, ravaged by disease, and shadows of their former selves.

Rather like her own husband.

She went through to the sitting room where Simon was sitting on the sofa watching some nonsense about truck drivers in America. The sports pages of the *Daily Mail* lay open on his lap. On the floor was a half-drunk mug of tea and a plate covered in crumbs. At least he'd managed to feed himself whilst she'd been away.

'You're back.' He muted the telly and struggled to rise to his feet. 'I was just going to do the washing up.'

'Don't worry,' said Rosemary. 'I'll sort it out and make us both a fresh cuppa.'

A look of relief spread over his face. 'Thanks, love.'

She took the dirty dishes through to the kitchen and added them to the rest of the unwashed plates piled in the sink. Simon didn't mean to be lazy, but he'd been off work ever since he fell off a ladder and hurt his back ten months ago. Now all movement was difficult for him, and there was no sign of him getting any better. She worried about him all the time when she was away from home, but what could she do? She had to go out to work, otherwise they would sink beneath a mountain of debt.

But there was a glimmer of hope on the horizon. She hadn't told Simon yet – she'd keep it to herself for a little while longer – but maybe she wouldn't need to work quite such long hours in the future.

She returned to the sitting room with two fresh mugs of tea and joined him on the sofa.

'I'm glad you're back,' he said, reaching across and giving her hand a squeeze. 'I missed you.'

'I missed you too. And I'm glad to get away from that place. That murder was a nasty business, and right after the funeral, too.'

'It must have been a dreadful shock,' he said. 'Did the police want to talk to you?'

Rosemary felt her heart begin to beat faster at the mention of the police. 'They did,' she said. 'I met the inspector in charge of the investigation this morning. I couldn't tell her anything, of course.'

'Of course not.'

The deliberate lie stuck in her throat and made her heart beat even harder. Her hand strayed to her cardigan pocket where she fingered the card that Detective Inspector Bridget Hart had given her. What to do about it? She pushed the thought aside. She'd deal with it later.

CHAPTER 11

'Everything in this room can be auctioned off,' said Tobias. 'There's nothing here I want to keep.' He gestured dismissively to a Regency mahogany side table and a nineteenth-century collector's cabinet with a dozen shallow drawers in which a Victorian ancestor of Henry Burton had carefully stored and catalogued hundreds of fossils, moths and butterflies.

Josephine noted the new squire's wishes in a jotter, adding these items to the growing list that already included a Victorian walnut extending dining table, six Edwardian dining chairs and a seventeenth-century French armoire, not to mention countless Persian rugs and paintings of landscapes and horses. Needless to say, the stag's head in the hallway would be going too.

For the past hour Josephine had accompanied Tobias on a tour of the house in which he had casually written off many items of great beauty that she had lovingly cared for over the years, using only the best beeswax to keep the surfaces blemish-free. Tobias, it seemed, was only interested in the monetary worth of each piece and how much it would fetch at auction. He had no appreciation of an item's history, or its association to the family going back generations. What a stark contrast to his father who had loved art for art's sake and who had cherished these antique pieces of furniture for what they represented – continuity, an unbroken chain to the past. Tobias's new hotel, as he'd made abundantly clear, was going to be furnished with the latest in contemporary furniture. He'd mentioned the name of a designer in London who was going to oversee a complete refurbishment of the manor house. Out with the old, in with the new. That was Tobias Burton's motto.

From the drawing room they moved on to the library. Henry Burton had loved collecting old books and had spent a lot of time in here. Leather-bound volumes with spines lettered in gold-leaf filled the glazed bookshelves. Once a month, Josephine had brushed a feather duster over the tops of the books, taking care not to damage anything.

'This lot's all going to the Bodleian Library,' said Tobias.

'Yes, I spoke to the Librarian this morning. They're sending a team round tomorrow.'

Tobias appeared not to be listening. 'Papa specified it in his will, would you believe it?' He made the idea sound completely hare-brained, the dying wish of a man who wasn't quite right in the head. Most probably he was thinking about the monetary value of the books, many of which were rare first editions and which could have fetched a tidy sum under the auctioneer's hammer.

'At least the collection won't be broken up,' said Josephine. She too was sorry to see the books go, but the Bodleian was probably the best place for them.

'Good, well I think that's everything for now.' Tobias looked at his watch, clearly eager to get away. He was always rushing off. He never took the time to talk properly, had never once asked her how she was feeling.

'Actually, there is something I'd like to say,' she said.

'Oh, yes? What's that?'

'Since all these old things are going' – she indicated the long list that she'd written down – 'I think it's time for me to go too. I've decided to retire at the end of the month.'

'Retire? Are you sure, Miss Daniels?' Tobias immediately launched into a charitable speech about how the place wouldn't be the same without her. He could certainly turn on the charm when the occasion demanded it, but through it all she saw the relief in his eyes. No doubt he had wanted to get rid of her too, along with the antique furniture and old books. But people weren't so easy to dispose of. Now, she realised, she'd made his life easy for him.

'I'm sure you'll be very happy in your retirement,' he concluded jovially.

'Thank you, Mr Burton. I'm sure I will.'

★

Bill Harris arrived early that evening to get things ready, setting out the chairs in a circle, then switching on the tea urn in the kitchen – normally tasks that Harriet Stevenson would have insisted on doing herself as if none of the others were capable. In addition to his belltower captain duties, Bill was deputy chair of Hambledon parish council. He liked having a reason to get out of the house, especially since his wife's death five years ago. It didn't do to sit at home on your own all the time. The council met in the village hall on the third Thursday of every month but tonight's meeting was inevitably going to be a rather sombre affair.

The wooden door creaked open and in bustled Alison Rawlinson, laden with an armful of files. As clerk to the parish council, it was Alison's task to handle all the paperwork, implement council decisions and maintain the council website, a role that she executed with care and diligence. Bill approved of the solemn notice that she had placed on the website homepage, announcing Harriet's untimely passing. There was now a casual vacancy on the council which, in due course, would have to be filled with an election. But in Bill's opinion it was far too early to be thinking about such matters. Harriet's body was barely cold. The police investigation into her murder had only just got started.

'Let me give you a hand with the tea,' said Alison, cheerful as ever. Bill knew she'd had a tricky working relationship with Harriet, who had liked to oversee every detail of council business, no matter how trivial. He'd once overheard Alison refer to Harriet as a "bloomin' control freak", which was harsh criticism coming from Alison's mild-mannered lips.

The rest of the councillors arrived over the course of the next ten minutes whilst Alison handed out cups of tea from the serving hatch. There was June Parker who ran the village shop and post office, Eric Fletcher the church organist, a retired bank manager by the name of Graham Ashton, and, resplendent as ever in a purple silk cravat and a pair of highly polished leather brogues, Maurice Fairweather, the local historian and all-round eccentric. Members of the public were always welcome to attend meetings of the parish council but by and large they didn't, and tonight was no exception.

When everyone had made themselves comfortable, Bill nodded a welcome to the assembled group and took his own seat. As deputy chair it was now his duty to step into Harriet's shoes and become acting chair, a responsibility he would rather have foregone. He felt it incumbent upon him to say a word or two about the tragic events of the previous day, but he wasn't one for making speeches and didn't really know where to start. Given that he'd been up in the belltower when the murder took place, the other councillors might expect him to know more about what had happened than he actually did. In truth he knew little more than the rest of them. He had lain awake half the night replaying everything from the moment Amy had started ringing the treble bell to the end of the quarter peal, when they had all trooped down the stairs and found the body. But try as he might, he was completely at a loss to explain how the murder had happened or who might have been responsible for such an appalling act of violence.

'Before we get the meeting underway,' he began, 'I just want to say...' But the words he had in mind seemed to trickle away as the others looked at him expectantly. He should really have prepared something and written it down.

June Parker came to his rescue. 'We're all very upset about what happened to Harriet Stevenson. I couldn't believe it when I heard the news. Shocking! And on the day of Henry Burton's funeral too! So tragic. Her death is a great loss to the council and to the community it serves.'

'Indeed,' said Bill, grateful to June for her intervention. 'We all owe a huge debt to Harriet for everything she did for the village. The place won't be the same without her.'

What sounded like a snort came from Maurice Fairweather. All heads turned sharply in Maurice's direction and June tutted audibly.

Maurice and Harriet had rarely seen eye to eye,

and some of their clashes over council business were legendary, such as the war that had raged over the number and position of dog waste bins on the village green. Harriet had considered them an eyesore and had argued they should be as discreet as possible. She clearly wasn't a dog lover herself. Maurice had argued that if the bins weren't clearly visible people wouldn't use them. In writing up the minutes Alison had managed to find tactful phrases such as "a lively discussion ensued" or "differences of opinion were expressed" which hardly did justice to the overheated arguments. Maurice and Harriet had frequently faced each other across a no-man's land of incomprehension and disagreement which other councillors had traversed with the utmost caution, fearful of setting off a landmine. Bill strongly suspected that Maurice secretly enjoyed riling the chair and just liked to be contrary.

He fixed Maurice with a stern stare to see if the rebel councillor had any comment to make, but wisely Maurice chose to say nothing on this occasion.

'Well, shall we make a start?' said Bill, keen to restore order and get the meeting moving. 'Does everyone have a copy of tonight's agenda and the minutes of the last meeting?' They all nodded and rustled their papers. 'Excellent. Any matters arising? No? In that case we'll move on to the first item.'

The agenda, prepared and circulated by Alison

three days before the meeting, had four main items, all of them pet projects of Harriet's. There was a proposal for a further reduction in speed limits and more traffic calming measures; the matter of the maintenance of the village green and the state of grass verges and publicly owned hedgerows; a proposal for a children's play area; and, last but not least, the future of the manor house. This item was by far the most controversial.

The first three matters were quickly discussed and passed *nem con*.

'Moving on to item number four,' said Bill, with an uneasy feeling in the pit of his stomach. 'Harriet wanted to organise a village protest against proposals to turn the manor house into a hotel. She had, as you know, called a provisional meeting for tomorrow evening to begin coordinating opposition.'

'Well, she's not here anymore, is she?' said Maurice with an unmistakable note of satisfaction in his voice. 'So I propose we scrap the whole idea. A hotel could be a good thing for the village. And, besides, it isn't as if Tobias Burton has even published his proposals yet. Harriet just liked to stir up trouble. Let's wait and see what Tobias is actually planning to do.'

June looked as if she wanted to protest, but then changed her mind. Alison threw Maurice a look of disgust but said nothing, and neither Eric nor Graham seemed to have any strong opinions on the matter one way or the other. Bill realised they were waiting for him to make a decision. Should they pursue the matter as Harriet had wished, or should they quietly drop it? In some ways it felt disrespectful to the dead woman to casually toss aside a matter that she had held so dear. But on the other hand, Bill didn't have the heart for a lengthy argument with Maurice Fairweather, or anyone else for that matter. After sleeping so badly the previous night he just wanted to bring the meeting to an end and go home. He decided, in the best tradition of the parish council, to opt for a compromise.

'I think it's best if we put this item on hold for now. In the coming days we'll have more urgent business to deal with regarding the casual vacancy that has arisen. In any case, without Harriet to lead the meeting tomorrow – and as a mark of respect to her – I think that we should cancel it.' He was gratified to see nodding heads all round. Maurice Fairweather sat there like a grinning cat.

Bill asked if there was any other business, and when no one spoke up, he drew the meeting to a close. Glancing at the clock on the wall, he was surprised to see that they'd finished in record time. It was certainly a welcome change from when Harriet had been in charge, and battles had often been fought long into the night. *Every cloud*, thought Bill as he restacked the chairs and helped Alison with the washing-up.

★

'What are you looking so pleased about?' asked Bridget.

Jonathan had a broad grin on his face when he arrived at her house that evening. He still had his own place in Iffley village on the other side of Oxford, but was spending increasing amounts of time at Bridget's. He had made his mark on the kitchen, throwing out Bridget's out-of-date herbs and spices, and upgrading her collection of knives with a professional set, fit for a cook of his ability. She'd even gone so far as to clear some space in her wardrobe for him to keep a spare set of clothes there. It was a welcome move as far as Bridget was concerned, and she was certainly enjoying Jonathan's company, as well as his famous scrambled eggs for breakfast. But Bridget's house, which had been cosy when it was just her and Chloe, was now feeling increasingly like a shoebox, and if they were ever going to move in together permanently they would need to look for somewhere bigger.

Jonathan produced a bottle of Prosecco from a canvas shopping bag. 'I made a whopping sale today. I thought we could celebrate.' Jonathan owned an art gallery on Oxford High Street, specialising in modern works by contemporary artists. Bridget would have loved to buy one of his paintings herself, but they were all too large for her tiny house, not to mention out of her budget.

'Prosecco on a weekday?' Bridget had been

trying – although admittedly not too hard – to limit her consumption of alcohol to the weekend in a bid to shed a few pounds before the upcoming wedding. The thought of Tamsin's judgemental eyes roaming over her curvaceous form and finding it altogether too generous, was a strong incentive to cut back on the calories. But on the other hand, Jonathan's good mood was infectious, and this sounded like the perfect excuse to break a rule that wasn't cast in stone anyway. 'Tell me about it,' she said, fetching two large wine glasses from the cupboard.

Jonathan filled the glasses and took a swig of the sparkling wine. 'A chap came into the shop today and chose a pair of large canvases for the lobby of his new hotel. He says he wants more by the same artist for all the bedrooms. I've arranged for him to meet the artist, to discuss a possible commission.'

Bridget was just about to congratulate him when she froze, her glass halfway to her lips. 'A new hotel. Did he say where this hotel is going to be?'

'Yes, it's in Hambledon-on-Thames. It's that lovely village with the charming pub where we went for a walk along the river.' He watched her face. 'What's wrong?'

'Was the name of this buyer Tobias Burton, by any chance?'

'That's him,' said Jonathan. 'You know him?'

'Let's just say that he's a person of interest in a murder investigation.'

Jonathan's face fell. 'Oh no, if I'd known...'

'You weren't to know, and anyway, what difference would it have made?'

'You're right. I was just so happy to make the sale. It's a lot of money.'

'In that case, congratulations,' said Bridget, raising her glass.

'Cheers!'

As Jonathan continued to talk excitedly about the sale, describing the paintings that had been sold, and the opportunity this could open up for the young artist, Bridget mulled over the news. It seemed that Tobias Burton was extremely confident about his plans for the manor house. As well he might. With Harriet Stevenson out of the way, who was there to stop him?

★

After running across Port Meadow to clear her head, then showering and making herself a mug of matcha green tea to help her focus, Ffion settled down with her laptop and books in readiness for a long evening of study.

For the last couple of months she'd been spending all her spare time immersed in books. Her exam for promotion to the rank of detective sergeant was now only eight days away and she was determined to be on top form. More than that, she had set herself the goal of obtaining the highest possible grade.

She opened her copy of *Blackstone's Police*

Manual, Volume 1 and turned to the section with the typically longwinded title of *Miscellaneous Offences Against the Person and Offences Involving the Deprivation of Liberty*, intending to pick up where she'd left off the night before. But tonight the words on the page refused to make sense.

Maybe a few moments of meditation would help still her mind. She closed her eyes and tried to focus on her breathing while letting her mind drift free.

Left to their own devices, her thoughts immediately turned to the new case in Hambledon, or more specifically to the team meeting that morning. When Jake had talked about bellringing and had said "my girlfriend, Amy", dropping her name so casually into the conversation, she had experienced a feeling that she wasn't proud of.

Jealousy.

It was an ugly emotion, unbecoming to her, but there it was nonetheless. She was only human, after all, even if she did sometimes prefer the company of computers to real people.

She had never met Jake's new girlfriend, but when he had rallied so passionately to Amy's defence after Andy had suggested that she might be a suspect, and when Ryan had dropped some crude sexual innuendo, Ffion's usual sangfroid had been pierced to the core. No one had noticed her reaction, as they were all so focused on Jake's description of the belltower. But it had caused her a moment of real pain.

She and Jake had been a couple, briefly, but that had ended messily after his ex-girlfriend, Brittany, had shown up on the scene during one of their murder investigations. Brittany had inveigled her way back into Jake's life and Ffion, in a fury of self-righteous indignation, had stormed off. Despite Jake's profuse apology, she had refused to forgive him. Now, she increasingly wondered if she had been too harsh on him.

She had found happiness for a time with a new girlfriend, Marion, a junior research fellow at the university. Voluptuous, French and full of fun, Marion had been just what she needed to get over the breakup with Jake. And when Marion had been offered a full-time lectureship in Edinburgh, she had begged Ffion to leave Oxford and go with her. But Ffion had chosen to stay in Oxford and the relationship with Marion was now a thing of the past.

Another regret. And perhaps another mistake.

When she had refused to go with Marion, Ffion had told herself she was staying in Oxford for the sake of her career, but had she been kidding herself? Was Jake the real reason she had stayed? But Jake was now unavailable and Ffion was alone again.

Her mind continued to swirl, taunting her with negative thoughts, but there was only one way to deal with that. Whatever mistakes she may have made, her actions belonged firmly in the past, and there was no room for regrets. The only thing now was to focus on the upcoming exam.

Miscellaneous Offences Against the Person and Offences Involving the Deprivation of Liberty beckoned for her attention. She took a sip of her tea and began to work through the chapter, making notes as she went.

CHAPTER 12

'Tobias Burton admits to being in the graveyard at the time of the murder,' said Bridget to her assembled team, 'but denies going back into the church after the burial.'

She had gathered everyone together for an early Friday morning briefing. With only one day to go before the weekend, she was hoping for some tangible progress.

'What was he doing in the graveyard?' asked Ryan. 'If that's not a silly question.'

'Spending a few moments in quiet reflection after burying his father,' said Bridget, 'or so he claims.' Despite Tobias Burton's portrayal of a difficult relationship with his father, and his desire to say goodbye to a man who had struggled to express himself emotionally, Tobias didn't strike her as the sort of person who would be capable of spending much time in contemplation. He had displayed clear alpha-type personality traits, and was the sort who rushed from one thing to the next, always busy, always achieving. In some ways he reminded Bridget of Vanessa. 'His estate manager claims that she saw him doing precisely what he said he was doing, but I'd be happier if we could find an independent witness to back that up. Lindsey Symonds is obviously working very closely with Tobias Burton on plans for the new hotel. It wouldn't be in her best interests if her boss was to become a murder suspect.'

'You want us to do a bit of digging,' said Ryan, 'no pun intended – and see if we can discredit her alibi?'

'Yes, please,' said Bridget. 'Or else find a second witness who can confirm it. How did you and Jake get on yesterday interviewing people in the village?'

'We spoke to dozens of people,' said Jake. 'The main topic that kept coming up was the schism in the village over the proposed plans for the manor house. Broadly speaking, the younger people are in favour of turning it into a hotel, and the older ones are against. They all spoke up in favour of the old squire and everything that he'd done for the village. The feeling was that the new squire is just a money grabber, and wants to abandon all the old traditions. They tended to think that Harriet Stevenson was right to oppose his plans.'

'Except for that old guy we met in the pub,' said Ryan. 'The guy in the silk cravat... Maurice Fairweather.'

'Him?' said Jake scathingly. 'He was a right waste of time. All he wanted to talk about was what happened in the village hundreds of years ago.'

'There was a consensus of opinion,' continued Ryan, 'that Tobias Burton would have had a real fight on his hands regarding his plans for the manor house if the churchwarden had still been around.'

'So for the moment, he remains the only suspect with a clear motive,' said Bridget. 'Pinning down his movements needs to be our top priority.'

'What about the other people who attended the burial?' asked Ffion. 'Do we have alibis for them?'

Jake consulted his notes. 'Mrs Burton and her two children made their way to the Eight Bells immediately afterwards. We have plenty of witnesses to confirm that. But I don't think we can confirm the movements of any of the others. That's to say, the vicar, the housekeeper, the nurse and the estate manager.'

'And the sexton, of course,' said Ryan. 'Which I discovered is a posh word for gravedigger.'

'Can the sexton confirm the whereabouts of any of the mourners after the burial?'

'He was too busy digging, apparently. The man takes his job seriously.'

Bridget directed her next question at Andy. 'Did you and Harry uncover anything we should know about Tobias Burton?'

Andy consulted his notebook. 'He's a property developer with a line in upmarket, exclusive hotels, mostly conversions of old properties, so converting Hambledon Manor sounds right up his street. His company is highly respected, although he ran into a bit of trouble a couple of years back.'

'Go on,' said Bridget, glad to be offered a morsel of information about the young lord of the manor.

'A former business partner made allegations about a shady deal. The case was due to go to court but at the last minute, Mr Burton agreed to an out-of-court settlement, and the case was dropped.'

Bridget digested this latest piece of information. Did it prove anything? Disputes between former business partners weren't uncommon, and it didn't necessarily mean that Tobias had done anything wrong. It certainly didn't suggest that he might go as far as to commit murder in pursuit of his business goals. It seemed that so far, two days into the investigation, they had very little to go on.

Andy was still consulting his notes. 'We've had an initial report back from forensics, ma'am. As you can imagine, a great deal of fingerprints were recovered from the crime scene. Basically the entire village had been in the church that day, so prints were everywhere. A few items of interest were recovered – two pairs of reading glasses, a mobile phone, and two folded umbrellas. The owners of the various articles have been identified, but for the moment we're holding everything as evidence.'

'What about the murder weapon?'

'Nothing found so far, I'm afraid. But we have a report on the footprints that were found at the scene. Vik was right when he said the marks came from a shoe with a smooth leather sole. Forensics have confirmed it as a man's size ten.'

'Okay,' said Bridget. 'Thanks to all of you for your work so far, but we have a lot more to do today. Our top priority has to be to corroborate the movements of everyone who was at the burial. They remain our primary suspects, unless we can identify anyone else who was in the vicinity of the church at the time of the murder. Jake, Ryan, go back to the village and carry on where you left off. Andy, Ffion, and Harry, I'd like you to start sifting through the witness statements. Look for discrepancies or confirmation of what Tobias Burton and Lindsey Symonds told us yesterday. See if you can identify anyone else who may have had opportunity. Everyone know what they're doing?'

'Yes, ma'am,' chorused the team.

Good, thought Bridget, who wished she could say the same about herself. It didn't take her long to discover what her next move would be. Chief Superintendent Grayson was beckoning to her from behind the large glass window of his office.

★

'I knew Henry Burton from way back,' said

136

Grayson, idly twirling his fountain pen between thumb and forefinger.

'Sir?' The Chief Super always seemed to know everyone of distinction and influence in the community. Bridget was willing to bet that his personal address book read like a *Who's Who* of Oxfordshire. Many of the people he rubbed shoulders with seemed to be keen golfers like him, but his social circles went far wider than that.

'Got to know him at the Rotary Club,' said Grayson. 'Very decent sort of chap. Generous to a fault. But I understand he'd been ill for some time. Absolute tragedy that this murder should take place on the day of his funeral.'

'Quite,' said Bridget. 'Although the two events may not be entirely unrelated.'

Grayson looked intrigued. 'How so?'

'Henry's son, Tobias Burton, is the sole inheritor of the estate. He has ambitious plans to turn Hambledon Manor into a luxury hotel. But the murder victim, Harriet Stevenson, was vigorously opposed to the idea and was gearing up to mount a campaign of opposition. With her out of the way, there's very little to prevent him going ahead with his plans.'

'Hmm, I see.' Grayson looked thoughtful. 'Do you have any evidence, apart from motive, to suggest that Tobias Burton might have killed her? Or had her killed?'

'Not at the moment,' said Bridget. 'We're making further enquiries.'

'Well, don't let him out of your sight,' said Grayson. 'I encountered Tobias once or twice in the company of his father, and I can tell you, he's not cut from the same cloth as the old man.'

'I got that impression, sir.'

Grayson had a habit of interfering in Bridget's investigations, and she waited to see if he had any further contributions or demands to make, but he seemed to have said all he wished to say. Perhaps he was beginning to trust her judgement at last.

'I'll keep you informed of any developments, sir,' she said, and with his words of wisdom ringing in her ears, she left his office.

★

'DI Hart, how nice to see you.'

'You too, Roy. All is well, I trust?'

'Nothing in particular to complain of.'

On leaving Grayson's office, Bridget had received a phone call from Dr Roy Andrews, informing her that he was bringing forward the post-mortem of Harriet Stevenson, and inviting her to join him at the hospital right away. With nothing more urgent to occupy her, she had accepted, despite her general aversion to blood and guts, and to autopsies in particular. As a detective, she couldn't afford to let her personal likes and dislikes hamper her investigation. And besides, she enjoyed spending time in Roy's company. Despite the senior pathologist's permanently downbeat air, there was always a soothing calmness to his gloom-laden outlook on life, brightened by his incongruous choice of colourful bow ties. Today, a particularly fine orange paisley peeked out above his white medical coat.

And yet there was something strange about Roy's appearance. Bridget couldn't be certain, but his expression seemed to hold all the characteristics of joy.

'You do look happy,' she said.

'Happy?' Roy folded his brow into a series of deep ruts. 'I do hope not. Happiness is a delusion caused by a lack of self-reflection. But you might say that I am suffering from a brief period of contentment before more sorrow comes my way.'

'I'm glad to hear it,' said Bridget. 'Any particular reason for the contentment?'

'Who can say?' said Roy, removing his wireframe glasses and squinting at his notebook. 'A reason would imply that life has meaning, which I think we can both agree, is not the case at all.'

'He's going on holiday,' said Julie, Roy's assistant, bringing in a tray of forceps, saws and needles.

'Somewhere nice?' asked Bridget.

'Western isles of Scotland,' said Roy with a grunt. 'We're hoping for rain.'

Bridget's interest picked up. '"We?"' she inquired nosily.

'Did I say "we"? A slip of the tongue.'

Dr Sarah Walker, mouthed Julie silently behind his back, confirming Bridget's suspicions.

The autopsy itself proceeded without any such interesting revelations. Roy merely confirmed what Bridget already knew – that Harriet Stevenson had died from blunt force trauma.

'A very nasty blow to the head,' he concluded. 'Quite considerable force was used. I think we can say that whoever did this intended the blow to be fatal.'

'And what kind of weapon was used?' asked Bridget.

'Heavy, obviously. But relatively compact. A metal bar, or a hammer, perhaps.'

'Thank you, Roy,' she said, on leaving the autopsy suite. 'And do try to enjoy your holiday with Sarah.'

★

Shaun Daniels knocked on the door of the estate manager's office.

'Enter.'

Enter, indeed! As if the woman was some kind of liege lord to whom he was expected to kowtow. Lindsey Symonds was an employee of the estate, just like him. She had no right to put on airs and graces. It had been different when the old squire was still running the show. Henry Burton would never have allowed his estate manager to treat his staff as if they were dirt. Shaun might have moaned once or twice about the old squire after a few drinks in the Eight Bells, but the old man hadn't been such a bad boss. Not like the new squire, who didn't give a fig about anyone. Now that he had taken over, Lindsey Symonds had been given free rein to treat Shaun however she pleased.

She'd summoned him – that was the only word for it – to a meeting first thing. He wondered whether Tobias Burton might also be present, to talk to him about the future of the house and garden, but Lindsey was sitting alone at her desk. So far, the new squire hadn't deigned to speak a word to him, the lowly gardener.

'You wanted to see me?' Whatever this was about, he hoped she'd make it quick. He didn't have time for meetings. There was always so much to do in the garden at this time of year. If you didn't cut the grass every few days it quickly got out of hand. Then there were hedges to trim, bedding plants to put out, and the vegetable patch to hoe. The runner beans were on track to produce a bumper crop this year, thanks to his care and attention, and the tomatoes in the greenhouse were already starting to ripen.

'Yes, come in.' She glanced down at his feet as he entered, as if worried he might leave a trail of mud all over the rug. In fact, he'd left his boots at the back door and was in his socks. But when he saw the look of disdain on her face, he began to regret it. Without his boots, he felt vulnerable, like a schoolboy standing before the headmistress.

Lindsey Symonds clasped her hands together. 'Thank you for coming to see me, Shaun.'

'So,' he said. 'What's this about?'

He never felt comfortable when summoned into the big house. Sometimes he slipped into the kitchen by the back door to see his mum when no one else was around, but he felt more at ease in his own little cottage or in the grounds. Once, he had lived in the manor house alongside Tobias, but that was many years ago. He was five years older than Tobias, and had played with the other boy when he was little. But Tobias had started acting like the lord of the manor from an early age, bossing Shaun around, and making it clear that he was no lord, but merely the son of the housekeeper. Shaun had quickly learned that it was better to play outdoors, alone.

'Mr Burton has asked me to inform you that your services as gardener will no longer be required beyond the end of the month.' Lindsey pushed a white envelope across the desk towards him. 'Everything is laid out in this letter. I think you'll find that Mr Burton has been more than generous in his settlement. You can be certain to receive an excellent reference from him, should you require one. Mr Burton would like you to move out of the cottage in four weeks' time. Do you have any questions?'

Shaun stood dumbfounded. Whatever he'd expected, it hadn't been this. What on earth was

Tobias Burton thinking? The garden would go to wrack and ruin in no time if left unattended. After a moment, he found his voice.

'What's the reason for this? I've been the gardener here all my working life. The old squire never had any complaint about my work.'

The estate manager held his gaze, but he thought he detected a slight heightening of colour in her cheeks.

'Shaun, no one is disputing the excellent work you've done in the past. But times are changing. Mr Burton has new plans for the house and grounds.'

'I know he wants to turn the house into a hotel,' protested Shaun. 'But the garden will still need looking after. I daresay it'll be even more important once there are paying guests staying here.'

Lindsey Symonds gave an exasperated sigh. 'Mr Burton has chosen to employ a firm of landscapers to oversee a complete redesign of the garden. They will also be responsible for its future maintenance.' She held out the envelope. 'Now, if you don't mind, I have work to be getting on with.'

He stared at her in disbelief, then snatched the envelope from her and stormed out of the office, letting the door slam shut behind him.

In the hallway he paused to catch his breath, not fully believing what had just happened. He tore open the envelope and pulled out the folded sheet of paper. There it was in black and white.

The termination of his contract. But did he even have a contract? Proper terms of employment? He'd been here all his life – he realised now how much he regarded Hambledon Manor as his home – and Henry Burton had never formalised his working arrangements. But now Tobias Burton was throwing him on the scrapheap. And the man didn't even have the decency to tell him to his face.

Thoughts whirled around Shaun's head. What rights did he have? Could he refuse to leave? Take Tobias Burton to court? He had no experience of such matters. Well, that wasn't quite true. He'd once found himself in the magistrates' court in Oxford on a charge of stealing the Sunday collection from the church, and that had gone badly for him. He didn't trust people in authority. Never had. And they didn't trust him.

He stuffed the letter roughly into his back pocket and was about to head outside for a smoke, when an idea struck him.

The door to the library stood ajar.

He crossed the parquet floor silently in his stockinged feet and slipped inside.

The serried ranks of books stood on the shelves, from floor to ceiling. As a boy he'd been allowed to help his mother clean them with a feather duster. And one day, Henry Burton had shown him something special.

The smell of the dust and polish in the library, and the fingers of warm sunlight reaching across the wooden floor brought that occasion vividly back to mind now.

'What do you make of this, Shaun?' the old squire had asked him, a playful glint in his eye.

He had reached for the book gingerly, not sure if he was allowed to touch it.

'Go on,' said the old squire encouragingly. 'It won't hurt you. I know you'll handle it with care.'

He had taken the book and held it in his hands, listening carefully to what Henry Burton said. The old squire was always full of stories.

Shaun remembered the location of the bookcase precisely. The fourth stack from the left, opposite the fireplace. He went there now and scanned the shelves, looking for the book that Henry Burton had shown him. It was a small volume, bound in brown leather, cracked and faded.

His eye lighted on a thin book wedged in between two sturdier titles. He eased it out of its slot and opened the creaking cover, holding it again just like he'd done all those years ago. Yes, this was it.

The title page was mottled with age, and a strong smell of musty paper rose to his nostrils. He recognised the funny title – he'd laughed at it as a boy. Written in old-fashioned lettering with the occasional odd spelling were the words:

TINTINNALOGIA:

OR,

THE ART

OF

RINGING.

Wherein

Is laid down plain and easie

Rules for Ringing

all sorts of *Plain Changes*.

Together with

Directions for Pricking and

Ringing all *Cross Peals*; with

a full Discovery of the Mystery

and Grounds of each Peal.

As Also

Instructions for *Hanging of Bells*,

with all things belonging thereunto.

By a Lover of that ART.

The date at the bottom of the page was 1668.

The old squire had explained to him that this was a very rare and valuable book. A first edition of a work dedicated to the ancient art of bellringing. Shaun wasn't a bellringer. He didn't know what was meant by *Plain Changes* or *Cross Peals* and didn't care. What he knew was that this book was worth a fortune.

His mother had told him that a team would be coming this morning from the Bodleian Library to collect the books and take them away. If he was going to act, this was his one and only chance. The librarians wouldn't miss one small volume among so many. No one would even know it was gone. And after the way he'd just been treated, he felt no qualms about taking something that no one would miss.

He slipped the book inside his jacket and went back outside.

★

Back at her desk, Bridget was about to call Chloe to make sure she'd got up in time for her afternoon exam when her phone rang.

Not recognising the number, she answered the call. 'Hello, Detective Inspector Bridget Hart here.'

'Oh, Inspector, I've caught you. Good.' The voice, a woman's, sounded breathy, rather nervous, and vaguely familiar.

'Who's calling please?'

'Yes, sorry, of course, it's Rosemary. Rosemary Carver, the nurse from Hambledon Manor. We met in the hallway yesterday as I was on my way out. You gave me your card and said to phone if I thought of anything.'

'Yes, I remember. Do you have some new information for me?' Bridget drew a pad of paper towards her and picked up a pen.

'I don't know if it's important. It could be something or nothing. But I thought I should mention it to you just in case.'

The pen in Bridget's hand hovered over the

paper. 'Please go on, Mrs Carver.'

'It's just that I saw Mr Burton... the son, that is.' She cleared her throat. 'Obviously I mean the son, his poor father being buried six foot underground by then...' The woman was clearly very anxious.

'Take your time,' said Bridget. 'You saw Tobias Burton. When was this?'

'After the burial.'

'Yes? And what was he doing?'

'He was running out of the church.' The words came out in a rush.

Bridget kept her voice as calm and level as possible, but excitement was coursing through her veins. 'What time was this exactly?'

'Not long after the burial had finished. About ten minutes afterwards.'

'You saw him run from the church,' said Bridget. 'Where were you at that time?'

'I was in the churchyard. Simon – my husband, that is – had left a message for me on my phone, and I was calling him back to check on him. He's poorly, you see. So I'd gone to a quiet corner in the shade of one of those big yew trees to speak to him. Anyway, while I was there, I saw Tobias Burton dash out of the church looking like he'd seen a ghost.'

'Can you describe exactly how he appeared?'

'Pale. Drawn. Frightened. He was in a big hurry to get away, I can tell you.'

'Did you see him enter the church?'

'No. Only coming out. I wasn't being nosey,

you understand,' she added quickly. 'I just happened to be looking that way, and there he was. He looked like he was going to be sick. I thought he might need some assistance, but by the time I'd finished talking to Simon, Mr Burton had gone.'

'Mrs Carver, can I ask why you didn't mention this to me when I spoke to you previously? At that time, you told me that you didn't notice anything suspicious?'

The line fell silent.

'Mrs Carver?'

'Am I going to get into trouble over this?' asked the nurse. 'I wondered if I was doing the right thing, calling you.'

'No,' Mrs Carver,' Bridget assured her. 'You're not in trouble. You did the right thing. I'd just like to know why you changed your mind?'

'Well, the truth is I was afraid.'

'Afraid of what?'

'Of Mr Burton. That man has a dreadful temper when he's cross about something. I hope you don't think me silly, but I didn't feel safe saying anything when I was in the manor house.'

'There's nothing to be afraid of now, Mrs Carver,' said Bridget. She thanked the nurse for the information and arranged for DC Harry Johns to call round to take a written statement.

As Harry left the office, Ffion approached looking triumphant. 'Ma'am? I've just found a witness statement that contradicts the estate manager's alibi for Tobias Burton. June Parker who runs the local shop reports speaking to Lindsey Symonds in the pub at the time Ms Symonds claims to have seen Tobias Burton taking a stroll around the churchyard.'

'Excellent work,' said Bridget. The investigation had begun to move quickly, and now the net was tightening around Tobias Burton. It was time to bring the young squire in for questioning.

CHAPTER 13

Jake checked his watch. Another morning spent interviewing witnesses and taking their statements had passed, and without much obvious progress. It looked like it was going to be another fruitless day. That's what police work was like as often as not. Slow, painstaking gathering of evidence, until a pattern emerged, or some small discrepancy led to a new line of enquiry. It wasn't like the detective books that Amy and her mum liked to read – all dashing about and sudden breakthroughs.

'Time for a pub lunch, I reckon,' said Ryan. 'I don't know about you, but I could murder another one of those bacon cheeseburgers.'

'Don't you think of anything except your stomach?'

'It's Maslow's hierarchy of needs,' said Ryan. 'We have to satisfy our basic requirements before we can move on to higher things. A burger is the route to self-actualisation.'

'You don't half talk a lot of rubbish,' said Jake. 'And how did you know the answer to that crossword clue that Maurice Fairweather asked us in the pub?'

'I'm a big fan of crosswords. They keep your mind sharp, and there's no better way to stay alert if you're on an all-night surveillance op. Anyway, that was a simple clue.'

'You'll have to explain it to me. I have no idea how these cryptic clues work.'

'Likelihood of person catching criminal?' said Ryan. 'It's an anagram. "Likelihood" is the clue. "Criminal" is the anagram indicator. "Person catching" is the anagram itself. *Sporting chance –* easy.'

They were crossing the village green in the direction of the pub when Jake's phone rang. 'Ma'am?' He listened with raised eyebrows as Bridget updated him on the latest developments.

'Well?' said Ryan when he'd finished the call. 'Don't keep me in suspense.'

'That was the boss.'

'I gathered that.'

'She wants us to bring Tobias Burton in for questioning. There's new information about his movements at the time of the murder. She's sending a marked car over to pick him up.'

'How long will it take to get here, do you reckon?'

'About ten minutes. It's coming from Abingdon.'

'Guess the burger will have to wait then.'

The grounds of the manor house appeared to be deserted. Jake pressed the button at the entrance and waited for the gates to swing open, before stepping through. He marvelled at the huge topiary that grew either side of the gravel path, and wondered how long something like that took to grow, never mind how much work was needed to sculpt it into such an intricate shape. He thought of his parents' small back yard in Leeds, in the terraced house where he'd grown up, and of the small collection of pot plants his mother tended. 'Impressive,' he said to Ryan.

'I've seen shabbier places,' agreed Ryan as they took in the grand old house with its many gables, leaded windows, tall chimneys and general air of gentility.

They rang the doorbell and were shown into a wood-panelled hallway by a woman who said she would fetch Mr Burton.

'This place is huge,' said Jake, looking around and comparing the manor house with his one-bedroom flat on the Cowley Road. The best thing to be said for his flat was that it was situated between an Indian restaurant and a Chinese takeaway, so he never had very far to go for a tasty meal. He wondered how easy it would be to get a takeaway delivered to Hambledon-on-Thames.

A man appeared on the upstairs gallery, dressed in a pair of chinos, a button-down shirt and linen jacket. He was clearly recognisable from the photograph pinned to the whiteboard in the incident room back at Kidlington. Tobias Burton descended the stairs briskly, seeming irritated by the intrusion into his home. 'Yes?

How can I help you?'

'Mr Tobias Burton?'

'Are you here about the books?'

'No, sir.' Jake held up his warrant card. 'Detective Sergeant Jake Derwent. And this is my colleague DS Ryan Hooper. We'd like to ask you to accompany us to the station to answer some questions regarding the murder of Harriet Stevenson.'

'There must be a mistake,' said Tobias. 'I spoke to your boss yesterday and told her everything I knew.'

'Fresh information has come to light,' said Ryan.

'Such as?'

'Sir, it would be in your best interests to come with us now.'

'What if I choose not to?'

Jake stepped in. 'Given the nature of the new information, it would be within our lawful rights to arrest you if you refuse to cooperate.'

'Then you don't leave me much choice,' said Tobias. 'But I insist on phoning my lawyer first.'

'That's fine,' said Jake. Then he remembered something. 'The shoes you wore to your father's funeral. Could you fetch them please?'

'What?'

'Your shoes, if you don't mind, sir,' said Jake. Outside, the sound of tyres crunching on the gravel announced the arrival of the marked police car.

Tobias Burton glared at Jake before stomping

back up the stairs. He returned carrying a pair of black, polished brogues.

'Thank you,' said Jake. As he slipped them into an evidence bag, he glanced at the soles, catching Ryan's eye as he did so.

The sole of the right shoe was stained an unmistakable rust-brown. Tobias Burton had been careless enough to step in some blood. What's more, he hadn't even noticed.

★

Tobias Burton sat very upright in his seat, as if determined not to give way to any questions that Bridget might pose. She had to admit that he presented an unshakeable appearance, assured of his innocence and ready to deny any accusation she might direct his way. But the evidence didn't lie, and Bridget found it very unlikely that two independent witnesses had also lied about what they had seen. Tobias Burton might have just lost his father, but Bridget had no intention of giving him an easy ride.

She recognised his solicitor, having encountered him precisely a year ago on a previous case, when he had represented a young tutor from Christ Church. Mr Raworth was a partner in an Oxford firm whose pedigree went back generations. Neat and correct in his customary three-piece suit, his silk tie held in place with a silver pin, Raworth sat poised with his leather notebook and gold-nibbed fountain pen at the ready. He greeted Bridget and Jake with a nod and a polite handshake, his professional demeanour overriding any past animosities.

'Mr Burton,' began Bridget, once Jake had read him the caution, 'when I spoke to you yesterday you told me that you attended the burial of your father's remains in the family plot at the church of St Michael and All Angels, and that the burial service finished at ten past one. Is that correct?'

Burton's reply was clipped and precise, and his eyes didn't linger from Bridget's for a second. 'Yes.'

'You also said that immediately after your father had been buried you spent some time alone in the churchyard.'

'Yes, that's right. I did.'

'Also among those present at the burial were your estate manager, Ms Lindsey Symonds, and the nurse who cared for your father during his final weeks, Mrs Rosemary Carver.'

'Correct.'

'When specifically asked, you denied going back inside the church after the burial.'

'I did,' said Tobias. 'If you remember, Ms Symonds vouched for me, confirming that what I told you was true.'

'She did,' said Bridget pleasantly. 'However, it would seem that Ms Symonds was not being truthful when she told us that. A reliable witness has made a statement that Ms Symonds was in the Eight Bells at the time she claims to have seen you in the churchyard.'

Mr Raworth made an entry in his notebook. 'As you will be aware, Inspector Hart, my client cannot be held responsible for what others may have claimed. Nor is he required to prove that he was where he says he was. The burden of proof lies with you.'

'Indeed it does,' said Bridget. 'Which is why I would like to introduce a second witness statement. Jake?'

Her sergeant referred to his notes. 'A second witness has come forward to say that they saw Mr Burton leaving the church some ten minutes after the burial service had finished. In fact, the witness states that Mr Burton was running from the church "as if he had seen a ghost." The witness went on to say that he appeared to be "in a big hurry to get away."'

The nurse's claim had the bombshell effect that Bridget had hoped.

Raworth looked abashed. 'May I have a moment alone with my client?'

'No,' said Bridget. 'I would like to hear what he has to say for himself. Was that you running from the church, Mr Burton?'

Tobias Burton adopted a pained look, as if Bridget had made an embarrassing *faux pas*. 'No comment.'

'May I remind you that you are under caution,' said Bridget, 'and that it may harm your defence if you do not mention when questioned something which you later rely on in court. I would advise you to think carefully about whether you wish to answer the question.'

A whispered conversation between solicitor and client ensued.

'Is there any further evidence that you intend to disclose?' asked Raworth.

Bridget nodded to Jake, who produced a photograph of Tobias's shoes. 'This pair of shoes, which was provided to us by Mr Burton this morning, is presently being examined by forensics.'

'Can you confirm that these are your shoes,' asked Bridget, 'and that you were wearing them at the time of your father's burial?'

'They are, and I was.'

'Then I can tell you that an initial examination of them has revealed the presence of blood on the soles, and that the size of the shoes – a size ten – matches that of bloody footprints found at the scene of the crime. We are waiting for confirmation that the blood is that of Miss Harriet Stevenson.'

A further bout of whispering took place between Tobias and his solicitor.

'All right, enough,' said Tobias at last, laying his hands flat on the table. 'This is how it was.'

Bridget braced herself for a confession, but it seemed that her suspect wasn't willing to give ground so easily. 'I did go back inside the church,' he said, 'but only for a minute. And I strongly refute the idea that I ran out. I may have been walking briskly, but I was expected at the wake. I didn't want to keep people waiting.'

It was a small admission, but at least he'd conceded something.

'Why did you go back inside the church, Mr Burton?'

'I had just buried my father – and let me tell you that's not something a man does lightly –and I wanted to visit the tomb of my ancestors.'

Bridget recalled the effigies of Sir Edmund and Lady Ellen Burton that she'd seen in the church, close to where the body of Harriet Stevenson had been discovered.

'You're referring to the tomb in the north transept?'

'Yes, I don't know exactly why I did it, but I suppose that the funeral had put me in a reflective frame of mind.'

'And when you went inside, did you meet Harriet Stevenson?'

A shake of the head.

'Could you speak your answer out loud for the benefit of the recording, please?'

'No! She was already dead! Or at least, I assumed that she was dead. There was blood everywhere. I approached the body, but there was no sign of life, and so I left immediately. I suppose that my shoe must have accidentally come into contact with her blood.'

'Why did you leave?' asked Jake. 'Why didn't you call for help?'

'There was nothing I could do to help her. And

I knew that people would leap to the wrong conclusion if they knew I had found the body.'

'What conclusion would that have been?' asked Bridget.

'That I murdered her.'

For a moment a silence hung in the interview room, which had grown stuffy in the summer heat.

The lawyer was the first to speak. 'In summary, my client has failed to report a crime. A moral failing, perhaps, but not a crime in itself, and entirely understandable under the circumstances. Your evidence that he is guilty of breaking any law is circumstantial, and I request that you bring this interview to an end.'

'I would like to remind you,' said Bridget, 'that Miss Stevenson's opposition to Mr Burton's plans to redevelop the manor house into a hotel gives him a clear motive for murder. He had motive and opportunity, and has been shown to have lied under questioning.'

Raworth shook his head. 'On the contrary, Inspector, my client has not yet submitted any such redevelopment plans, as he has been at pains to stress. And even if he had, there is a formal procedure for obtaining planning permission. To suggest that Miss Stevenson's opposition to any such plans might have given my client a motive for murder is preposterous.'

He fixed Bridget with an indignant stare. 'And might I enquire if a murder weapon has been recovered from the scene?'

'It hasn't,' admitted Bridget.

'Then was my client seen leaving the church carrying such a weapon?'

'The witness wasn't clear on that point.'

'I didn't think so,' said Raworth, screwing the lid back onto his fountain pen and rising from his seat. 'I think we're finished here.'

CHAPTER 14

The Reverend Martin Armistead crossed the churchyard slowly, his head bowed low in contemplation. He had left his wife pruning the roses, and was reasonably confident that she would be safe engaged in that task, the sharp blades of the secateurs notwithstanding.

Emma was calmer when she was outside in nature, tending to the flowers or simply sitting on the lawn, her face turned to the sun, watching the bees at work as they moved from rose to penstemon to astrantia. The garden at the vicarage was a blessing for which he constantly gave thanks.

It had been a habit of his for many years to practice gratitude, seeking out the small things each day that brought joy to his life. When effort was applied consciously to list and catalogue such blessings, it was astonishing how quickly the list grew. A murmured "thank you" from a parishioner; a breath of cool wind against his face on a hot and humid day; a fleeting smile across Emma's face. Life could be a treasure trove of joy, if only one devoted a little effort to recognising it.

And yet the week's events had left him in a state of deep anxiety, bordering on despair.

When he and Emma had been offered the chance to relocate from the inner city to a small, rural parish in South Oxfordshire, he had jumped at the chance. A fresh start was precisely what they needed. A simpler, slower-paced life in a friendly, close-knit community. All right, if he was being entirely honest with himself, which he always tried his utmost to do, in a safer, more *middle-class* community, far away from the social problems of Birmingham's rougher neighbourhoods. He'd imagined Emma making friends with other women in the village, maybe joining a book club, perhaps getting involved in running the village fête, and teaching in the Sunday School. For his own part he'd hoped for a small but devoted congregation, probably consisting mainly of elderly ladies. He'd sketched out the kind of sermon he would give – relevant, yet not overtly challenging – and looked forward to being invited round to tea with the churchwarden or perhaps even the lord of the manor himself. For Hambledon was the kind of village that – extraordinarily, in the modern era – still had a manor house whose occupant could trace his ancestry back to Tudor times and beyond.

Such a contrast to the social deprivation and human misery he had faced in the previous posting to which God had called him.

But their problems hadn't gone away. Emma, although at first calmer and outwardly happier in her new surroundings, had quickly sunk into a lethargy from which she was impossible to rouse. She hadn't made any friends in the village – had not even made an effort, despite his gentle encouragement, and the many opportunities presented by being vicar's wife in a small village – and the idea that she would enjoy organising the raffle at the village fête now seemed like a childish pipedream.

As for himself, far from finding a compliant and welcoming congregation, he had encountered Harriet Stevenson. His former churchwarden had a will of iron and had placed so many demands on him, he had grown to dread his meetings with her.

And her effect on Emma had been calamitous, causing her fragile mental health to deteriorate further.

After Harriet's death, he had felt a huge relief, to be replaced almost immediately by a sick feeling of dread. Prayer offered no consolation. God had resolutely refused to answer his pleas.

He pushed open the door of the church and stepped inside the north porch.

It was the first time the police had allowed him back inside the church since the murder, and he paused for a moment by the font, resting his hand against the rough stonework.

He had expected the church to feel different in some way after what had happened, as if an echo of the violence that had taken place here might still be palpable in the vibrations of the air, or in the very fabric of the building.

But instead, his overwhelming impression was of the infinite immutability of the place. The stone walls, the sturdy pillars, the stained-glass windows, the arching roof that mirrored the vault of Heaven; all these had stood the test of time. If these stones could speak, what stories would they tell? They had witnessed religious persecution, Civil War, two world wars, and now a murder in cold blood.

But they gave nothing away.

He crossed over to the southern wall of the church and walked quickly down the aisle, his footsteps ringing out and following him like a ghost. He resisted the urge to look behind to see if he was being followed, and he deliberately averted his gaze from the north transept. Was the floor there still stained? He didn't wish to know.

From the chancel he descended a couple of stone steps and pushed open the wooden door of the vestry, a small, cluttered room that contained a wardrobe for hanging cassocks, shelves piled high with hymn books, old copies of the Book of Common Prayer, and cupboards stashed full of minutes of church meetings dating back to the 1970s. It was the room in which he got himself ready before taking the Sunday morning service each week. Now that the police had finished their work in the building, he'd come here to return the spare set of keys.

A small wooden cupboard on one wall contained a set of hooks on which hung keys to the north and south doors, the belltower, the organ vestry, and the crypt. Opening the cupboard now, he saw that the key to the crypt was missing.

He stopped and stared at the empty hook.

Why would the key to the crypt be missing? He was certain it had been there the last time he looked. Hardly anyone ever went down to the crypt. It was a cold, dark place, and when he'd been down there himself he'd been very glad to come back up.

He wondered what to do about it. It would be a simple enough matter to get a new key cut from his own, back in the vicarage. But instinct told him that a missing key wasn't something he could ignore. He ought to tell someone what he'd found.

He took out his phone and dialled.

★

The library at Hambledon Manor was far more extensive than Amy had imagined. The large room with its walls of glazed bookcases, leather armchairs for reading, and an antique globe on a wooden stand, was Amy's idea of paradise. She would be spending most of the day here, supervising the clearing of the shelves and the packing of the books into crates, making sure that everything was properly labelled for future reference.

Full of eager anticipation, she had met the removal men from the Bodleian outside the manor house that morning. This was the first time she'd been inside the house, although after all the summer fêtes she'd been to over the years, she was already familiar with the grounds. The housekeeper, Miss Daniels, had shown them into the library and offered to bring tea.

Amy was delighted that the Librarian had assigned this job to her, and she had spent the morning thoroughly engrossed in the world of books. She had experienced the visceral thrill of holding in her gloved hands first editions of works such as *A Vindication of the Rights of Woman* by Mary Wollstonecraft of 1792, Mary Shelley's *Frankenstein* from 1818, and Charles Darwin's *On the Origin of Species*, dated 1859. Needless to say, the library also contained other classics such as the complete works of William Shakespeare, Jane Austen and Charles Dickens. Cataloguing the collection would be like compiling an index of the greatest works of English literature.

There were a few surprises buried among the more obvious works too. She had found a section dedicated entirely to bellringing, and to her amazement had uncovered a copy of Charles Troyte's work of 1869, *Change ringing: An Introduction to the early stages of the Art of Church or Hand Bell Ringing.*

But, thrilling though they were, it wasn't the

leather-bound first editions that Amy was most excited about. Being inside the manor house would give her an opportunity to do some real-life investigative work. Under the guise of making polite conversation, she hoped to make some discreet enquiries into the murder of Harriet Stevenson and uncover something that she could pass on to Jake.

Returning the empty cups to the kitchen finally gave her the excuse she was looking for to explore a little of the house, and to engage the housekeeper in conversation. She found Josephine Daniels standing at the Belfast sink, doing the washing up, gazing out at the vegetable garden.

'Let me give you a hand with the drying,' said Amy, grabbing a tea towel.

'There's really no need,' said Josephine.

'It's all right. The men know what they're doing. They won't miss me for ten minutes.' She picked up a plate and began rubbing it vigorously to ward off any further attempt to dissuade her from helping. 'Do you know what's happening with the summer fête this year?' she enquired casually. Although she hoped that the new squire would keep up the old tradition, she had no great interest in the summer fête one way or the other, but had already decided to approach her main subject from an oblique angle. It wouldn't do to come across as too obvious if she wanted to elicit some vital nugget of information that the police might have missed with their direct questioning.

'I don't know,' said Josephine, her hands in the sink. 'It'll be up to the new squire, but he hasn't said anything about it to me.'

'I just thought, you know, after the murder and all that, it might be cancelled?' Amy set the plate on the table and picked up another.

'I doubt that it's a priority for Mr Burton,' said Josephine. 'He has other matters on his mind. The best person to ask would be Bill Harris. I hear he's acting chair on the parish council now.'

'Yes, of course. So, have you heard anything about how the investigation is going? Has there been any news?'

'Not to my knowledge.'

This was proving harder than Amy had hoped. She didn't know Josephine Daniels all that well. Maybe she wasn't the gossipy type. But in the pub and the village shop, the murder was the only subject anyone was talking about. She couldn't understand why Miss Daniels wasn't as eager as she was to discuss it.

She decided to try a more direct tack. 'I expect that the police were keen to speak to Mr Burton about what happened?'

'Why do you assume that?'

'Well, isn't it an open secret that Harriet Stevenson was determined to put a stop to his plans for the house?'

Josephine put the last cup on the draining board and pulled the plug from the sink. The water made a noisy gurgle as it drained away. 'Mr Burton's plans for the house are no business of mine, especially since I've decided to retire at the end of the month.'

'Oh, have you?' said Amy. 'I didn't realise you were that old. I hope you don't mind me saying.' The words weren't mere flattery; Miss Daniels really didn't look old enough to take retirement.

Her comment drew a faint smile from the housekeeper's lips. 'I'll be sixty-eight next March, and I've been working in this house since I was a girl. So I think I've earned a chance to take life easier at last.'

'Oh, of course,' said Amy. 'Absolutely.'

Josephine dried her hands on a clean tea towel. 'I daresay that a number of people in the village don't approve of young Mr Burton's plans for the estate, but that's hardly a good reason for him to kill one of them.' She held Amy's gaze with her own unwavering one.

'Oh, no, certainly not,' said Amy quickly. 'That isn't what I meant at all.'

'Or perhaps you think they ought to have questioned my son?'

'Your son?' said Amy. 'You mean Shaun, the gardener?' She knew Shaun Daniels as a regular at the pub. He was a handsome man, in a brooding, saturnine way, but she had always kept her distance from him. A hot temper ran through his veins, and after a few beers he could become rather frightening. 'Why would they suspect him of being involved?'

'No reason.' To her relief, Josephine seemed not to have taken offence at Amy's rather clumsy probing. 'How are you getting on in the library?' she asked in a friendlier tone.

'Good, thanks. Although actually there was one thing that was puzzling me.'

'Oh?'

'On one of the shelves, there appears to be a book missing.'

At that, Josephine looked surprised. 'Really? What makes you say that?'

'Well, of course I can't say for sure, because there's no catalogue for the collection – it'll be my job to produce one – but there's definitely a small gap on one of the shelves. I might not have noticed it, but the other books are all so tightly packed together, it just seemed odd that there would be a space. It's in the campanology section.'

'No one has used the library for months,' said Josephine. 'I'm sure there can't be anything missing. I would have noticed it when I was cleaning.'

'You're probably right.' Amy hung the tea towel back where she had found it. Her attempt to elicit information from Miss Daniels had been a complete flop, but at least she didn't seem to have fallen out with the housekeeper. She gave Josephine a quick parting smile. 'I'd best be getting back to work.'

★

The Reverend Martin Armistead seemed even

more jittery than when Bridget had first met him on the day of the murder. He was waiting for her beneath the lychgate, his hands thrust into the pockets of his jeans, his shoulders hunched, his eyes darting around the village green, while his front teeth bit down on his bottom lip. Unshaven, his shirt slightly crumpled, he didn't look like a man to inspire confidence or to administer pastoral care and spiritual guidance to his flock. He looked more like he was in need of a strong drink and a long holiday. Only the dog collar around his neck marked him out as a man of the cloth. He greeted Bridget with a nervous smile.

'You said on the phone that one of the keys to the church is missing,' she said, as she accompanied him along the path to the north door of the church.

'The key to the crypt. I can't think who might have taken it. I'm sure that it was there on the morning of the funeral. Of course, there might be a simple explanation and I apologise in advance if I've called you all the way out here for nothing, but I thought...'

Bridget waved away his concerns. 'You were right to call me. When a crime like this has taken place, we have to look into anything out of the ordinary. This might turn out to be important.'

Her words of reassurance seemed to calm him, and he let out a long sigh. 'It's been a tough couple of days. I find myself starting to imagine all manner of things. In fact, I don't mind admitting to you, I was rather anxious going back inside the church for the first time since the… the murder.'

'I can imagine,' said Bridget. 'You know, there are people who can provide counselling after a traumatic event like this. I can put you in touch with someone, if you like.'

He laughed. 'Ah, I'm very familiar with counsellors, believe me.'

'I'm sure you are. But even so…'

He threw her a good-natured smile. 'Trust me, if I need help, I know who to turn to.'

'Could you show me where the key is normally kept?' she asked as they entered the church.

'Of course.' He led her to a small room to the south side, immediately before the altar. It was the first time for Bridget to venture this far into the church. The last time she'd been here, the place had been crawling with Vik's white-suited SOCO team, and she had tried to stay out of their way. Now she stopped to take in the details of the lovely old chancel.

'This is the oldest part of the church,' said the vicar. 'It dates back to the eleventh century. There was an older Anglo-Saxon church on the site, but the present building is of Norman origin.' He pointed back the way they had come. 'The nave was built in the twelfth century, and the north and south transepts were added by the monks of Abingdon in the early fifteenth century. The belltower was built in the following century, and the Victorians installed the stained glass in the East window.' He swung back round to indicate the fine image that took centre-stage above the altar. The coloured glass depicted St Michael vanquishing Satan in the form of a green devil.

'There's a cupboard in the vestry,' he continued. 'The key is always there. No one ever goes into the crypt, you see. There's no reason to.'

She followed him into the vestry where he opened the door to a small wooden cupboard mounted on the wall. Inside were two rows of hooks with keys on them. Each hook was labelled with a small handwritten sign sellotaped to the back of the cupboard: *north door, south door, belltower, organ vestry, crypt*. The hook labelled *crypt* was empty.

'Is this cupboard kept locked?' asked Bridget.

'No, it doesn't have a lock,' said Armistead, looking sheepish. 'I suppose that's an oversight in retrospect.'

'What about the vestry itself? Is it locked when you're not here?'

He shook his head with a dejected air. 'I don't normally bother to lock it up. If the church itself is locked, it doesn't seem worth locking this room as well. Hambledon is such a safe village. At least it felt that way before... I mean, I know there was that incident a few years back with the theft of lead from the roof, but the thieves didn't need a key to get up there.'

'So anyone could come in here and help

themselves to the key to the crypt?'

'Well, theoretically yes, but most people never come into the vestry.'

'Who does come in here? Who would know about the key cupboard?'

'Well, there's Eric Fletcher the organist, Bill Harris the tower captain – in fact all of the bellringers, come to think of it. Obviously, there was Harriet Stevenson. And, I suppose...' He hesitated.

'Yes?'

'I was going to say Emma, my wife, but I can't remember the last time she ever came into the vestry. There's simply no reason for her to do so. She's probably forgotten all about the key cupboard, if she ever knew about it. Anyway, I can't imagine for the life of me why Emma would want access to the crypt. Forget I mentioned her, she's not relevant here.'

Everyone is potentially relevant, thought Bridget, *including you.*

'You said that the key to the crypt was here on the morning of the funeral?'

Armistead considered the empty hook. 'Well, I think it was. I'm certain it was there on Sunday morning, at least.'

'And what about Wednesday? The day of the funeral?' *And the murder.*

He hesitated. 'I'd like to say that it was there, but I can't be a hundred percent certain. You could ask Bill Harris. He came in that morning to get the key to the belltower. We do make a

175

point of keeping the belltower locked. We wouldn't want unauthorised people wandering up there and falling on the spiral stairs or damaging the bells.'

'You told me on the phone that you thought you had a spare set of keys at the vicarage. Did you manage to find them?'

'Yes.' He produced a bunch of keys from his pocket.

'And this includes a key to the crypt?'

He brandished an old iron key, with an air of triumph.

'In that case, let's take a look inside the crypt, shall we?'

He led her to a small arched doorway located in the south transept, and after fumbling to turn the key in the lock, he eventually managed to get the door open. A steep and narrow flight of stone steps led down.

'It's best if I go first,' he said, producing his phone and switching on the flashlight. 'The treads are very uneven, and there's no lighting. No one ever comes down here.'

Bridget followed him into the gloom, his body a dark silhouette against the light from the phone. Only a faint white gleam flitted over the stone steps and walls. The temperature dropped quickly as she descended into the dark, chilly vault where sunlight never penetrated. Bridget shivered.

The descent into the darkness didn't last long. Soon she felt level ground beneath her feet again, and a damp, earthy smell filled her nostrils. She switched on her own flashlight and shone it around to try and get an understanding of the space she had entered.

The crypt was large, the far walls disappearing into darkness so that it was impossible to accurately gauge the size of the place. Thick, stone pillars supported the vaulted ceiling, from which long ropes of cobwebs trailed like Hallowe'en decorations. She felt one touch her face, and quickly stepped back and brushed it away. Reluctant to venture too far from the steps, she swept her phone back and forth, until its feeble light picked out a row of stone masses huddled together in the middle of the room.

'What are those?' she asked, holding the light on them.

'Coffins,' whispered Martin. 'They're hundreds of years old.'

'And are they...'

'Yes, I believe that a number of bodies are interred in here.'

Bridget moved the light around the stone shapes, making large shadows rise and fall. A dull glint between the two nearest sarcophagi caught her eye. She moved forward a little and crouched down to examine it. A large, brass candlestick was wedged between the gap in the coffins. About eighteen inches in length, with a solid, tiered base, the candlestick bore a dark stain that in the cold light from the phone looked like rust.

'I think we might have found the murder

CHAPTER 15

Amy followed Bill Harris up the steep and winding belfry stairs. It was eight o'clock on Saturday morning, and they had come to prepare the bells for the wedding of Jamie Reade and Kayleigh Simpson. The church had been out of bounds due to the police investigation, and so they hadn't yet had a chance to remove the mufflers after Henry Burton's funeral. It had looked at one point as if the wedding might have to be postponed but, much to everyone's relief, they had been given the go-ahead at last.

In the ringing chamber, the eight bell ropes were neatly looped to the walls, out of harm's way, their upper ends vanishing through holes in the ceiling. Amy had recruited one of her Oxford bell-ringing buddies to take Jamie's place on bell number five. The groom could hardly be expected to ring the bells at his own wedding.

'I'm getting too old for this,' said Bill, eyeing the wooden ladder that led up to the next level of the tower.

'Nonsense,' said Amy. 'You're as fit as a fiddle.' But looking more closely, Bill did seem

179

tired, not quite his usual sprightly self. The murder had taken a toll on all of them, and Bill was now the acting chair of the parish council on top of his other duties, something he could probably have done without.

'I'm sure I can manage it myself,' said Amy, 'if you want to stay here.'

'No, no, I'll be fine,' said Bill, shrugging off his earlier weariness. 'After you.'

With a firm grip and a steady foot, Amy quickly climbed the rungs that led up to the bell loft. She'd never been a big fan of school games lessons, but when it came to belltowers, she had a natural agility, not to mention a head for heights, that stood her in good stead.

On the next level, the bell ropes emerged from sally-holes in the floor and disappeared once again through corresponding holes in the ceiling. Mounted on the west wall of this room was a case housing the clock mechanism. One more ladder to climb, and up through a trap door, and she was in the bell chamber itself, Bill not far behind, despite his protestations of becoming too old for this job.

The view from up here was breath-taking. Through the slats of the south-facing window she could see the manor house, and the riverside path where she had walked arm-in-arm with Jake the other evening. The village was spread out before her like a scale model. Beyond the village lay miles of open fields, all the way to the Ridgeway, the ancient path that crossed England from east to west. To the north lay Abingdon and beyond that Oxford, and the Bodleian Library where she worked.

But what Amy loved most about the bell chamber was being up close to the huge bells, the largest weighing almost half a ton, and being able to touch the smooth, cold bronze, cast to perfection at the Whitechapel Foundry in London. The eight bells with their wheels and pulley mechanisms sat in a square metal frame, the original wooden frame having been replaced by Whites of Appleton as part of the Millennium refurbishment. The bells had been here for centuries and there was no reason to suppose they wouldn't still be ringing hundreds of years from now. They were like old friends, each one with its own personality. Now they waited, motionless and mute, but before long they would be singing in celebration.

To access each bell it was necessary to climb a small stepladder that was kept in the bell chamber for that purpose. Amy was happy to do the honours. She fetched the ladder and positioned it beside the treble bell. Then, climbing up she unwrapped the leather muffler that half-enclosed the clapper and handed it down to Bill.

Her hand traced out the inscription stamped onto the bell. She had often wondered about these mysterious markings. The gothic lettering wasn't easy to decipher, and they didn't seem to make much sense. She asked Bill about them now.

'Ah, yes,' said Bill. 'Each bell has its own inscription. If you read them all, from the treble down to the tenor, they make a short rhyme.'

'Really?' said Amy.

'Read them if you don't believe me,' said Bill with a chuckle. 'And then you can try and work out what it means.'

Amy leaned in closer to the bell, running her finger along the intricate lettering. Some of the spellings were a little archaic, but it wasn't too hard to read once you got used to the style of font.

Bee it knowne unto all men far and wyde

Her curiosity sparked, she tapped the inscription into the notes app on her phone, then moved the ladder round to the next bell. She removed the muffler, then quickly deciphered the words that ran around its curved form.

That in this place a secret doth reside

'Now I'm hooked,' she said to Bill with a grin. 'I love secrets.'

By the time she had removed the mufflers from all eight bells and noted the inscriptions on her phone, she had an eight-line verse:

Bee it knowne unto all men far and wyde

That in this place a secret doth reside
Where mortal bones are set to rest within
And blind wormes creep and lay their eggs hidd'n
'Gainst northern wall in wynter's chill embrace
To iron girde and stone then turn to face
Descend into my chamber cold and darke
Therein thou shalt thy reward come to marke

'What does it mean?' she asked.

Bill shook his head. 'I wish I knew. Maurice Fairweather has a theory that the poem refers to buried treasure, but if there was once any treasure buried in the village, it's long gone now.'

Buried treasure!

Amy's mind was buzzing with possibilities.

Buried treasure, here in Hambledon!

She could hardly wait to tell Jake about her discovery. A legend about buried treasure was obviously a clear motive for murder.

★

Shaun Daniels hopped off the bus just outside Oxford Crown Court and walked the rest of the way up St Aldate's. Saturday shoppers and tourists thronged the wide pavements; double-decker buses clogged the narrow road. He didn't come into the city very often and had forgotten how overcrowded it could be. Tom Tower, gleaming golden in the bright June sun, rose tall and proud above the hubbub of the street below,

183

but Shaun had no time for architectural niceties. He had come here with a single purpose in mind, and when it was done he would catch the next bus back to Abingdon and from there to Hambledon.

He found the place he was looking for quickly enough, having already checked it out online. A small, independent bookseller that specialised in rare and second-hand books. His research hadn't been able to pin down how much *Tintinnalogia* could be worth, but given that inscribed first editions of *Harry Potter* could sell for tens of thousands of pounds, he reckoned something of this age and rarity must be worth a lot more. The fact that he hadn't been able to find any other examples online must mean that it was extremely rare indeed.

He regretted now not nicking another couple of books while he'd had the chance, but it was too late now. A van had come to the manor the previous day and some men in overalls had carted off the entire contents of the library to the Bodleian where the books would no doubt sit in some gloomy corner for the next hundred years and no good would come of them, except for a handful of students and dons who might be interested in the old squire's dusty collection.

He pushed open the door of the shop and a bell tinkled overhead. Inside, the atmosphere was quiet and scholarly. An Oxford-type in mustard corduroys and a tweed jacket was browsing a shelf of leather-bound volumes. He turned to

Shaun and gave him a bespectacled stare. Shaun stared back and the man returned to his book browsing. *Arrogant prick.* Just because Shaun was dressed in jeans, trainers and a zip-up jacket didn't mean he wasn't as good as mister tweed jacket.

He marched up to the counter where a slim, balding man in a check shirt and sombre tie was fussing about. He offered Shaun a snooty greeting. 'May I be of assistance?'

'Yeah,' said Shaun. 'You may.' He produced the copy of *Tintinnalogia* from inside his jacket. 'I have a book to sell. A very old one,' he said, laying it flat on the counter.

The bookseller produced a pair of rimless reading glasses from his top pocket, placed them carefully on his nose and lifted the book with long, delicate fingers.

Shaun watched carefully, keen to gauge the man's reaction. He was pleased by what he saw. The bookseller must be used to handling rare and valuable volumes, yet his eyes nearly bulged out of his head when he opened the book and turned to the first page. His finger hovered over the title of the book, and then over its publication date. 1668. He turned a page, and then another, his gaze locked on the words that flowed across the yellowed paper. Shaun let him have a good look. The longer the look, the better the price, he reckoned.

'How did you come by this book?' asked the bookseller eventually, after he'd spent a good while immersed in it.

'It was left to me,' lied Shaun. 'In a will. An old man I work for died recently, and he left me this. He once told me it was worth a lot of money.'

He'd already decided on this story before leaving home that morning. A mix of fact and fiction always worked better than barefaced lying. It was the same with the yarns he liked to spin in the Eight Bells on a Friday night. Mix in a few facts, and no one could tell where the truth ended and the cock and bull began.

'I see,' said the bookseller.

'So, I was hoping you'd be able to give me a price for it.'

'I certainly can,' said the bookseller. 'But this is an extremely rare and valuable book. I've never come across one quite like it before, so I would need to do some research and consult with colleagues in London before coming to a final price. If you could leave it with me for a couple of days, I'd be able to give you an accurate figure then.'

'Leave it with you?' Shaun was immediately on his guard. Was he being tricked? He reached out his hand and there was a tense moment as both men stood facing each other across the counter, their palms laid firmly on the book, looking each other in the eye. The bookseller's irises were pale blue and watery, almost grey. The man was thin and weedy. He would never be able to stop Shaun taking the book back and walking out of the shop. But what would be the point of that? He needed the money.

'I'll be wanting a receipt,' he said. 'A proper one, mind you. No funny business.'

'Of course,' said the bookseller. 'I can assure you that everything will be entirely above board. I am a highly respected buyer and seller of rare works.'

Shaun relaxed a little at the man's reassuring words and he released the book. 'All right, then. But no longer than two days.'

The bookseller wrote him a receipt, carefully noting down the title, author, publisher and date of publication of the book. Shaun checked it all thoroughly before pocketing it.

'I'll be back on Monday,' he said in what he hoped was a polite but vaguely threatening tone.

'I'll look forward to seeing you then,' said the bookseller with a timid smile.

Shaun left the shop, throwing a final glare at the man in corduroys and tweeds as he went.

CHAPTER 16

Jake sat at the back of the church clutching his order of service and trying not to feel too out of place. He was here as Amy's "significant other half", but as usual she was up in the belltower preparing to ring the bells. Although he recognised quite a few faces in the congregation, there was no one he knew well enough to sit with.

The pamphlet in his hands was printed on marbled white card and decorated with silver-embossed hearts and bells. *Order of Service for the marriage of Kayleigh Simpson and Jamie Reade.* Two names he had never even heard of just two months previously. He smiled, thinking how much his life had changed. If Ryan hadn't persuaded him to give online dating a shot, he would never have met Amy. He'd very nearly thrown in the towel on the whole internet-dating business after his first two dates had gone badly wrong – one with a desperate older woman, and one with a woman who had turned out to be married and whose bruiser of a husband Jake had needed to handcuff after he'd stormed into the wine bar to confront his faithless wife. He cringed with embarrassment as he recalled the toe-curling experiences. But then, incredibly, Amy had breezed into his life like a breath of fresh air. Now here he was, a guest at the wedding of two of her friends. He hardly recognised himself.

It felt odd being here for a wedding. The last time he'd been inside St Michael and All Angels he'd been standing over a dead body lying in a pool of blood. Now, the church was awash with stunning floral displays in red, pink and white, and the atmosphere was joyous. People waved cheerily at their friends and called out greetings; women in colourful summer dresses fanned themselves with their orders of service in the summer heat; the organist played something gentle and soporific in the background.

But the crime was as yet unsolved, and for all Jake knew the murderer might be among today's guests. He looked around, but could tell from the happy faces that no one apart from him had murder on their mind. Not today, at least. Yet he couldn't help glancing towards the tomb of Sir Edmund and Lady Ellen Burton in the north transept. He pictured the corpse of Harriet Stevenson lying at the foot of the tomb, her blood leaking over the floor. He hoped that Vik's team had cleaned up thoroughly, otherwise the bride's friends and family, who were seated on that side of the church, would have a very nasty reminder of what had taken place here only days before. Jake himself was sitting on the south side of the aisle, as he felt he knew Jamie better than Kayleigh. He shifted along the pew to make space for a couple of women whose partners were also in the belltower. They smiled and said hello, recognising him as one of their own. That's what he was now: a bellringing groupie.

The groom, looking splendid in grey tails and a burgundy waistcoat with a white rose in his lapel, entered, escorting a middle-aged woman in a floaty lilac dress and big hat – presumably the mother of the bride – to her place in the front pew on the north side of the church. Jake's thoughts turned inevitably to his own parents living in Leeds. He hadn't seen them since Christmas when he'd been on the verge of applying for a job in Halifax. Thankfully, he had chosen to remain in Oxford.

His mum had been pestering him for weeks now to bring Amy "up north" so they could meet her. He did want to introduce Amy to his parents – he was sure they would like her – so why hadn't he done it yet? It was true, he couldn't take time off work right in the middle of a murder investigation, but there was more to it than that. His mother wanted nothing more than for him to settle down with the right woman – and give her lots of doting grandchildren. And wasn't that just the problem? Jake was happy as he was. He was getting on great with Amy, but settling down and getting married was another step entirely. Where would they live, for one thing? Amy still lived at home with her parents, and his flat above the launderette was hardly suitable for married life. And Oxford was so expensive. A little voice inside told him he was making excuses, but he brushed it aside. Marriage was a big step and he needed to be absolutely sure that he was doing the right thing. He'd had his heart broken before and didn't want to be hurt again.

He was jolted out of his brooding by a sudden shift in the atmosphere. The buzz of conversation died away, and the organist struck a louder, more confident note. *The Arrival of the Queen of Sheba by George Frederick Handel*, the order of service informed him. As per their printed instructions, the guests rose to their feet and heads turned to watch as Kayleigh Simpson, looking elegant in a simple silk gown, walked down the aisle on the arm of her proud-looking father, trailed by half a dozen bridesmaids in peach silk, aged from mid-twenties to about five years old. Jake swallowed, wondering how Jamie was feeling at the sight of such an imposing delegation coming his way. Make no bones about it – marriage was definitely not a matter to be taken lightly.

The Reverend Martin Armistead led the service, welcoming everyone to St Michael and All Angels on this happy occasion. Except that the vicar didn't sound particularly happy to Jake's ears. His voice was strained and Jake had the distinct impression he was trying too hard to sound cheerful. There was an awkward moment when the vicar asked if anyone present knew of any reason why these two people may not lawfully marry and a toddler chose that moment to shout something unintelligible. But the tension was quickly broken by general laughter, and from then on, the wedding service flowed without a hitch. The singing was notably more robust and sonorous on the bride's side of the church thanks to a contingent of sopranos, altos, tenors and basses from an Oxford choir that Kayleigh sang with. The singers more than made up for the lack of musical ability on the groom's side. Jake himself mumbled along to the hymns, doing his best to keep in tune.

Half an hour later the happy couple were walking arm-in-arm back down the aisle to – according to the order of service – the jolly-sounding *Hornpipe from Handel's Water Music*, and right on cue the bells began to ring, beginning with the treble and descending to the tenor before embarking on some complicated pattern that Jake couldn't follow. No doubt Amy would try to explain it to him later. Glad to be out of the church at last, he found a bench in a quiet corner of the churchyard and sat in the early afternoon sun, happily listening to the bells.

★

Bridget swore as she struggled, and failed again, to zip up the dress she was trying on. She had always managed to fit perfectly well into a size sixteen in the past, so why not now? It was impossible that she could have gone up a whole dress size, especially while she'd been watching the calories so closely in the run-up to Ben and Tamsin's wedding. And why did clothing designers always assume that generously proportioned women must also be taller than average? Even if she could have squeezed into this dress she'd have been constantly tripping over the hem. Was there nothing in the whole of Oxford for a woman of her size but under five foot three? She'd lost count of the number of dresses she had tried on that morning and was rapidly closing in on despair. Finally, she abandoned her efforts and pulled the dress off, tugging it over her hips and letting the slinky fabric pool around her ankles.

'How's it going in there?' On the other side of the changing room curtain, the shop assistant remained hopeful despite the increasingly obvious futility of her task. She was a real trier, and Bridget was grateful that one of them still seemed to believe that the perfect dress was out there somewhere. 'Can I fetch you anything else?'

A slice of chocolate gateau and a large glass of wine, thought Bridget glumly. Dieting had done nothing for her cause, and she was tempted to believe that the supposed link between calorie intake and bodyweight was nothing more than a cruel hoax, designed to sell slimming products to desperate women.

'I don't think any of these are quite right,' she

said, drawing aside the curtain and handing back the large collection of dresses that had been tested and found wanting.

'Perhaps something a little more…' began the assistant, but even she now seemed to be out of ideas.

'I think I'll leave it for now,' said Bridget. There's still a week to go before the wedding.'

She left the shop empty-handed with a growing feeling of impending doom. It was her own fault, of course. Chloe had been pestering her for weeks about her dress, and yet she'd left it until the last minute.

'I'm far too busy at work,' Bridget had told her whenever questioned. But they both knew that wasn't the real reason. She had simply wanted to pretend that the wedding wasn't happening. Now her plan appeared to have backfired catastrophically. She would arrive at the event wearing… what? She had no idea. Humiliation was guaranteed.

Jonathan had told her not to worry, that it wasn't the least bit important. But what did men know? Weddings were easy for them – they simply had to get their suits dry-cleaned and polish their shoes.

Oh, my God, shoes!

That was the other thing – accessories. It wasn't sufficient just to buy a dress, assuming she could ever find one that wasn't too tight, too long or too low-cut. She needed all the right accessories to go with it: shoes (and Bridget had never mastered the art of walking properly in high heels), clutch bag (fine for the days when women only carried a lipstick and a powder compact, but totally impractical for the modern specimen with her phone, car keys and a wallet full of credit cards), and then there was the question of a hat.

Bridget's helpful shop assistant had provided her with a bewildering plethora of advice on the subject. Some sort of headgear was definitely appropriate for a contemporary wedding, it seemed, especially for a posh one of the type that Ben and Tamsin's was sure to be, and a hat was perfect for a more mature woman. Bridget had levelled the assistant with a stern gaze at that point, and she had hastily added that for a younger woman, a fascinator would make a good choice. Bridget had been coaxed into trying on one or two of the ridiculous things before giving them up as a bad job. They reminded her of insects' antennae.

Nevertheless, a hat was the least of her problems. As she tried to put the failed shopping expedition behind her, her other worries immediately came crowding in.

Chloe, who ought to have been revising for her last few exams, had instead chosen to take the day off and go out with Alfie. 'It's the weekend, Mum! A break will do me good. Alfie's mum said so.'

Bridget was of the opinion that last-minute cramming never did anyone any harm – she had relied on it to get her through Oxford – and could make all the difference between a middling and a top grade. But if Alfie's mum was on Chloe's side, then the argument didn't seem to be a fair one. In the end they had come to a truce on the understanding that Chloe could take Saturday off but would study on Sunday.

But it was yesterday's discovery in the crypt of St Michael and All Angels that was really distracting her. She had called Vik straightaway after the find, and he had brought the SOCO team back to the church to collect the murder weapon and to examine the crypt for further evidence. The team's initial foray, it appeared, hadn't included the crypt, as no key for it was to be found and the underground chamber hadn't seemed relevant to the investigation. Bridget was now waiting for forensics to confirm that Harriet Stevenson had been killed with the candlestick. The brass ornament was certainly heavy enough to have dealt the fatal blow, and the dried blood on its base left little room in her mind for doubt.

In the north transept with the candlestick.

It sounded like a clue from a murder mystery game. But who had wielded the candlestick? Someone who knew where to find the key to the crypt. But that could have been one of many people, and not only the names that Martin Armistead had given her. The vestry and cupboard hadn't been kept locked, and so in principle anyone could have retrieved the key. Security had clearly not been a top priority in the

196

church. Maybe that would change now.

Bridget had interviewed Bill Harris, the tower captain, and he had confirmed that the key to the crypt had been hanging on its hook when he had arrived on the morning of the funeral to collect the key to the belltower. So that must mean that it had been taken immediately before or just after the funeral. If before, that implied premeditation. If after, that suggested that the person responsible might have panicked and thrown the murder weapon down into the crypt before fleeing the scene.

Just like Tobias Burton had been sighted – running from the church, with blood on his shoe.

She checked her phone in the vain hope that Vik or someone from the forensics lab might have tried to get in touch. She'd asked them to call her as soon as they had any news on the candlestick. But there was nothing, at least not from work. Vanessa had sent a message checking that Bridget would be coming for Sunday lunch as usual. It was tempting to decline, using pressure of work or the need to supervise Chloe's revision as an excuse, but she was trying to be a better sister, being more supportive of Vanessa's efforts to relocate their ageing parents to a retirement home. She sent a quick confirmation and then, worn out from her morning – shopping was far more exhausting if you didn't buy anything – dropped in at her favourite café on Turl Street for a restorative cappuccino and a chocolate brownie.

To hell with the diet, and to hell with wedding outfits.

★

Jake carried two pints of Old Speckled Hen over to the far end of the pub garden, where Amy was waiting for him at one of the picnic benches that overlooked the river. It was a quiet corner, or at least as quiet as anywhere in the vicinity of the Eight Bells could be this evening, given the cries and squeals of small children running over the grass, and the laughter of their parents and the other wedding guests. The day had been a lot of fun, but he was looking forward to spending some time alone with Amy, for despite attending the wedding together, they'd hardly had a private moment to themselves all day.

The bellringers had rung the bells of St Michael and All Angels throughout the taking of the wedding photographs, first in the churchyard and then moving on to the village green. Jake had been happy to remain in the churchyard listening to what he now regarded as a pleasant sound rather than a cacophony. He had listened out especially for the highest pitched bell, knowing that Amy was in her usual place on the treble. He had tried to make sense of the pattern of changes, but although he could now tell the difference between the opening "round" – in which the bells were rung in order down the scale from treble to tenor, and the "rows" that followed, in which each of the eight bells sounded once, but in a different order each time – he still couldn't identify precisely what changes were being applied to produce the resulting variations. No doubt Amy would tell him later whether it was a "Primrose Surprise Major" or an "Avon Delight Maximus" or something even more elaborate.

The wedding photographs took an age to complete, with the photographer seemingly engaged in a quest of his own to capture every possible permutation of guest: bride and groom; bride and bridesmaid; groom and best man; bride with family, groom with mother-in-law, and so on, and so forth. Jamie's smile never once wavered, yet Jake felt a sense of relief that he was an observer and not a participant in this complicated and protracted ritual of marriage.

When the bellringers finally appeared, everyone gave them a round of applause. And then the guests proceeded on foot to the pub where the wedding reception was held in a marquee on the lawn. The afternoon had unfolded in a sequence of drinks, food and speeches, and by the end of it, Jake had the feeling that he'd chatted to more folk than when he'd made his round of the village taking witness statements after the murder. The conversation had certainly been a lot more pleasant this time.

Now he was looking forward to having Amy to himself for a while, and he was wondering if he might even pluck up the courage to invite her up north to visit his parents.

'Cheers.' Amy took a swig of her beer, then swiped her phone to unlock it. 'Look at this. I've been waiting all day to show you.'

He was expecting her to show him some photos from the wedding, but when she passed him the phone, he saw what looked like a poem. 'What's this?'

'Read it.' He could tell she was excited about it.

He read it aloud, stumbling over one or two of the peculiar words. 'Is it Shakespeare or something?' Since coming to Oxford, Jake had grown used to Shakespearean love sonnets popping up in the middle of murder investigations. But this was hardly a love sonnet. The references to "mortal bones", "blind wormes" and "my chamber cold and darke" were sinister, to say the least.

'Not Shakespeare,' said Amy, 'but you're in the right century. Those lines are the inscriptions written on the bells of St Michael and All Angels. One line on each bell, from the treble down to the tenor. When you put them together you get this eight-line verse, written in iambic pentameter.'

Jake scratched his nose. He had learned about iambic pentameter back in school, but couldn't remember for the life of him what it meant, and had hoped never to hear about it again. 'So what does it mean?' he asked. 'It says, "in this place a secret doth reside". What secret? And what's this "reward" it talks about?'

'Well,' said Amy, taking back her phone, 'it's a secret! But some people think it's talking about buried treasure. Hold on, I'll send it to you.' She tapped at her phone and pressed send.

Jake's phone beeped to acknowledge receipt of the message, but he made no move to look at it. First Shakespeare, now buried treasure. Even by Oxford standards, this was pretty wild. Against his better judgement, he asked, 'So where's this treasure buried? And who buried it?'

'Duh, that's the mystery!' Amy grinned at him. 'But don't you think this might be the reason Harriet Stevenson was murdered?'

'Now you've totally lost me.'

'Look,' said Amy, 'if there really is treasure hidden in the village, perhaps even in the church itself, isn't it possible that someone might have discovered its location? Or perhaps it was Harriet who found out where it is, and that's why she was killed.'

'I still don't understand the logic.'

'I don't understand it myself yet,' said Amy crossly. 'But I was hoping that you'd be able to find out more. You're supposed to be a police detective.'

It was the closest that they had ever come to exchanging angry words, and Jake was dismayed that they seemed to be falling out over something so ridiculous. He struggled to find a way to diffuse the disagreement, but his thoughts were interrupted by the sound of shouting coming from across the lawn.

Amy looked anxiously in the direction of the pub. 'That's Dad's voice. What's going on?'

Jake jumped to his feet, relieved by the interruption. 'I'll go and see. You stay here.'

He ran inside and found Robert Bagot in an altercation with Shaun Daniels, the gardener from the manor house. A quick assessment of the situation told him that the latter had drunk far too much and that Robert was attempting to oust him from the premises, without much success.

'I've ev'ry right to be 'ere,' bellowed Shaun, his words slurring. 'This is a public bar, and I demand another drink.'

'You've had quite enough already, Shaun,' said Robert.

Shaun swayed dangerously. 'I'll be the judge of that. Not you. Not anyone! People 'ave been judging me my whole life. Bastard, they call me, because my father ran away. But I'll show them!' He turned to face the rest of the pub, who were all watching. 'I'm as good as any one of yer!'

'Hey,' said Jake, stepping into the fray. 'Cool it, mate.'

Shaun turned in his direction. 'Cool it? Who are you to tell me what t'do? I'll do what I damn well want! And what I want is 'nother drink!' He slammed his empty glass on the bar.

'I think it's time you called it a day.'

Shaun stumbled forwards, brandishing the pint glass. 'I told yer, I'll do what I please.' He prodded Jake in the chest with a thick finger. 'You dunno what it's like growing up in a place like this.' He gestured expansively with his arms. 'Y'can't do a thing here without someone poking their nose into y'business. Well, I've had a belly full o' that, I can tell you. It's all going to be diff'rent from now on. Soon, I'll be rich! I'll be as rich as any of you, and I'll be able t'do whatever I bloody well like!'

He lurched to one side, knocking into a table and sending drinks flying. A woman leapt up with a shriek, her white dress covered in red wine.

'That's enough,' said Jake. 'Now put that glass down and let me walk you home.'

'Get yer hands off me!' shouted Shaun. He hurled the empty pint glass at the bar where it smashed into the row of optics, making Sue Bagot scream in fright.

'Right, that's it,' said Jake. He grabbed Shaun's arms behind his back and slapped on a pair of handcuffs which he'd handily forgotten to take out of his suit pocket. 'Shaun Daniels, I'm arresting you for being drunk and disorderly in a public place. Let's see how you enjoy spending a night in the cells of Abingdon police station.'

CHAPTER 17

Dear Lord and Father of mankind,
Forgive our foolish ways;
Reclothe us in our rightful mind;
In purer lives Thy service find,
In deeper reverence, praise,
In deeper reverence, praise.

As the voices of the congregation swelled to fill
the rafters, the Reverend Martin Armistead
gazed out upon the faces of his flock and
wondered, not for the first time, if he could in all
conscience continue as vicar of St Michael and
All Angels, or whether it might be time to step
aside.

The pressure of carrying on, and endeavouring
to keep up appearances and pretend that nothing
was wrong when inside all was agonising turmoil
was becoming unbearable.

Mouthing the familiar words of the hymn, he
replayed in his mind the conversation he'd had
with his wife the previous evening. A
conversation that had shocked him to the core,

and given him yet another sleepless night.

He had believed, or at least he had persuaded himself to believe, that in the last few days she was looking more herself. A rosy glow had appeared in her cheeks, which he had interpreted as renewed vigour. And she had been spending more time outdoors, enjoying the warm sunshine, instead of staying in her room, the curtains closed against the light, her face pale and drawn.

And then it had happened. Over a simple meal of spaghetti accompanied by a glass of wine, Emma had announced, quite serenely, that she was glad Harriet Stevenson was dead. That in fact, the woman's murder had brought her a great deal of comfort.

'You don't really mean that,' he'd said in response.

'I do,' she said, lifting up her wine glass. 'I hated her.'

For a moment he thought she was going to raise a toast to the killer of the churchwarden, but she had calmly taken a sip of her wine and then carried on with her meal as if she had said nothing out of the ordinary.

Martin hadn't known at the time what to make of this pronouncement and he still didn't. Now, the words of the hymn sounded hollow to him. *Reclothe us in our rightful mind.* The fact was, Emma wasn't in her rightful mind and hadn't been for a long time.

He gripped the edge of the pulpit for support

as his own mind flashed back to the awful series of events that had unfolded in Birmingham. First joy at learning they were expecting their first child, and then – four months later – the trauma of losing it: the blood, the panic of the rush into hospital, his gut-wrenching wait as Emma underwent an emergency operation, and then the ensuing months of her depression, as black as anything he had ever witnessed.

The gracious calling of the Lord…

He had prayed fervently throughout that period, but no good had come of his hours spent kneeling. No easing, nor comfort, nor grace. Instead, Emma had almost died in a suicide attempt.

That had been the final straw.

He had requested, and been granted, a transfer to a quieter parish, a place where Emma might gradually heal, away from the stresses of the inner city.

O sabbath rest by Galilee!
O calm of hills above…

But living in Hambledon hadn't helped Emma in the way he'd hoped. She had remained withdrawn at best. Her depression had continued, as frightening as ever. And when she said such horrible things as she had the previous day, his worry grew even deeper. She simply wasn't the Emma he knew. She had been such a kind person before.

They reached the final verse of the hymn. It had been one of Harriet Stevenson's favourites, which was why he'd chosen it today. When he glanced toward the pew she had always occupied, he still expected to see her there, singing her heart out. But of course, the pew was empty.

Breathe through the heats of our desire
Thy coolness and Thy balm;
Let sense be dumb, let flesh retire;
Speak through the earthquake, wind, and fire,
O still small voice of calm,
O still small voice of calm!

If only he could rediscover that *still small voice of calm*. But he feared it was lost to him forever.

★

Leaving Chloe immersed in her English Literature revision and with a frozen pizza to heat in the oven, Bridget drove round to her sister's house in Charlbury Avenue for Sunday lunch. It was the one day in the week when she could be guaranteed a home-cooked meal using all the finest ingredients instead of the microwavable fare that was her staple diet.

She felt guilty leaving Chloe at home while she went out for lunch, but this was the bargain they had struck – that in return for a day off on Saturday, Chloe would work all through Sunday. 'But you will remember to eat, won't you?' Bridget had asked.

'Duh. Of course, Mum. I'll be fine. Don't worry.'

'And you won't spend all your time chatting with Alfie or Olivia?'

'No, I promise.'

Jonathan was busy this weekend preparing for a new exhibition, so Bridget went to her sister's alone. She parked her Mini on the driveway behind Vanessa's Range Rover and rang the bell of the large, detached house. The garden looked amazing, the borders blooming with so many flowers that it looked like an exhibit from the Chelsea Flower Show. Bridget could only marvel at her sister's achievements. It helped that Vanessa's husband, James, ran a successful business, leaving Vanessa free to raise their two children, Florence and Toby. But even so, she clearly worked tremendously hard to keep her house and garden so perfect. Bridget could scarcely imagine maintaining her own life in such immaculate order. Perhaps when she retired.

'Bridget,' said Vanessa with surprise as she opened the door, scanning the driveway. 'Is it just you today?'

An incredible aroma of roast beef wafted from the kitchen, making Bridget's stomach rumble.

'Just me,' she said. 'Jonathan's busy at the gallery, and Chloe's revising her English Literature.'

Rufus, the family's Golden Labrador, hurtled down the hallway and thrust his nose against Bridget's legs. She patted him on the head. A dog was another thing she had no time for. Perhaps that was something else she might consider for her retirement, but right now any kind of pet was out of the question unless it could feed and entertain itself all day long.

'How are the exams going?' asked Vanessa as she ushered Bridget into the kitchen.

'Just one more to go. I'll be so glad when they're over. It's been so stressful. All the time I worry whether she's working hard enough.'

'I'm sure she'll be fine,' said Vanessa breezily, checking on the vegetables and stirring the gravy. Vanessa could be remarkably cool about things that didn't directly involve her. Perhaps that was the flipside to the obsessive control that she exerted over everything she did consider to be her domain. 'Chloe's a bright girl. You know, James and I have started thinking about where Florence and Toby will go to school when they're thirteen.'

'But they're only nine and seven,' said Bridget. She hoped Vanessa wasn't going to spend the next four to six years agonising over senior school choices the way she obsessed over everything else. Both children were currently day pupils at Oxford's prestigious Dragon School, a preparatory school with outstanding extracurricular opportunities. Private education was well beyond Bridget's means, but Chloe had always been happy enough in the local comprehensive.

'Can you carry these for me?' asked Vanessa, passing her a tureen of potatoes.

Bridget helped her carry the food through to the dining room where the children were dutifully laying the table, supervised by their father.

'A glass of red?' asked James, holding up a bottle of wine.

'Just a small one for me, please,' said Bridget.

'So,' said Vanessa, once everyone was seated and the plates had been piled high with succulent roast beef, roast potatoes crisped to perfection, steamed broccoli and carrots, and thick, brown gravy made with juices from the meat, 'how did your shopping trip go yesterday? I want to hear about everything you bought.'

Bridget groaned. It had been a mistake to tell Vanessa about her shopping plans. At five foot nine and a size ten, Vanessa always found it easy to buy clothes that showed off her figure to advantage. She could never understand Bridget's inability to do the same.

'I didn't actually buy anything. Nothing fitted,' said Bridget, popping a roast potato into her mouth.

'Oh, Bridget! You're hopeless! I knew I should have come with you. I'll tell you what, I'll drop everything tomorrow and come with you. I'm sure that together we can sort you out.'

'No,' said Bridget, who had no desire to be "sorted out" by her sister. 'I've got far too much on at work at the moment.'

'Well, you're going to have to make time soon. The wedding's less than a week away. And you'll want to look your very best in front of Ben's new wife, won't you?'

'Thanks for reminding me,' said Bridget sullenly.

'More carrots, anyone?' asked James into the uncomfortable silence that had fallen on the table.

It was afterwards, over coffee, when Florence and Toby had disappeared off to the living room to do some jigsaws, that Vanessa launched into her prepared speech which she'd obviously been saving up for the appropriate moment. She brought a glossy brochure to the table and pushed it in Bridget's direction. The picture on the front showed a white-haired couple smiling beatifically at each other in landscaped grounds with a row of white houses in the background.

'I finally persuaded Mum and Dad to visit the retirement village in Witney,' said Vanessa, 'but you'd have thought I was proposing to send them to a prison camp, they were so unenthusiastic about it.'

'What didn't they like about it?' asked Bridget.

'I've no idea,' said Vanessa, bewildered. 'I mean, just look at the brochure. They've got a spa, a library, a restaurant and a café. They offer arts and crafts sessions, lectures, music, croquet and bowling. They arrange trips to the local garden centre and places of interest. And Mum and Dad would be well cared for. It's ideal.'

'Maybe it's just all too different to what they're used to,' said Bridget, flicking through the brochure. The range of activities on offer was quite exhausting.

'I don't know how many times I've told them they need to put their house on the market,' said Vanessa, blithely ignoring Bridget's comment. 'Now's the perfect time. They don't want to leave it till the winter when the weather's rotten. It's always blowing a gale on the coast.'

'What do you want me to do?' asked Bridget with a sinking feeling in her stomach. She could already guess the answer.

'I want you to back me up,' said Vanessa, 'and properly, this time. Like you mean it. I need you to speak to them and make them see sense. They won't be able to keep resisting if we show a united front.'

A united front. Vanessa made it sound like they were preparing for battle. Perhaps they were. Her parents could be pig-headed at times – and they definitely weren't the only ones in the family like that. Bridget's default position of claiming that she was too busy at work – which was almost always true – wouldn't keep Vanessa off her back much longer.

But perhaps there was another way of solving

the dispute. 'I think the problem is that Mum and Dad don't want to give up their independence,' she said.

Vanessa arched her eyebrows in affront. 'But they wouldn't have to. They could still have their freedom. It's just that everything would be taken care of for them... meals, cleaning, gardening –'

'Exactly,' said Bridget. 'Dad loves his garden, and Mum's very houseproud. They don't want to be looked after all the time.'

'That's just silly. It would enable them to get so much more from life.'

'Here's a suggestion,' said Bridget, an idea taking form as she spoke, 'what if they came to live with you?'

'With me?'

'With you and James, I mean. Your house is plenty big enough, isn't it?'

'I suppose.'

James nodded his approval. 'We could make the guest suite available to them and still have a spare room if anyone else wanted to stay over. Couldn't we, Vanessa?'

'Hmm...'

'And,' concluded Bridget, sensing the possibility of triumph, 'you could keep an eye on them, while allowing them to look after themselves as much as they want.'

Bridget could tell that Vanessa was giving the suggestion serious consideration. 'You know, Bridget, it's not a *terrible* idea. It's certainly better than your proposal to do *nothing*. I'll have to put it to them and see what they say.'

Bridget caught James's eye and thought she detected a note of relief that the two sisters had appeared to agree on something. 'That's decided then,' he said cheerfully. 'More coffee everyone?'

CHAPTER 18

Monday morning, and Bridget was glad to be back at work. Weekends were supposed to be a time to relax, but hers had left her feeling exhausted. She had failed to buy a dress for the rapidly-approaching wedding, battled with her daughter over exam revision, and clashed with Vanessa over their parents. She had longed for Jonathan to console her, but he'd been busy all weekend, just putting in an all-too-brief appearance on Sunday evening.

Now, back at work, all she had to worry about was whether there had been any progress on the investigation. She was still waiting for forensics to get back to her about the candlestick.

'Does anyone have anything to report?' she asked at the morning's team briefing.

'It might not be relevant,' said Jake, 'but I was in Hambledon on Saturday for the wedding of Jamie Reade and Kayleigh Simpson.'

'Go on,' she said.

'Well,' said Jake, 'in the evening, I arrested Shaun Daniels, the gardener at the manor house, for being drunk and disorderly. He was in the pub, mouthing off about how everyone had looked down on him all his life, but now he was going to be rich. He wasn't making a lot of sense to be honest.'

'What happened to him?'

'He was released after a night in Abingdon cells.'

'It's funny you should mention Shaun Daniels,' said Andy, 'because earlier on Saturday, St Aldate's police station logged a report of a possible stolen book in connection with him.'

'A stolen book?' asked Bridget, puzzled.

Andy flicked through his notebook. 'I was cross-checking witness statements with the police database to find out if any of the people we'd spoken to had a criminal record. Shaun's name came up in connection with an offence of theft committed in 1993.'

'That's going back a good few years,' said Ryan. 'What did he nick?'

'The Sunday collection from the church. He was arrested again four years ago on suspicion of stealing lead from the church roof, but was released without charge because of insufficient evidence. What's interesting about that is that the witness who accused him of theft was none other than Harriet Stevenson.'

'That is interesting,' said Bridget. 'What about this stolen book?'

'Well,' said Andy, 'it seems that Shaun was in Oxford on Saturday morning, trying to sell an extremely rare and valuable book to an antiquarian bookseller. Apparently, this book is so rare that only three copies of its first edition are known to exist. Well, four now, if this one turns out to be genuine. Anyway, the bookseller immediately became suspicious and contacted the police.'

'What's the name of this book?' asked Bridget.

'It's a funny one.' Andy furrowed his brow as he struggled over the pronunciation. '*Tin...Tin...*'

'*The Adventures of Tintin*?' suggested Ryan with a wink.

'*Tintinnalogia*,' said Andy, eventually spitting it out.

Bridget shrugged. 'I've never heard of it. What is it?'

To her surprise it was Jake who answered. 'It's a famous book about bellringing.' He turned to Ryan. 'That historian bloke in the pub, Maurice Fairweather, he mentioned it.'

'But how on earth could Shaun Daniels have got his hands on such a rare book?' asked Bridget.

'Maurice told us that Henry Burton's grandfather, Francis, was a keen bellringer and a collector of books on the subject. So perhaps Shaun stole it from the library at the manor house. Come to think of it, Amy did mention something about a missing book.'

'So this is why Shaun was boasting about becoming rich,' said Ryan. 'He must think this book is going to make his fortune.'

'All right,' said Bridget. 'I think we can all agree that this sheds fresh light on the case. Shaun Daniels appears to be a habitual criminal with a previous conviction. Stealing the Sunday collection wasn't a big-time crime, but this book sounds like it might be extremely valuable, and the business of stealing lead from the church roof also sounds relevant. I know that Harriet Stevenson was concerned about the state of the roof. If she suspected that Shaun was responsible, then...' She left her speculation hanging.

'You want to bring him in for questioning, ma'am?' asked Ffion, looking keen to get involved.

'Definitely.' But in light of everything she now knew about the surly gardener, Bridget felt that she could use a little extra muscle on her side. 'Jake, since you're on familiar terms with Mr Daniels, maybe you'd like to join me?'

★

There was no gardener tending the topiary hedges of Hambledon Manor when Bridget and Jake arrived at the house that morning. Instead the grounds were deserted.

'Let's try his cottage,' said Bridget. 'It's down by the boathouse.'

She knocked on the door and waited, but there was no answer.

She was about to give up and take a look around the back of the house when the door creaked open and Shaun Daniels's face appeared, unshaven and with bloodshot eyes. He was wearing a baggy T-shirt with loose-fitting jogging pants, his feet bare. As soon as he saw Jake, he glowered.

'What do you lot want now? This is harassment.'

'May we come in, please, Mr Daniels?' said Bridget.

He shot a resentful look in Jake's direction, and Bridget thought he was about to refuse, but then the fight seemed to go out of him and he stepped away from the door. She followed him inside.

The entrance opened directly into a small front room with a flagstone floor, and walls finished in cracked and damp-looking plaster. Shaun hadn't been lying when he'd said the cottage was cold and damp. There appeared to be no heating other than the open fireplace that was piled high with logs. The grimy windows were small and let little light inside.

The place was a tip, with empty pizza boxes and beer cans over the floor, chairs and side table. Shaun took a seat on an old, brown sofa in front of the TV. He muted the television but didn't turn it off. Nor did he offer Jake or Bridget a seat.

Bridget looked around, but every available surface appeared to be covered in junk. She perched on the edge of an armchair, while Jake remained standing.

'Not working today, Mr Daniels?' she enquired. It was already ten o'clock in the morning, and she imagined that a gardener would start work early to make the most of the day.

A fresh scowl stretched his features. 'I've been sacked. Can you believe it? Thrown out of my job and kicked out of my home, after all those years of loyal service.'

This was news to Bridget. But perhaps it explained why he had got so drunk the other night. 'I'm sorry to hear that,' she said.

'Are you? Are you really? The fact is, nobody cares a jot what happens to me. They never have.' He picked up the remote and turned off the TV. 'So, why have you come to talk to me? Is it about Saturday night? Listen, I meant no harm, I just had a little too much to drink, that's all.'

'We're not here about Saturday night,' said Jake.

Shaun's bloodshot eyes jerked up. 'What, then?'

'We'd like to speak to you about the matter of a book that you' – Bridget hesitated over her choice of verb – '*acquired* recently and which you took to a bookseller in Oxford on Saturday morning.'

Shaun seemed startled by her words. He was immediately more alert, sitting forward, hands clenched on his knees. 'What's all this about a book?'

'We've received a report that the book in question may be stolen goods. Can you explain how you came to be in possession of it?'

Shaun's face screwed up in dismay. 'Did that damn bookseller tell you it was stolen? That scheming bastard. I knew I couldn't trust him.'

'You don't deny attempting to sell the book, then?'

'I don't deny it at all! I've even got a receipt for it. I've got it here, somewhere.' He began to rummage through his pockets.

'There's no need to show us a receipt,' said Bridget. 'The fact that you offered the book for sale doesn't appear to be in dispute. What does concern us is how you came to be in possession of such a rare and valuable item.'

He nodded. 'It is valuable, then? How much?'

'I don't know,' said Bridget. 'Tell me what you know about the book.'

He shot her a calculating look, as if trying to work out how much he could tell her without incriminating himself. 'It belonged to the old squire,' he said at last.

'And how did it end up in your possession?'

'He gave it to me.'

'When?'

'Before he died.'

'Can you be more specific?'

'It was a few months ago, maybe six.'

'And why did he give it to you?'

'Perhaps because he appreciated me,' said

Shaun. 'He was a decent bloke, the old squire, not like that son of his.' His eyes darkened. 'Throwing me out of my own home. After all these years. Can you credit it! Now I've got no work. How am I supposed to pay the rent on a new place?'

'Can you prove that Henry Burton gave the book to you?' asked Jake.

A rebellious flash animated the gardener's features. 'Can you prove he didn't?'

'Mr Daniels,' said Bridget, 'we are aware that you have a previous conviction for theft.'

'That was years ago,' he protested. 'I was just a youngster then. I learned my lesson and put all that behind me.'

'Harriet Stevenson didn't think so,' said Jake. 'She accused you of stealing lead from the church roof.'

'That old cow was always on my case. If as much as a bar of chocolate went missing from the village shop, she was convinced that I'd taken it.'

'So you deny any involvement in removing lead from the church?'

'Of course I do!'

'And you deny stealing the book?'

'I do deny it.'

Bridget tried a different tack. 'Are you aware that Henry Burton bequeathed his entire collection of books to the Bodleian Library?'

'Yes,' said Shaun sullenly. 'I saw the van come to the house the other day and take them all away.'

'And do you have a particular interest in bellringing?'

'Bellringing? No!'

'So why did he choose to give you what may have been the most valuable book in his entire collection, but not to mention it in his will?'

The gardener appeared to have no good explanation. 'He's dead and buried now, so you can't ask him.'

'Was anyone else aware of this gift? Your mother, for example?'

'I don't know. You'd have to ask her.'

'Don't worry. We will. But tell me this, did Harriet Stevenson find out that you'd stolen *Tintinnalogia*, and is that why you killed her?'

Now a look of terror seemed to seize him. 'No!' he blurted. 'She was already dead when I took the book!'

Bridget allowed the silence that followed this pronouncement to fill the room. Shaun looked aghast as the realisation of what he'd just revealed sunk in. He buried his face in his hands.

'So,' said Bridget, 'you do admit to taking the book?'

Shaun slumped back on the sofa. 'What does it matter, anyway? The rest of the collection has been given to the Bodleian. Haven't they got enough books already? They're not going to miss one little book about bellringing.'

'So you thought you'd just help yourself,' said Jake. 'To something that didn't belong to you.'

Shaun shook his head miserably. 'I had no

choice. I'd lost my job, my home, I had nothing left. I've worked here all my life, and then that bitch of an estate manager just goes and tells me to bugger off, as if I'm nothing. Tobias couldn't even be bothered to give me the news himself. The money from selling that book would have kept me off the streets. I didn't want much for it, just enough to tide me over and get me back on my feet. I reckon it's no more than I deserve after all the work I've put in maintaining that garden. What will happen now?' he asked miserably.

Bridget couldn't help but feel a touch of sympathy for the wretched man. 'What will happen now, Shaun, is that you'll be arrested for theft and taken to Kidlington for questioning. Added to the drunk and disorderly charge from Saturday night, I'm afraid it's not looking too good for you.'

'Can I say goodbye to my mum before I go?'

'All right.' Bridget nodded to Jake, who cuffed Shaun Daniels for the second time in three days, then called for a marked car to come and pick him up. They led him to the manor house, where Bridget rang the bell.

When Josephine Daniels answered the door, she gasped at the sight of her son in handcuffs. 'What's going on?'

'I'm sorry, Mum.'

It was distressing to see a man of fifty years reduced to such a pathetic state. 'Miss Daniels,' said Bridget, 'I'm afraid I have to inform you that your son is under arrest on suspicion of theft.'

The housekeeper wrung her thin hands together. 'Oh, Shaun! What have you done?'

'I took a book, Mum. One belonging to the old squire. I'm sorry.'

Josephine Daniels turned to Bridget. 'Inspector,' she appealed, 'I know that Shaun doesn't always make the right choices, but please don't be too hard on him.'

'He's a grown man,' said Bridget. 'He ought to know the difference between right and wrong.'

'He's had a hard life,' said his mother. 'It's not been easy for him.'

Bridget kept her voice level. 'The judge may take that into consideration, but as far as the police are concerned, he'll be charged and treated just the same as anyone else in his position. Good-bye, Miss Daniels.'

The marked police car arrived just on time and Jake bundled Shaun into the back.

Bridget breathed a sigh of relief.

'Don't feel sorry for him, ma'am,' said Jake. 'He should be grateful we're only charging him with theft, and not murder.'

'You think he might have killed Harriet Stevenson?'

'I don't know,' said Jake. 'But he's a very dodgy character and I've seen for myself how violent he can be.'

CHAPTER 19

It was late morning when Amy received a summons from the Librarian. She'd just been about to embark on the mammoth task of cataloguing the books that had been transferred from Hambledon Manor to the Bodleian and she expected that Professor Danvers would be wanting an update on the project. So on entering his office, she was rather surprised to find a uniformed policeman standing there. Her thoughts jumped immediately to the murder enquiry and to Jake.

The concern must have shown on her face because Danvers said, 'No need to look so alarmed, Amy. This is good news.'

'Sir?'

'This policeman has just dropped by to return a book to us.' He held out a small volume for her to take.

She glanced at the title and felt a rush of excitement. 'Wow,' she said, before collecting herself. 'Sorry, it's just that *Tintinnalogia* was the first book ever written on the art of bellringing.' She turned to the title page and could scarcely believe what she was seeing. 'But this is a first edition!'

'I thought you'd be happy,' said Danvers. 'When she's not working here,' he told the policeman, 'Miss Bagot is a keen bellringer.'

'I see, sir,' said the policeman.

'But I don't understand,' said Amy. 'Only three copies of the first edition of *Tintinnalogia* are known to exist. One is at the British Museum, one is at Cambridge University Library, and the other is owned by the Central Council of Bellringers.'

'And now a fourth copy has been unearthed, and it belongs to us here at the Bodleian,' said Danvers with an indulgent smile.

Amy couldn't have been happier if she'd been holding Shakespeare's handwritten manuscript of *Hamlet*, complete with all the bard's inkblots and crossings out. She carefully turned another page of the ageing book. It really was in remarkably good condition. She beamed at Professor Danvers. 'This is wonderful news. But where did it come from?'

Danvers gestured to the policeman. 'Would you care to explain?'

The policeman cleared his throat. 'We have reason to believe that this book belongs to the collection of the late Henry Burton of Hambledon Manor. It was stolen and offered for sale to an antiquarian bookseller in the city who realised its significance and brought it to our attention.'

'I thought there was a book missing,' said Amy. 'There was a small gap on one of the shelves, which seemed very odd because all the other books were so tightly packed.'

'An amateur sleuth, I see,' said Danvers with a twinkle in his eye, 'as well as a keen bellringer and an excellent librarian in the making.' He was clearly in a good mood today, as well he might be, having just been presented with a copy of one of the world's rarest books to add to the library's collection. The Bodleian might have over twelve million documents in its collection, but as a true booklover Amy could appreciate the value of one small book that had been lost and now was found.

'I'll add it to the rest of the collection,' she said, holding the book tightly against her chest. 'Thank you!' she said to the policeman.

'My pleasure, ma'am.'

She carried the book back to her desk, unable to stop herself from beaming with pleasure. Her job at the library involved a lot of routine work which, if she was honest, could be quite tedious, but moments like this more than made up for the monotonous hours of shelving and cataloguing books.

'What are you looking so happy about?' asked Evan, who was tapping away at a nearby computer.

'This,' said Amy, showing him the book, and injecting as much passion and enthusiasm into her voice as she could muster.

'What is it?'

'Only a first edition of the first book ever written about the art of bellringing!'

'Oh, right,' said Evan, showing polite but brief interest before returning to his work.

Some people, thought Amy as she sat back down. She spent the next quarter of an hour carefully turning the pages of *Tintinnalogia,* delighting in the archaic text with its odd spellings and peculiar way of expressing things. 1668 was the date of its publication. A century after the founding of the bells in St Michael and All Angels.

The wording of the inscription on the bells was even more eccentric than the text of *Tintinnalogia.* She had spent much of the weekend pondering the meaning of the eight-line verse, but her internet searches had proven to be of no help whatsoever in understanding its meaning. What was the secret? And how was it related to the murder of Harriet Stevenson? She had been disappointed by Jake's reluctance to take it seriously. But being back at work had given her an idea.

Stopping early for lunch, she unwrapped her sandwiches and logged on to the library's main catalogue. A project that had been started back in 2015 now made it possible to view digital versions of thousands of the library's more fragile items, including manuscripts, prints, maps and photographs. The oldest, dating from around 500 BC, was a fragment of a letter from a Persian prince to his steward, written on leather in Aramaic.

But Amy was specifically interested in anything relating to Hambledon in the sixteenth or early seventeenth centuries. She narrowed the search to manuscripts and maps from 1500 to 1650 and entered the keywords: Oxford, Abingdon and Hambledon. The results appeared instantaneously.

Scrolling through them, she found some exquisitely drawn maps of Oxford giving a bird's-eye view of the city, with the handful of colleges that existed at that time delineated in painstaking detail. The city had been much smaller in those days, surrounded by fields and contained almost entirely within its ancient walls, against which the houses of the townsfolk crowded and jostled. The basic medieval street plan was unchanged, and she recognised the central crossroads of Carfax, the church of St Mary the Virgin, the cathedral of Christ Church, and the Bodleian's Divinity School. But the city was dominated by the castle, which in the mid-sixteenth century still retained its moat, curtain walls, towers and keep – most of which were now gone or ruined.

She continued to scroll through the results. Abingdon's heyday, she noted, had been largely before the sixteenth century, when the cathedral-like abbey had been one of the wealthiest in the country. In fact the monks of Abingdon had been making books and teaching students long before the first scholar arrived in Oxford. But by the time Henry VIII dissolved the abbey in 1545, the town of Abingdon had already fallen under Oxford's shadow. As for Hambledon, it seemed that the village had been too small and insignificant for any medieval cartographer to have bothered to produce a map of it.

And then, just when she was about to give up the search – her lunchbreak was almost over – she stumbled across a map of Hambledon-on-Thames dated 1585. Clicking on the link, she zoomed in for a better view.

Although originally drawn by hand in the sixteenth century, the map had been engraved in copperplate nearly two hundred years later, and it was a print of this engraving that the Bodleian held in its collection. Amy peered at it in fascination. It was like something that JRR Tolkien might have drawn to illustrate a scene from *The Lord of the Rings*. A large bend in the river Thames looped around the village, almost turning it into an island. The church and manor house were drawn in exacting detail, with a few other buildings, including the pub – which in those days had been a coaching inn – appearing like little model houses. The town of *Abbington*, as the cartographer so quaintly called it, lay to the north, with Dorchester to the east.

'Is that a Ralph Agas map?' asked a voice behind her.

Amy jumped. 'Evan, I didn't know you were there.'

Evan leaned over her shoulder, peering at her

computer screen. 'It looks like his work. I recognise his style. Amazingly skilled draughtsman. Just look at the detail.' Her colleague was clearly more enthusiastic about old maps than he was about books on bellringing.

'It sounds like you're quite the expert,' said Amy, giving him a quizzical look.

'I did a lot of the donkey work digitizing those maps when I first joined the library,' he said, sitting back down at his desk. 'What's your interest?'

'Oh, nothing in particular,' said Amy casually. 'Just looking to see what my home village looked like years ago, that's all.'

'Fair enough.' Evan accepted this explanation with a nod and returned to his work. But Amy's heart was thumping with excitement. Her lunch hour had come to an end, and she'd need to take a closer look when she had time, but she had spotted something on the map of great interest. She clicked the download button and entered her email address. It would take a few hours for the file to be sent to her, but it ought to be available by the time she finished work. She could hardly wait. She picked up the next book in the pile and returned to cataloguing Henry Burton's collection.

★

On Bridget and Jake's return to Kidlington, Andy greeted them waving a sheet of paper.

'Good news, ma'am. Forensics have got back to us with a report on the candlestick.'

'About time,' said Bridget. 'Did they find any prints?'

'Unfortunately not,' said Andy. 'However, they confirmed that the dried blood is a match for Harriet Stevenson's, and they also found a silk thread stuck to the stem of the candlestick.'

'So in all likelihood the murderer used a silk handkerchief or something similar to conceal their fingerprints.'

'Maurice Fairweather likes his silk cravats,' said Ryan.

'I think you mentioned him before,' said Bridget. 'Remind me who he is.'

'He's a local historian,' said Jake. 'Old chap. Bit of an eccentric. Ryan and I met him in the pub and had to listen to him droning on about a murder that took place in the church in the sixteenth century. But I think Ryan took a bit of a liking to him.'

'Well, he certainly knows his history,' said Ryan, 'not to mention his crossword clues. But he's not simply the harmless old eccentric he appears.'

'Oh?' said Bridget.

'June Parker, who runs the local shop and post office, and who sits on the parish council claimed that Maurice is a troublemaker.'

'In what way?'

'Well, I'm not saying that he goes around causing mayhem on the streets of Hambledon or anything like that, but he clashed repeatedly with Harriet Stevenson in her role as chair of the parish council.'

'Do you have any specifics?'

'Let me check.' Ryan consulted his notebook, which appeared to be surprisingly well-organised. 'Okay, he seemed to enjoy winding her up generally, opposing motions just for the sake of it, but he's been pursuing a campaign for some years to open up one of the tombs in the church to search for buried treasure.'

'Buried treasure,' repeated Bridget. She'd heard it all now. People's imaginations were clearly running away with themselves.

'I'm not saying there's anything in this buried treasure business,' said Ryan hurriedly. 'No doubt it's a load of old nonsense. My point was just that Fairweather and Stevenson didn't see eye to eye over it.'

'We're going to need more than that to bring him in,' said Bridget. 'Even if he is in the habit of wearing silk cravats.'

'Um, ma'am?' Jake was looking embarrassed, his pink ears sending out a tell-tale signal.

'What is it?'

'This buried treasure business…'

Bridget groaned. Had all her sergeants taken leave of their senses?

'It's just that Amy mentioned something about this to me the other day.'

'What?'

He passed her his phone, showing a message.

'These eight lines are inscribed on the bells of St Michael and All Angels. Amy was up in the belltower on Saturday preparing for the wedding, and noted them down. The legend is that this verse refers to treasure buried somewhere in the village.'

Bridget read the words aloud.

Bee it knowne unto all men far and wyde
That in this place a secret doth reside
Where mortal bones are set to rest within
And blind wormes creep and lay their eggs hidd'n
'Gainst northern wall in wynter's chill embrace
To iron girde and stone then turn to face
Descend into my chamber cold and darke
Therein thou shalt thy reward come to marke

'Sounds like a riddle,' said Harry.

'More like a set of directions,' said Ryan.

'I'm not saying there's anything in it at all,' said Jake. 'But if Maurice Fairweather wanted to open up a tomb, he must have taken it seriously. And if Harriet Stevenson was preventing him from doing that...'

'Maurice loves solving crossword clues,' said Ryan. 'And he's an expert on the history of the village. If you ask me, he's just the sort of person who'd want to get to the bottom of something like this.'

'Would he kill someone who was standing in his way?' asked Bridget.

Jake shrugged. 'Who knows? People like that can become obsessed when they get an idea in their heads.'

Bridget weighed her options. So far their enquiries hadn't led them very far, or at least, every lead had come to nothing. Now, with the discovery of the silk strand on the murder weapon, and a tentative – if far-fetched – motive, it seemed like it might at least be worth interviewing this local historian.

'Where can I find Maurice Fairweather?' she asked.

Jake looked at his watch. 'It's lunchtime, so I'd say the Eight Bells in Hambledon is a good bet. Do you want me to phone the landlord and check for you?'

'Please,' said Bridget. At the very least, lunch at the village pub was preferable to whatever they were serving up in the staff canteen.

CHAPTER 20

Monday lunchtime at the Eight Bells was clearly not the busiest time of the week, and that suited Bridget just fine. She had come here for a quiet chat with the historian, nothing more at this stage. She ordered some coffee from the bar for herself and Jake, and then asked him to introduce her to Maurice Fairweather who was sitting at a table near the fireplace, the *Times* crossword, an empty plate and a half-finished pint of beer in front of him. As Ryan and Jake had described, he was wearing a silk cravat – this one featuring a Paisley print in shades of turquoise, blue, purple and yellow.

He glanced up with a bemused expression as they approached the table. 'Detective Sergeant Jake Derwent,' he said, looking first at Jake before switching his attention to Bridget. 'And this must be your superior officer. Detective Inspector Bridget Hart, if I'm not mistaken.' He rose from his seat to shake her hand.

'That's correct,' said Bridget. 'I see that you're well informed. Do you mind if we join you for a chat?'

'Not at all. I would be delighted to assist the forces of law and order in their quest for truth.' He gestured for them to sit down with a smile that showed his yellowing teeth.

'Thank you, Mr Fairweather,' said Bridget. 'We won't take up any more of your time than is absolutely necessary.'

'Take as much of it as you like,' said Fairweather. 'I'll only fritter it away on the crossword otherwise.'

'I understand you're an expert on local history.'

'I dabble in the story of Hambledon,' said Fairweather. 'At my time of life, a man needs interests to keep the mind sharp.'

'You've more than dabbled,' said Jake. 'You've written a book on the history of the village.'

'Years ago, dear boy,' said Fairweather with a wave of his hand. 'It's long out of print now, although no doubt a copy of it will be gathering dust somewhere in the depths of the Bodleian archive. Did you know that they keep a copy of every book ever published? Even mine!' The idea seemed to amuse him greatly.

'So you'd be the right person to ask about the village and its legends,' said Bridget.

He gave her a sharp look. 'Legends? I do hope you haven't come here in search of the Holy Grail, because I can assure you, you'll be disappointed on that score.' He chuckled to himself and took a sip of his beer.

'I was thinking more about buried treasure in

the church.'

'Ah, yes, the famous Hambledon hoard. Who told you about that?'

'We dabble in history ourselves,' said Bridget. 'We know about the verse inscribed on the church bells. And we're also aware of your campaign to open up a tomb in the church.'

Maurice looked impressed. 'I see that you've been doing your homework, Inspector. And I thought that modern policing was all about DNA analysis and mobile phone records. So dry and dull.'

'My job is to uncover facts,' said Bridget. 'And one of the facts in this case is that you clashed with Harriet Stevenson over your desire to search for treasure in the church.'

'Hardly a clash,' said Maurice. 'Just local democracy at work. Someone had to stand up to that dictator, or she would have had her way on every matter that came before the parish council.'

'According to a witness statement,' said Jake, 'you and Miss Stevenson had a particularly vicious row over the matter of Sunday licensing hours at the Eight Bells.'

'I expect you heard that from June Parker,' said Maurice. 'And as a result of that you think I murdered Harriet because we took opposing sides in debates? I think, Inspector, that you may have mistaken Hambledon Parish Council for the Florentine Republic, and got me mixed up with Niccolò Machiavelli.'

239

Maurice sat back in his chair, seeming very pleased with himself. He sipped his beer and waited for Bridget to respond.

'Tell me about the inscription on the bells,' she said. The way to get the most out of Maurice Fairweather, she had decided, was to let him speak and not to challenge or contradict him. He clearly relished any opportunity to argue his corner.

'Well, where to begin?' he said. 'How much do you know about England in the sixteenth century?'

'Quite a bit as it happens,' said Bridget. 'I read Modern History at Oxford and my tutor, Dr Irene Thomas, was a Tudor specialist.' She'd had the pleasure of consulting with Dr Thomas on a recent case when her tutor's knowledge of Elizabethan revenge tragedies had provided valuable insight.

Maurice beamed at her. 'In that case, I don't need to tell you all about the religious persecution that took place in that turbulent period of our country's past.'

'No need to explain how the Protestants were persecuted under Mary, and how Elizabeth was convinced there was a Catholic plot lurking around every corner,' said Bridget, 'but what has all that got to do with Hambledon?'

'Quite a lot,' said Maurice. You see, the lord of the manor in those days was one Edmund Burton. He was a staunch Protestant and a supporter of the English Reformation. He was also a rather astute political mover and managed to survive Mary's reign by keeping his head down and playing his cards close to his chest.'

As Fairweather warmed to his subject he started to lose his tendency towards facetiousness. Bridget suspected this was a defence mechanism, perhaps to cover an innate shyness. Maybe his brightly-coloured clothing served much the same function.

'Edmund was a rich man when he died,' continued Fairweather. 'He was favoured by Elizabeth I and opened his house to her when she travelled the country on her famous progresses. In 1570, seven years before he died, he paid for the bells to be installed in St Michael and All Angels.'

'So was he responsible for the inscriptions on the bells?'

'No, they were added after Edmund's death by his son, Thomas, who claimed they were his father's dying wish. It was as if Edmund was leaving behind a riddle for future generations to solve.'

'And what do you think the riddle is telling us?'

Fairweather leaned across the table as if he were about to impart a secret that might threaten the stability of the realm.

'The verse strongly suggests that something of considerable value was buried with Edmund when he died. Let's consider the meaning of the lines. *Bee it knowne unto all men far and wyde, That in this place a secret doth reside.* I'm sure you'd agree that this is a straightforward declaration of intent. *Where mortal bones are set to rest within, And blind wormes creep and lay their eggs hidd'n.* To me, that clearly indicates that the "secret", whatever it may be, has been placed inside a tomb. *'Gainst northern wall in wynter's chill embrace.* Now we have to speculate a little. Which wall does this refer to? I would suggest that since we are searching for a tomb, then this must be the northern wall of the Church of St Michael and All Angels. Are you still with me?'

Despite her own scepticism, Bridget found herself intrigued by the mystery and by the historian's enthusiasm in explaining it. She nodded.

'Good. Then, consider the next line. *To iron girde and stone then turn to face.*' Maurice's face brightened with a smile. 'You've been inside the church often enough now, Inspector, to know its layout. Picture yourself standing against the northern wall. If you turned around, where might you expect to come face to face with an iron "girde" or grid, as we might say in modern English?'

The church's interior came easily to Bridget's mind, and she pictured herself standing with her back against the wall of the north transept. Before her stood... 'The tomb of Lord Edmund and Lady Ellen Burton.'

'Exactly. The effigy is carved from stone, and an iron grid is set into its base, revealing a tantalising glimpse of the stone slab that covers the tomb itself.' He smiled. 'The rest is elementary. *Descend into my chamber cold and darke, Therein thou shalt thy reward come to marke.*'

'But what kind of reward?' asked Jake.

'Well, that's the most intriguing aspect of the whole mystery, don't you think?' said Maurice.

'And if I understand you correctly,' said Bridget, 'you'd like to open the tomb to find out what that mystery is.'

'Wouldn't you?' asked Maurice. 'Wouldn't anyone?'

'Not Harriet Stevenson, it would seem.'

Fairweather snorted derisively. 'Well, that should tell you all you need to know about the woman. She was a puritan, determined to put a stop to everyone else's fun.'

'What about Martin Armistead, the vicar? Any excavation work at the church would surely require his approval. What does he have to say on the matter?'

Maurice exhaled in exasperation. 'Not a lot. He doesn't want to get involved, and he certainly wasn't willing to stand up to Harriet Stevenson. I can't blame him for that, I suppose.'

'And what about the late Henry Burton? What was his position?'

'Henry wasn't keen either,' he admitted. 'I raised the matter with him on a couple of occasions. I really thought that he'd be interested. But the old squire could be very conservative at times. I suppose that was due to his upbringing. Imagine being raised as lord of the manor and being able to trace your family back for fifteen generations! Anyway, for whatever reason, he was adamant that he didn't want his ancestors' tomb to be disturbed.'

'So he and Harriet Stevenson were in complete agreement in that regard.'

'Oh, Henry Burton often took Harriet's side. In part, I suppose, because of their own shared history.'

'Sorry?' said Bridget. 'I don't understand. What shared history?'

'You don't know?' said Fairweather. 'Well, I suppose there's no reason why you should. There are few people left in the village old enough to remember.'

'Remember what?'

'That Harriet Stevenson and Henry Burton were engaged to be married.'

Bridget looked at Jake to see if he'd heard this before, but he shook his head, nonplussed. 'They were engaged?' she repeated.

'Oh, not recently,' said Maurice, catching the look of amazement on her face. 'No, this was back in the sixties. It would have been '67, or perhaps '68. The era of sexual liberation and free love. Not that much of that ever came my way.'

'But they didn't marry?'

'No, Harriet called it off. She was determined to pursue a career as an academic, and as forward-thinking as Henry Burton was, it simply wouldn't have been acceptable for the lady of

Hambledon Manor to have pursued a career of her own, not even in the swinging sixties.'

Bridget took a moment to digest the new information. 'Can you think of any reason why Harriet's engagement to Henry Burton might have led to her being attacked straight after his funeral?'

'That,' said Fairweather with a sardonic smile, 'is for you to determine. I merely offer it up as a morsel of truth to add to the cauldron of suspicion and speculation that is brewing in the incident room at Kidlington.' The facetious Fairweather was back with a vengeance.

Bridget thought for a moment and then asked, 'Do you know where the key to the crypt is normally kept?'

Maurice looked surprised. 'The crypt? I should imagine it's kept in the vestry. Why do you ask?'

'Has the key ever been in your possession?'

'No. I've only ever been down into the crypt once, and that was many years ago, when I was researching my book.'

'The key that normally hangs in the vestry has gone missing. Do you know anything about that?'

'No.'

'When did you last go into the vestry?'

'I probably haven't been in there for years. Cramped, untidy little room. Have you seen the state of the place?' He flicked an imaginary speck of dust off his cuff.

He was certainly a fastidious dresser. If he had

killed the churchwarden, he would have taken pains to ensure that he left no incriminating fingerprints or DNA evidence behind. Her eyes shifted to the silk cravat covering his scrawny neck.

'Do you always wear a cravat?'

'Most certainly.'

'Were you wearing one on the day of Henry Burton's funeral?'

'Yes. I was wearing this one. Why do you ask?' His tone was suddenly wary.

'It would help with our enquiries,' said Bridget, 'if you could provide us with your cravat for forensic analysis.'

'What? Now?'

'If you wouldn't mind.'

Jake produced an evidence bag and held it open. Fairweather hesitated, but in the end he undid the cravat from around his neck and deposited it into the bag. 'Whatever it takes to get to the truth, I suppose.'

'Thank you,' said Bridget. Without his neck covering, Fairweather looked frailer and more vulnerable. But he was still fit and strong enough to have wielded a candlestick. And was it possible that after years of being frustrated in pursuit of his obsession, he had seized the moment and taken the opportunity to remove the one person who stood in his way?

'And now, if you'll excuse me' – he nodded at Bridget and Jake – 'I must be on my way.' He finished his beer, scooped up his newspaper, and strode out of the pub.

'Well,' said Bridget, watching his retreating back. 'I've met some eccentrics in my time, but Maurice Fairweather is close to the top of the list.'

'I'm glad you said that, ma'am,' said Jake. He checked his watch, a hint of desperation in his eye. 'And now, do you think we could order some food before they stop serving?'

'Good idea,' said Bridget. The encounter with Maurice Fairweather had lasted longer than she'd been expecting, and she could definitely use some restorative carbohydrates.

★

Rosemary Carver gave her husband her arm to lean on as they walked slowly home from their local pub, the Marsh Harrier, where they'd spent a pleasant evening enjoying traditional British fish and chips washed down with pints of London Pride. It had been nice for the pair of them to go out together after all the time Rosemary had spent in Hambledon leaving Simon to fend for himself. She didn't want to leave him on his own again. It was clear that he needed her around the house. He wouldn't even have been able to make it to the pub and back without her help.

She'd bought him a walking stick a while back. It was one of those extendable ones that he could fold away when not in use. But he hated to be seen using it in public. Simon was a proud man, and was unwilling to acknowledge just how much he'd come to depend on her. He was only fifty-eight, and he'd worked all his life before the accident. It was easy for her to forget that when she saw him now.

It didn't matter. Rosemary was strong enough to support her husband. She'd grown brawny working as a nurse, helping patients sit up in bed, lifting them in and out of wheelchairs. She could easily bear Simon's weight. And perhaps it didn't matter if he never worked again. In fact, if everything went as well as she hoped, she might even be able to take early retirement herself.

She turned her key in the lock and pushed open the front door of the house. Simon reached for the doorframe, taking the weight off her arm. 'I can manage from here, love,' he said.

She was about to tell him to go and make himself comfortable in the sitting room while she put the kettle on for a cuppa, when she stopped on the doormat. A sixth sense, or whatever you wanted to call it, made the back of her neck prickle.

'What's the matter?' asked Simon.

She wrinkled her nose, sniffing the air. 'What's that funny smell?'

'I can't smell anything. You didn't leave the gas on, did you?'

'No, it's not gas, it's something...' She couldn't place it, although it seemed vaguely familiar. 'I don't know, it's more like a man's aftershave.'

Simon shook his head. 'I'm sure it's nothing.'

But it wasn't nothing. It was something.

Rosemary scanned the hallway. The door to the sitting room was ajar. Had she left it like that when they went out? It was possible, but she usually made a point of keeping the doors closed to keep out draughts – a habit learned from many years of caring for the elderly and infirm. She pushed the door open tentatively.

'Oh my goodness!' She clutched at the wall for support, feeling her legs go weak.

Simon was right behind her, a protective hand on her shoulder. 'What the bloody hell...'

The sitting room, which Rosemary had cleaned and tidied only the day before, was in total disarray. The doors of the inbuilt cupboards to either side of the gas fire were thrown open, the contents – photograph albums, letters and birthday cards, results of medical tests, Simon's disability benefit details – strewn across the floor higgledy-piggledy. A pile of unopened letters – bills and final demands no doubt – that she'd left on the coffee table to sort through later had been ripped open and tossed aside. The handful of paperback books – mostly romances and the odd thriller – that she kept on the shelf beside the telly were lying on the floor, their pages open, as if someone had rifled through them.

Simon unfolded his walking stick. 'If the bastard who did this is still here, I'll...'

'No, Simon, stop.' Rosemary laid a restraining hand on his arm. In that moment, she loved her husband for his bravery and his defiance, but she knew that he would come off worse in a confrontation between himself and the person who had broken in and done this.

She put a finger to her lips and indicated that they should listen. The house was quiet. Something told her that the intruder had been and gone.

She led the way back into the hallway and through to the kitchen. It was the same story there. Cupboards and drawers open, her neatly ironed and folded tea towels pulled out and tossed on the floor. Cookbooks cast aside. The back door stood open, the lock having been forced. So that was how the intruder had got in. She'd been meaning to get a locksmith to fit a better lock for months, but it was one of those jobs she'd just never got round to.

Upstairs in the bedrooms, drawers and cupboards had been opened, their contents rummaged through. Her jewellery box, where she kept the handful of items she'd inherited from her mum, was open, but to her relief nothing had been taken.

That was when she knew for certain.

'I'm calling the police,' said Simon.

'No, wait, love.' She sank down on the bed, suddenly feeling very tired. 'Whoever did this wasn't trying to rob us. They were looking for something. Something that belongs to them.'

'What?' Simon sat down on the bed beside her, his bulk causing the soft mattress to sag.

'This is all my fault,' she said. 'I did something wrong.'

'What? What could you possibly have done that could lead to this?'

She felt tears coming then. She wasn't one for weeping. She couldn't afford to be in her job. But now the tears ran down her cheeks, making her mascara run black. 'I should never have agreed to do it. I knew it was wrong at the time, but I was under so much pressure, and...' The tears were coursing in rivers now, choking off her words.

Simon reached for a box of tissues from the bedside table and passed her a handful. 'Here you go, love.' She wiped her eyes and blew her nose. 'Now,' he said, taking charge. 'Let's go downstairs and put the kettle on. And then I think you'd better tell me what this is all about.'

CHAPTER 21

On Tuesday morning, Bridget dropped Chloe off at school. The day of her final exam – English Literature – had come at last, and Bridget was almost giddy with relief. For better or worse, by noon today her daughter's future prospects would be determined, and no amount of revision – or lack of – would change the outcome. Bridget would be pouring herself a very large glass of Pinot Noir tonight to mark the occasion.

'Good luck,' she whispered as Chloe hopped out of the car. Then, 'Wait!' she called. 'Have you got enough spare pens?'

'Yes!' said Chloe in exasperation. 'Now go and catch a killer.'

Bridget watched her daughter heading into school, greeting her friends. She'd be sixteen in a matter of days, as unbelievable as that seemed. It felt like only yesterday that Bridget was dropping her off for her first day at school. Soon she would be starting sixth form and studying for her A-levels.

If she passes her exams.

Bridget's heart contracted at the thought. But

she quickly expelled the idea of failure from her mind. She had work of her own to be getting on with. *Go and catch a killer*, Chloe had told her. Yes, that's what she had to do.

She set off towards the Oxford ring road, but on reaching it, instead of continuing north towards Kidlington, on impulse she turned south down the A34 in the direction of Hambledon.

Her conversation in the Eight Bells with Maurice Fairweather had left her with misgivings. Was he really just a harmless eccentric with a penchant for tall tales and improbable legends, or was there something more sinister behind his genteel façade? And what about this business of Harriet Stevenson having been engaged to Henry Burton? No one else had mentioned this. Was it true or had Maurice invented it as a smokescreen? Bridget wanted to hear what the Reverend Martin Armistead had to say about relations between Maurice and Harriet. How deep had their divisions run? Could they have been a motive for murder? And how, for that matter, did the lord of the manor fit into all this, if indeed he did?

When she knocked at the vicarage door some twenty minutes later, Martin Armistead didn't seem surprised to see her. He invited her once more into his study, overlooking the back garden. There was no sign of Emma this time, either in the garden or the kitchen, but the vicar himself appeared rather preoccupied. Like the previous time Bridget had encountered him, his eyes were rimmed in dark shadows. He rubbed at his forehead distractedly.

'Is everything all right?' she enquired.

'Yes. Why shouldn't it be?'

'Only you seem–'

'I'm sorry,' he said apologetically. 'It's just that after everything that's happened... especially with the murder taking place in the church... and then that business with the missing key...' He wrung his hands together, his eyes fixed on some spot to the left of Bridget's head.

'This must be a very stressful time for you.'

'Yes. Yes, it is. People expect... you know... as vicar... that I have all the answers.'

'Whereas,' said Bridget, 'you know no more than anyone else.'

'Precisely.' He seemed relieved to have been understood. 'Sometimes it feels like, well, that my shoulders aren't broad enough to bear the weight they have to carry. I hope that doesn't sound too melodramatic, or self-pitying.'

'Not at all. I understand entirely.'

He nodded. 'So, how can I help you, Inspector?'

'I'd like to ask you a few questions about Maurice Fairweather.'

'Maurice? Well, I'll tell you as much as I know, but I'm not especially close to him.'

'Can you describe the nature of his relationship with Harriet Stevenson?'

He considered the matter thoughtfully before responding. 'People often use the word "relationship" to mean a romantic attachment. In the case of Maurice and Harriet, I'm certain there was nothing of that nature. In fact, they were often at odds. Every time I encountered them together, they seemed to be at war with each other, squabbling about some issue or other. If Harriet was in favour of something, you could bet that Maurice would be against it. It was almost as if they enjoyed sparring, you know, as if one of them couldn't exist without the other. I don't know what Maurice will do now she's gone. There'll be nothing for him to cause a fuss about.'

'One of the issues they disagreed about was the matter of the tomb of Lord Edmund and Lady Ellen Burton.'

Martin groaned. 'Oh, that! Maurice had this absurd idea of opening it up to search for buried treasure. Can you imagine? Of course, everyone else thought it was ridiculous.'

'Everyone?'

'Well, Harriet mainly. But most other people on the parish council agreed with her. And Henry Burton too, of course. He was very much against it.'

'What about you?'

'Me? Fortunately I didn't have to get involved. The proposal was voted down unanimously before it got that far.'

'Maurice seems to blame Harriet for that.'

'Well, you could say that Harriet spearheaded resistance to the idea. But she didn't have to work terribly hard. I mean, really... buried treasure in a tomb!'

Through the study window, Bridget saw Emma Armistead emerge into the garden. She was barefoot again, almost floating across the lawn in a white summer dress, with a broad-brimmed straw hat shading her pale face. She carried a pair of secateurs in her hand.

Martin's head swivelled to follow her.

Emma proceeded to wander languidly around the garden, occasionally stooping to smell a flower, looking for all the world like a quintessential English rose.

'I also wanted to ask you about Harriet's relationship with the late Henry Burton,' said Bridget.

Martin dragged his attention back to her. 'Relationship? What do you mean?'

'I was hoping you might be able to tell me.'

'I'm not sure what there is to tell,' said the vicar. 'I believe they were friendly. Harriet was born in the village, so they knew each other from way back. She was some ten years younger than him, and of course she spent most of her life living and working in Oxford, but yes, I would say that they were on good terms.'

'Were you aware that they had once been engaged to be married?'

His eyebrows rose. 'I didn't know that. It must have been when she was very young. Henry got married in his thirties, I believe, when Harriet would have been studying for her degree at

Oxford, and his wife died a few years before Harriet retired and returned to Hambledon.'

His eyes drifted once again to the window. Bridget followed his gaze to where Emma was now snipping flowers from their stems, letting the cut blooms tumble and fall at her feet.

'Is something the matter?' asked Bridget.

When his face met hers, she saw that his eyes were filled with pain and grief. Whatever was disturbing him, it was more than just the murder of his churchwarden. He had tried to hide his feelings, but now he seemed to have abandoned all pretence. Maybe it was his wife's odd behaviour that had prompted the change, or perhaps the simple fact of Bridget asking the question had given him permission to drop his guard and reveal his true feelings. Like police officers, vicars were expected to be strong, and to offer solace to others.

'It's Emma. I'm worried about her.'

'What is it?' asked Bridget gently.

'She's... she's been going through a very difficult time. We both have.'

He sat for a moment with his elbows on the desk, his head buried in his hands. When he looked up, his eyes glimmered with tears. 'We lost a baby.'

'I'm very sorry to hear that.'

'Thank you. It was before we moved here, when we were in Birmingham.' Now that he had started talking about his troubles, he seemed unable to stop. Bridget guessed that he had been bottling up his feelings for a long time, unable to unburden himself to anyone. 'It was a terrible thing for both of us, but Emma took it especially hard. She blamed herself, although of course that was irrational. The doctors assured her that miscarriage is a common problem. She was given counselling and support, and everyone did their best to reassure her and to convince her that she hadn't done anything wrong. But it was no use. She healed physically, but sank into a depression. At one point' – he stopped, steeling himself before going on – 'she even tried to take her own life. That's when I knew we had to make a change. And so I requested a transfer. We had wanted to devote ourselves to a challenging parish, but inner-city Birmingham was too much for us. I simply couldn't handle other people's problems on top of Emma's. That's why we moved out here, you see. A quiet life in a rural parish. I hoped it would give her the time and space she needed to come to terms with what had happened.'

'But it hasn't worked out like that?'

Armistead shook his head. 'She's still on medication, and as you can see' – he gestured towards the window – 'half the time she's in her own world, oblivious to those around her. She just drifts through life and doesn't seem able to connect with anything.'

'How has the murder of Harriet Stevenson affected her?' asked Bridget. 'It would be understandable if an event like that had a negative impact on someone who was already fragile.'

Martin shook his head. 'That's just the thing,' he said, a note of desperation creeping into his voice. 'It's almost had the opposite effect. At first I thought I detected something of the old spark in her, but then she said...'

'What?'

'She said she was glad that Harriet Stevenson was dead. She told me that she hated her.' There was real fear in Armistead's eyes as his words hung between them.

'Why would she say that?' asked Bridget. 'Why would your wife have hated Harriet?'

'I don't know,' he whispered. 'I know that Harriet could be a difficult person. She had very clear ideas of right and wrong and could be rather judgemental. Maybe she said something unkind to Emma...'

'I think I need to speak to your wife,' said Bridget. 'Would it be all right for me to go outside and talk to her now?'

He seemed hugely relieved that she had made the suggestion. 'Yes, yes, of course.' He glanced once more through the window. 'Just one thing.'

'Yes?'

'Ask her to put down the secateurs before you ask her any questions.'

★

The Reverend Martin Armistead waited

anxiously in his study while Bridget went out to the garden at the back of the house. Emma Armistead was at the far end, picking sweet peas from a wigwam covered in a mass of pink, purple and white flowers. Their fragrant scent reminded Bridget of her parents' house in Woodstock where there had always been a vase of sweet peas on the table in summer.

'Emma? It's Detective Inspector Bridget Hart. Is it all right if I talk to you for a moment?'

Emma stopped what she was doing and turned to look at Bridget. Her features were half-hidden behind the long golden hair that fell in quiet disarray around her face. She brushed it aside to reveal wide, childlike eyes. She was standing barefoot on the soil, the soles of her feet black, the secateurs in one hand.

'Why don't we sit down together?' said Bridget, indicating the wooden bench on the paved area next to the house.

Emma nodded and followed her over, dropping the sweet peas behind her on the lawn, but continuing to clutch the secateurs.

'Why don't you put those down for now,' suggested Bridget, once they were seated.

Emma looked at them, seeming unaware that she was still holding anything. Then she placed them on the patio. Close up, the scarring across her wrists was clearly visible.

'Your garden is very beautiful,' said Bridget.

'Yes.'

'It must be a lovely place to sit and enjoy the

sunshine.'

Emma nodded, raising her chin to the heavens as if she was seeing the sun for the first time. She dipped her head again, clothing her face in shadow.

'I wanted to ask you about Harriet Stevenson,' said Bridget.

A faint crinkle appeared on Emma's forehead at the mention of the dead woman's name. 'What about her?'

'Did you see much of her?'

'She was the churchwarden,' said Emma simply. 'I'm the vicar's wife.'

'Did she come to the vicarage very often?'

'To speak to Martin, yes.'

'And did you see her at other times?'

'At church. And in the village shop.'

'I get the impression you didn't much like her,' said Bridget.

Emma's eyes narrowed and Bridget saw a steelier character come to the fore, like dark clouds crossing the sun. 'No one liked her. She was a horrible woman.'

'Why do you say that?'

Emma's serene features twisted into a grimace. 'She was evil. Mean; cruel. I hated her.'

'Why was that?'

Emma frowned.

'Did she say something to you?' asked Bridget.

'I thought I could trust her. I thought she would understand.'

'Did you tell her about your troubles?'

Emma's eyes were on Bridget's, but her gaze was elsewhere. 'She asked me why we had come to Hambledon. I told her about my baby.' She fell silent, and Bridget waited patiently. A bumble bee passed by, buzzing gently as it went about its work. 'I thought she would show sympathy. I hoped... that she might be someone I could talk to.'

'But she wasn't?'

'She had a kind manner about her at first, but it was just a front. Politeness; not compassion. Inside, she was pure poison. She told me to pull myself together. She said that a vicar's wife needed to show more backbone. She told me that the problem these days was that everyone was too sensitive, and that it was about time someone told me to snap out of it.' Emma's eyes were dry but her face looked ready to crumple.

'When was the last time you saw Harriet?'

'I... it was the day of the funeral.' The old Emma had returned after her brief outburst, vague and hesitant, groping her way through her words as if cutting a path through an overgrown briar.

'Tell me what happened that day.'

'I... Martin couldn't be with me. He was busy, because he had the funeral to attend to. He asked me if I wanted to come to the church or stay here. He said it would be all right if I didn't come, because of... because of the baby.'

Bridget nodded, waiting.

'I didn't know what to do. I wanted to be there

for Martin's sake, but I was frightened.'

'Frightened? Why?'

'I was frightened I might get upset. When that happens…' She trailed off, then started again. 'In the end, I decided to come. I waited until the very last minute, when everyone was already inside, so that no one would see me, and then I crept inside.'

'Good,' said Bridget. 'You're doing very well. Go on.'

'Harriet was there,' said Emma. 'She was sitting right at the back of the church. When she saw me, she turned to look at me, and I could see what she was thinking.'

'What was she thinking, Emma?'

'That I was a disgrace. That I had let my husband down again. She didn't say anything, because the funeral service had already begun, but I could see it in her eyes.'

'And then what?'

'And then… I was back here, and it was all over. The funeral, I mean. It was over and Martin was back. I was so glad to see him, but there was something in his expression that scared me. I said, "Is everything okay?" But he said, "No, Harriet's dead."'

Bridget waited for more, but Emma seemed to have come to a halt. 'I'm sorry,' said Bridget. 'I don't quite understand. You said that you were in the church with Harriet, and then you were back here with your husband. "It was all over," you said. But what happened between your arrival in the church, and returning here to the vicarage?'

'I don't know,' said Emma, her voice so quiet that Bridget had to strain to catch it. 'I have these gaps. Blanks in my mind. But... I have dreams.'

'Tell me about them.'

'Sometimes when I'm awake, I think I'm dreaming because nothing seems real anymore.' Emma looked about the garden, taking in the vivid colours and scents as if they were all just a creation of her own imagination. 'All this. I have no taste, no feeling, nothing. But when I dream, that's when I come to life. Everything feels real again and I can forget all my sorrows. Sometimes when Martin comes home, I tell him what I've been doing, but he says, "No, darling, that wasn't real, it was just a dream." So I can't always tell if what I remember actually happened, or if it was just my mind playing tricks.' She looked up, as if struggling to tell whether Bridget was real or a phantom of her own invention.

'Did you have a dream on the day of the funeral?' asked Bridget.

'I dreamed... I dreamed that I was in church, and there was noise all around. It was the bells. They were ringing, and they were so loud, I couldn't hear myself think. But then Harriet was in front of me, and she was saying things to me. Horrible things. Cruel things, about my baby. And then I –'

'I think that's quite enough for now.' Martin

Armistead had appeared at the back door of the house. Bridget didn't know how long he'd been listening. 'Emma's upset. She needs some quiet time to herself.' There was a determination in the vicar's voice that Bridget hadn't heard before. He sat down next to his wife and threw a protective arm around her. 'She doesn't know what she's saying.'

Bridget stood up. 'I'm sorry if I upset you, Mrs Armistead. But I might need to call back and ask more questions later.'

'If you do, we'll want a solicitor,' said Martin.

'Of course,' said Bridget. 'That won't be a problem. Thank you for your time.'

She was walking back to her car when her phone rang. The voice at the end of the line sounded upset. 'Inspector Hart? It's Rosemary Carver here, the nurse from Hambledon Manor.'

'Yes, Mrs Carver? How can I help you?'

'Well,' said the nurse. 'It's more a question of how I can help you. You see, Inspector, I want to confess.'

CHAPTER 22

'Is that the Ralph Agas map you've got there?'

Amy looked up to see Evan peering over her shoulder. She'd been so intent on studying the map that she hadn't noticed him get up from his own desk and come over to hers. She really must say something to him about not being so nosey. But she had to admit that the ancient drawing of Hambledon-on-Thames held a fascination that was hard to resist. She'd always loved maps, and the thought that she might be holding a real-life treasure map in her hands was almost too thrilling to handle. Not that she was going to tell Evan about that. He would almost certainly laugh at the notion.

'Yeah, I thought I'd take it home to have a closer look,' she told him.

It wasn't the original sixteenth-century document she had on her desk, of course. That was stowed safely in the library's climate-controlled archive. She had downloaded a digital copy and printed a full-size version to study. Spread out across her desk, it measured almost two feet by one and a half.

The amount of detail contained in the drawing was quite astonishing and it appeared to be a realistic and accurate representation of the layout of the village. There was the pub, smaller than Amy knew it, as it was lacking the "modern" extension added in the eighteenth century, but with every window and gable precisely reproduced. She could even see her own room, looking out across the river in the direction of Hambledon Lock. There had been no lock when the map had been drawn. That was a nineteenth century development, built to enhance navigability as river traffic increased at the beginning of the industrial age. In Agas's day, the Thames upstream of Burcot had been almost impassable to barges. But the old Toll Bridge that linked Hambledon to the nearby village of Appleford looked exactly as it did now.

The village itself seemed to have about half the number of houses in 1585 as it did presently, but they were drawn in sufficient detail that Amy could recognise each one. There was the village shop; there was the tiny cottage that Kayleigh and Jamie had saved up to buy together. The school where Kayleigh taught had not yet come into existence; nor had the vicarage; and the village green appeared to be nothing more than a patch of grass where no one had thought to build. Occupying a large swathe of land in the bend of the river was the manor house, which was slightly smaller then, having been extended in the seventeenth century, and lacked the various outbuildings that had been added over the years.

But the church appeared exactly as it was now, with belltower, north and south transepts all present, and unchanged in over four hundred years. It was the church that Amy was most interested in, and in particular whether the map might shed any light on the tantalising prospect of a treasure hoard buried there.

Jake had told her what Maurice Fairweather had said about the treasure being concealed beneath the Burton tomb in the north transept. He had even gone through the lines of the verse one by one, explaining what each meant.

'So you believe me now, do you?' she'd asked him.

'I didn't say I believed in the treasure. I'm just telling you what Maurice Fairweather said.'

Amy stuck out her tongue at him. 'You're so sceptical! Call yourself a detective! Don't you have any curiosity?'

She was determined to prove Jake wrong. Edmund Burton had been a very rich man. Everyone in the village knew that. And the sixteenth century had been a dangerous period, especially for a prominent supporter of the English Reformation like Edmund. So it wasn't hard to believe that he had hidden some of his wealth in the tomb where his wife was buried. Although it wasn't so clear to her why he would have instructed his son to have a riddle inscribed on the bells, instead of simply telling him where the money was. But perhaps he didn't like his son particularly, and had decided to leave his wealth to whoever was clever enough to decipher the secret message. *Bee it knowne unto all men far and wyde.*

Whatever the reason, the meaning of the riddle seemed clear enough. Or did it?

On studying the map carefully, Amy was struck by an interesting observation. There were two north-facing walls within the church. One above ground and one below, and both were marked on the map.

Against Maurice's assumption – that the treasure was located beneath the tomb of Lord Edmund and Lady Ellen – an equally valid interpretation was that it was buried in the crypt beneath the church.

Where mortal bones are set to rest within, And blind wormes creep and lay their eggs hidd'n. It was obvious that this could just as well apply to a crypt as to a tomb. *'Gainst northern wall in wynter's chill embrace.* As the map clearly showed, the crypt also had a northern wall. *To iron girde and stone then turn to face.* This part was trickier. Amy had never been into the crypt, so she couldn't say with certainty what was down there. But there was sure to be stone of some description. And if there were iron bars too, then that would be just as likely a candidate for the location of the hidden treasure as the tomb in the church. *Descend into my chamber cold and darke. Therein thou shalt thy reward come to marke.* A cold

269

shiver ran along her spine, making her tingle all over. The crypt itself was doubtless a cold, dark chamber. But if there was a reward waiting there to be claimed, Amy was sure she could pluck up enough courage to go and take a look for herself.

★

After receiving the phone call from Rosemary Carver, Bridget drove straight to the nurse's house in Cowley. On the phone, Rosemary had sounded tearful, almost panicky. And what precisely did she intend to confess to? Bridget squeezed the Mini into a tight parking spot between a van and the markings for a zebra crossing, and rang the bell of the pebble-dashed semi that stood back from the busy road.

Rosemary must have been watching out for her arrival, because the door to the house swung open within seconds. The nurse stood in the hallway, anxiously wringing her hands together.

'Oh, thank you so much for coming to see me,' she said. 'I'm sorry to drag you out like this, I know you must be very busy, but I wanted to talk to you face to face. It's so much easier that way, isn't it? And what with Simon being as he is, I didn't want to leave him on his own. Do you know what the buses are like? I'd have to catch one into town, and then wait for another one to get to Kidlington. And you can never be sure if they'll come on time, it's–'

'It's really no problem,' said Bridget,

interrupting Rosemary's stream of chatter. The woman was clearly a bag of nerves.

'Well, come and make yourself comfortable in the sitting room,' she said, stepping back to allow Bridget inside. She led the way into a small but tidy front room dominated by an oversized beige suite facing a small television. On the mantelpiece above the fireplace, an excess of fussy ornaments battled for space. A man sitting on the sofa began to struggle laboriously in an effort to get to his feet.

Bridget quickly moved forwards to shake his hand. 'No need to get up.'

'This is Simon, my husband,' said Rosemary. 'He's on long-term sick.'

'Fell off a ladder,' said Simon. 'All my own fault. Silly thing to do.'

'Let me fetch you a hot drink,' said Rosemary. 'Tea or coffee? I can rustle up a hot chocolate if you like.'

'There's really no need,' said Bridget.

But Rosemary was determined not to be deflected from her hospitality. 'I insist,' she said. 'It's no bother.'

'Tea, then, please.' Bridget waited quietly in one of the deep armchairs while the tea was being made. Simon, unlike his garrulous wife, seemed content to say nothing until the task was complete.

Rosemary bustled back a few minutes later, bearing a tray laden with cups of tea and a plate piled high with assorted biscuits. She placed the tray on a side table and handed out the cups. 'Have a biscuit,' she told Bridget. 'The jammy ones are nice. Don't you think so?'

'Lovely.' Bridget politely accepted one, then waited for Rosemary to finish fussing about. 'Now, then, you said on the phone that you had something to tell me?'

Rosemary immediately reverted to her nervous hand wringing. She seemed suddenly at a loss for words. It was Simon who spoke. He took his wife's hand in his and said, 'Why don't you just tell the Inspector, love, exactly what you told me last night? You know it's the right thing to do. Get it all off your chest.'

Bridget gave her an encouraging look.

Rosemary nodded. 'The truth is, Inspector, and there's no easy way to say this, I did something wrong. I ought never to have done it, I know that now, but at the time... well, I can't have been thinking straight. And if it hadn't been for that Lindsey Symonds...'

'Lindsey Symonds, the estate manager?' queried Bridget.

'That's right. If it hadn't been for her, I tell you, I never would have done it. I said to Simon—'

'Sorry,' said Bridget, interrupting. 'You never would have done what?'

Rosemary exchanged a quick glance with her husband, who gave her a reassuring nod. 'He wrote a new will,' she blurted out.

'Who did?'

'Henry Burton. The old squire. Just before he died. He wrote a new will and he got me and Lindsey to witness it.'

'I see,' said Bridget. 'I think you'd better start at the beginning. Take your time and tell me exactly what happened.'

Rosemary took a deep breath. 'Yes, yes, I'm rushing it, I know. It's because I'm all het up.'

'You're doing fine, love,' said Simon, patting her hand. 'Just take your time. There's no hurry.'

She nodded. 'This is how it happened, Inspector. Mr Burton was very ill. He knew he hadn't got long left, but he still had all his marbles.' She tapped the side of her forehead. 'It was only the morphine that made him a bit vague, poor soul, but most of the time he knew exactly what was what. Anyway, one day, it was about four days before the end, he asks me to go and fetch Ms Symonds, the estate manager. Well, I never had much to do with her, she was always busy in the office with something or other, or she was out with the young Mr Burton, doing I don't know what. That son has all manner of grand plans for redeveloping the house, I expect you've heard about that. A hotel, they say. Rushing about all the time he was, and with his father lying on his death bed. If you ask me –'

'So you went to fetch Ms Symonds?' prompted Bridget.

'Yes, I found her in her office and I say to her, "Mr Burton would like to see you." She didn't take kindly to being interrupted in her work, I can tell you. "What about?" she asks, all snooty like. I found her a bit standoffish to be honest, not a bit like Josephine, the housekeeper. You know the type. All airs and graces, even though she was no better than you or me. "I don't know what it's about," I say to her. "But he says, can you bring a pen and paper with you." So anyway, she makes a big show of how she's got important work to do but she'll grant him five minutes of her precious time. So we go upstairs and Mr Burton is propped up on a pile of pillows and he says, "I want to make a new will." Well, I could see that even *she* hadn't expected that. So I fetch the bed table, which he used for all his meals, and I make sure he's comfortable and can write easily. And he goes ahead and writes out a new will, just like that, as if he already knows exactly what he wants to say, all the legal bits right and proper too. And then he asks me and Ms Symonds to act as witnesses and sign it. Well, of course, I could hardly refuse, could I? It was a dying man's last wish, and you have to respect the wishes of the dying.'

She paused for breath and Bridget asked, 'Who was the beneficiary of the new will?'

'Oh, I never said, did I?' Rosemary laughed at her omission. 'He left everything to his son.'

Bridget frowned in puzzlement. 'I'm not sure I understand. Henry Burton's will already left everything to his son, apart from the books in his library.'

Rosemary put a hand to her mouth. 'Of course, how silly of me, you don't know, do you? I forgot to tell you.'

'Tell me what?'

'The new will left everything to his *other* son.'

'His other son?'

'That's right. It was news to me, and I could tell that Lindsey could hardly credit what she was hearing either. The gardener, Josephine's boy. You know the one I mean. Big chap, can't say I liked him that much, very surly, not like his mother. I said to Simon–'

'Wait, you're telling me that Shaun Daniels is Henry Burton's son?'

'Exactly!' said Rosemary. 'Would you believe it? Now that I know, I can see the likeness. They're both handsome men, Tobias and Shaun, just like their father was in his younger days. They had different mothers, but boys often take after their father, I find. I knew this one family –'

'Stop, love,' said Simon. 'You're running off at a tangent again. The inspector doesn't want to hear about some other family.'

Bridget's mind was whirring furiously. Now that Rosemary had delivered her bombshell, it was clear that Tobias and Shaun had quite similar looks. The thick hair, so dark it was almost black; the strong brows; the intense eyes; the thin mouths, almost cruel in their appearance... Shaun was about five years older than Tobias, who had been born shortly after

Henry Burton married, so the dates held up. If the news was true, then Shaun would have been born just two years before the old squire married his wife. Could Henry have had a brief affair with his housekeeper, resulting in a son born out of wedlock? Bridget couldn't think of any reason why not. Back then, in the late sixties, there would still have been a sense of shame in fathering an illegitimate child. A man in Henry Burton's position might well have felt pressured to conceal the truth. Or perhaps he hadn't wanted to acknowledge it.

'Are you absolutely sure that Henry Burton said Shaun Daniels was his son?' she asked.

'Absolutely. He wrote it in his will, for all to see.'

'Did he explain why he was changing his will at such a late stage?'

'He said that he ought to have treated Shaun better, and that Shaun deserved to know who his father was. He said something about Tobias having plenty in his life, and Shaun having nothing. I think he was trying to make amends, you know, for not having been a better father to Shaun. But he swore me and Lindsey to secrecy. He didn't want any of this to come out while he was still alive.'

'Josephine had never said anything to you about this? I understood that you two became quite close.'

'We did,' said Rosemary, 'but I suppose she'd kept it a secret for so long, she wasn't going to suddenly blurt it out to me who'd only just got to know her.'

'Do you think that Shaun suspected the truth?'

'I don't think so. He was never very close to the old squire, as far as I could tell. And he used to talk about how his father had run off and abandoned his mother. I don't think she ever told him who his father really was.'

Bridget nodded. Josephine Daniels would need to be questioned, and the truth, or otherwise, of Shaun Daniels's parentage could be verified through a DNA test. As for the existence of a new will... 'You said on the phone that you wanted to make a confession?' she said to Rosemary.

The nurse's face fell. 'Well, like I said, I'm not proud of what I did. But it was all Lindsey Symonds's idea. After old Mr Burton finished writing his will, and she and I had both witnessed it, she took it away. She told him she would keep it safe for him and make sure it was delivered to the solicitors, and I had no reason to doubt her. By that stage the old squire was getting tired very quickly, and after all the excitement of making a new will, he was quite exhausted, God bless him. It was just about the last time he had all his wits about him.'

'So Ms Symonds kept the will for safekeeping?' said Bridget.

'Yes. I didn't speak to her about it again until after Mr Burton had died. Then she asked to speak to me, in confidence.' Rosemary stopped.

'This is the difficult part. Are you sure you wouldn't like another cup of tea? I can fetch you one, it's really no trouble.'

'I'd just like to hear what happened next,' said Bridget.

'Right you are. Well, it was the day that old Mr Burton finally passed away. Even though I'd known it was coming, I was quite upset, I can tell you. Such a dear old man. Anyway, she wasted no time. I'd only just notified the doctor about the death when she summons me into her office. "All right," I say to her, "I can spare you five minutes," and I follow her into the office. "Shut the door behind you," she says. "This is just between me and you." "What's this about?" I ask her, knowing full well that something's not right. I can see the new will lying on the desk, and she'd promised she was going to take it to the solicitors. "We both know that Mr Burton wasn't in his right mind when he wrote this will," she says. "He can't possibly have wanted to disinherit his only son." "He seemed perfectly all right to me," I tell her, "that's why I agreed to witness it. I've seen folk go doolally plenty of times, and Mr Burton wasn't like that at all." "But all this nonsense about Shaun Daniels being his son," she says, "you can't believe that?" "I don't know what to believe," I say. "If old Mr Burton wanted to leave his money to his gardener, it's not for the likes of us to stand in his way." But she's having none of it. "What would Shaun Daniels do with a house like this?"

she says. "He wouldn't know where to start with it. And all that money in the hands of a man like that? It'd be gone on drink and women and gambling within a year. Whereas Tobias has great plans for this place. Plans that will bring a real economic benefit to the village." She goes on like this at great length, all hoity-toity, I can't remember everything. I tried arguing with her, but she wasn't having any of it. "Here's the thing," she says at last, after I've refused to go along with her scheme. She picks up the will and says, "This is an extremely valuable document, in the right hands." So I ask her what she means by that, and she says, "Tobias Burton will pay both of us good money to keep this document hidden." And then' – Rosemary was beginning to cry now – 'she goes on about Simon and how difficult it must be for me to have a husband who can't work anymore, and how much of a difference it would make to have a little extra money coming in each month. The bottom line is, I agreed to go along with it. "I'll speak to Tobias," she assures me. "You won't have to do a thing. Just keep quiet, and everything will be all right."'

Rosemary was crying properly now, her head buried in her hands, her husband saying, 'There, there, love. It's better to get it out in the open at last.'

'So,' said Bridget, 'you and Lindsey Symonds started blackmailing Tobias Burton.'

'It sounds horrible when you put it that way,'

said Rosemary. 'I didn't think of it as blackmail, just keeping quiet and not upsetting the apple cart. After all, Tobias was Mr Burton's son, too. And Ms Symonds was right – Shaun Daniels would probably have made a mess of everything. You hear about these folk who win the lottery and fritter all their money away on silly things. It never makes them happy.'

'Rosemary knows that she did wrong,' said Simon, 'and she wants to put things right. That's why she called you.'

'Oh, Inspector, if I could put the clock back, I would,' said Rosemary. 'I feel thoroughly ashamed of myself now, but Lindsey Symonds can be very persuasive, and at the time I thought that if I took the money, life would be better for once.'

'What made you change your mind?' asked Bridget. 'Why did you decide to speak up now?'

'We had a break-in last night,' said Simon. 'While we were down the pub. Nothing was taken, but we came home to find the place turned upside down. I said we should report it to the police. But then she told me what she's just told you. We think Tobias Burton, or someone working for him, was looking for the will. If he could find it and destroy it, then he wouldn't have to keep paying Lindsey and Rosemary to keep quiet about it.'

'Where is the will now?' asked Bridget. 'You said that nothing was taken?'

'Lindsey Symonds still has it,' said Rosemary.

'I don't know what she's done with it, but you can be sure it's somewhere safe. She knows that Tobias hasn't got any choice other than to keep paying. If he stops, or if he tries to do anything, she'll take it straight to the solicitors and he'll lose everything. I can't say I like the man, but you can't help feeling a little sorry for him, can you?'

Bridget wasn't sure how much sympathy she felt for Tobias Burton, but she had none whatsoever for Lindsey Symonds. Together, the estate manager and her employer had conspired to keep Shaun Daniels's rightful inheritance from him, not to mention the knowledge of his father's identity. But at least that was something that could be put right.

CHAPTER 23

On returning to the station, Bridget sent Jake and Ryan to go and arrest Lindsey Symonds on suspicion of blackmail.

'Shaun Daniels is the old squire's son?' said Jake incredulously, when Bridget explained what the nurse had told her. 'Bloody hell! And he's spent the last thirty years working as gardener on the old man's estate.'

'Boy, is he going to be mad!' remarked Ryan, whistling.

Bridget had no desire to find out what a mad Shaun Daniels might be like, knowing how badly he had behaved in the Eight Bells on Saturday night. 'Just go and bring that woman in, and let's see if we can begin to sort out this mess,' she told her two sergeants.

An hour later, Lindsey Symonds was sitting opposite her and Jake in interview room number two, accompanied by a lawyer from the firm used by Tobias Burton. Bridget suspected that once the nature of the allegation was made clear, Ms Symonds might be in the market for a new lawyer. The same firm could hardly represent the interests of both Tobias Burton and the person who had blackmailed him.

Lindsey appeared much as she had done when Bridget had first encountered her at the restaurant in Oxford. Dressed in a cream blouse beneath an olive business suit that coordinated nicely with her blonde hair, she showed little sign of nerves. She made a stark contrast to her co-conspirator, Rosemary Carver. Bridget wondered how long that veneer of confidence would survive under the weight of the accusations that had been made against her.

With the formalities out of the way and the recording machine rolling, Bridget launched straight into the attack. 'Ms Symonds, it is our understanding that the late Mr Henry Burton wrote a new will, approximately four days before he died. Do you know anything about that?'

'No comment,' said Lindsey, looking unruffled by the question.

'We also believe that you acted as a witness to that will.'

'No comment.'

'In that will, Henry Burton named Shaun Daniels as his son, and left the entirety of his estate to him.'

'No comment.'

'DI Hart,' said the solicitor, 'Do you have any evidence to support these claims, or is this simply speculation?'

Bridget nodded to Jake, who produced a typed document. 'We have just taken a signed statement from Mrs Rosemary Carver,' he said to Lindsey Symonds. 'In it, she asserts that you and she together acted as witnesses to the new will, and that you took the will for safekeeping. She also alleges that after the death of Mr Henry Burton, you persuaded her to keep silent about the will, and that the two of you conspired to demand money from Mr Tobias Burton to keep the will a secret.'

'No comment,' said Lindsey, although Bridget thought she now detected an edge of alarm in the estate manager's blue eyes.

'Ms Symonds,' she said. 'It will be a simple task for us to establish from DNA profiles whether Shaun Daniels really is the half-brother of Tobias Burton, and also very easy for an examination of your bank account to reveal whether you have recently received any unexplained payments from Mr Burton. We have already examined Mrs Carver's bank statements and found a payment of five hundred pounds from you to her.'

Instead of another "no comment", Bridget was gratified to find that this resulted in a whispered exchange between client and solicitor. After a minute, the solicitor made a note for himself and said, 'My client wishes to make a statement.'

'Ms Symonds?' said Bridget.

If the solicitor had been expecting a reasonable and judicious response from his client, he was sorely disappointed. Lindsey's reply was heartfelt and vicious. 'That stupid woman,' she spat.

'I should never have trusted her. She was half-hearted from the outset. All she had to do was keep her big mouth shut, and she couldn't even manage that.'

'So you admit to conspiring to keep the will a secret, and to blackmailing Tobias Burton?'

'My client believed she was acting with the best of intentions,' interjected the solicitor before Lindsey could say anything.

'The best of intentions?' queried Bridget. 'How so?'

Lindsey seemed to have recovered some of her poise. 'Inspector, you can imagine my reaction when I realised that Henry Burton was planning to leave everything to Shaun Daniels. That would have been a disaster for the estate, and for everyone involved.'

'It wasn't your place to decide that,' said Bridget.

'It was clear to me that Mr Burton couldn't have been in his right mind at the time he made the will.'

'Rosemary Carver claims that he was perfectly *compos mentis*. She has said so in her statement, and she has a great deal of experience of caring for people at the end of their life.'

'Yes, well,' said Lindsey dismissively, 'I'd worked for Mr Burton for more than a decade, and I feel that I knew him very well. I can tell you that during all that time he never so much as hinted that Shaun Daniels was his son.'

'A DNA test will prove that one way or the

other.'

Lindsey shrugged. 'If Shaun really is Mr Burton's son then that was long before my time. But I thought him to be an entirely unsuitable choice of person to be taking on such a large, historic house. What does he know about preservation of a grade II listed property?'

'That's quite irrelevant,' said Bridget. 'What does concern me, however, is that yesterday a break-in occurred at Mrs Carver's house. Nothing was taken, and there is a strong possibility that the intruder was searching for something that they were unable to find. Do you know who might have broken into her house and what they may have been looking for?'

'My client is not obliged to speculate on such matters,' said the solicitor.

But Lindsey looked very uncomfortable at the news. 'I don't know,' she muttered.

'Do you think that Tobias Burton might have broken into her home, searching for the will?'

'I don't know,' repeated Lindsey, but now a look approaching fear had entered her eyes.

'Where is the will now?'

Once again, Lindsey conferred briefly with her solicitor. 'In a safe deposit box,' she said.

'And how much money has been paid out in blackmail by Tobias Burton?'

'Five thousand pounds, which I shared with Rosemary Carver.'

Bridget raised an eyebrow. 'Mrs Carver has received five hundred pounds.'

'I didn't say it was an equal share,' said Lindsey, some of the earlier defiance back in her attitude. 'Ten percent seemed more than fair, given that it was entirely my idea and I did all the work.' Her solicitor appeared horrified by what she had just said, but Lindsey didn't notice his expression, and it was too late to retract her words now.

Bridget had heard quite enough. She charged Lindsey Symonds with blackmail and intent to defraud and sent Jake to escort her down to the cells.

★

'What now, ma'am?' asked Jake after returning from the cells.

'Now we pay another visit to Hambledon Manor,' said Bridget. She had already sent Harry to retrieve the will from Lindsey Symonds's safe deposit box. The youngest and most junior member of Bridget's team, Harry had been delighted to be assigned such a responsible task.

Now, having read the will through and verified that everything Rosemary Carver had told Bridget about its contents was true, it was time to deliver the news to all involved.

It was Josephine Daniels who opened the door to the manor house. 'Inspector, come in.' Her manner was polite, but constrained. She was again wearing the black dress Bridget had first seen her in. The dark material served only to accentuate the paleness of her skin and the slenderness of her frame. 'Mr Burton is in his office,' she explained. 'If you'll wait in the drawing room, I'll tell him you're here.'

'Actually,' said Bridget, 'I would like to see Mr Burton afterwards, but first I'd like to speak to you and your son together.'

'Me and Shaun?' The housekeeper appeared mystified. 'What about?'

'It'll be better if I explain in person,' said Bridget. 'But I hope, for once, it will be good news.'

'You'd better wait in here,' said Josephine, showing them into a well-proportioned panelled room at the front of the house. 'I'll go and fetch Shaun from his cottage.'

Bridget and Jake made themselves comfortable on a deep Chesterfield sofa overlooking the garden. The room was imbued with a strong scent of leather, furniture polish and age. Bridget wondered how many generations of the Burton family had sat or stood in this very room. She wondered also how Tobias Burton would respond to the news that he was no longer lord of the manor, but that his lowly half-brother was about to replace him.

Through the leaded windows, she could see the intricate box hedging of a knot garden. Despite his shortcomings, Shaun Daniels had certainly done a fine job of maintaining the grounds of the manor house for all these years. Bridget guessed that the old squire had given him the job partly out of charity, and partly out of a desire to keep his son close, despite being unable to acknowledge him openly.

Who knew how mother and son might react to what she was about to unveil? Suddenly finding yourself the owner of a sixteenth-century manor house and acres of land might seem like a dream come true, but Rosemary Carver had been right when she'd said that lottery winners often found their lives upended, and not for the better, by the sudden change in their circumstances. And then there was the question of what Shaun Daniels would do upon learning the truth of his parentage. That revelation alone was likely to produce shock waves, the outcome of which Bridget couldn't predict.

The housekeeper and gardener entered the room after a few minutes, the son towering over his mother like a giant. He looked bleary-eyed as if he'd been roused from his bed, and wore a pair of old jeans and a loose shirt, the sleeves rolled up to the elbows to reveal meaty forearms. He acknowledged Bridget and Jake with a scowl. 'What have I done this time?' he demanded. 'Aren't you lot ever going to leave me in peace?'

'Hopefully this will be the last time we need to speak to you,' said Bridget with a smile.

Josephine looked on anxiously. 'You said this was going to be good news, Inspector?'

'I hope so,' said Bridget. 'But perhaps you'd like to sit down before I say anything.' She gestured at the sofa opposite, and waited for mother and son to take up position, Josephine's hands folded neatly on her lap, and Shaun with his legs apart, his arms spread out insolently along the back of the leather sofa.

Bridget removed the will from her bag and unfolded it. It was a simple document, handwritten on a single sheet of paper, and unambiguously clear in its intentions. Shaun Daniels, the man sitting opposite her with a look of undisguised loathing on his face, was to be the sole inheritor of Hambledon Manor and all it contained.

As concisely as she could, Bridget explained to her audience that Henry Burton had written a new will four days before he died. 'This will,' she said, watching closely for their reactions, 'names you, Shaun, as Henry Burton's son, and leaves his entire estate to you.'

For a moment, neither mother nor son said a word. What little colour Josephine had in her cheeks faded away, leaving only a ghostly pallor. Shaun simply looked stunned, as if he couldn't understand what Bridget had said.

Eventually he turned to his mother. 'You told me that my dad ran off before I was born,' he exploded, rising to his feet. 'Now I find that he was here all along and neither of you had the decency to tell me?'

'Shaun –' said Josephine.

'Why didn't you tell me the truth?' Shaun ran his hands through his hair, causing it to stand on end, and for a moment Bridget glimpsed the lost little boy inside the grown man, the adolescent who had never had a father figure to look up to, the man who would always yearn for something he had never known.

'I'm sorry,' said Josephine in a small voice. 'Your father, Henry Burton, was a good man. He provided a home for us, he gave you a job, but he couldn't acknowledge that he was your father. A man in his position, back then, it simply wasn't the done thing.'

'It was the nineteen seventies, not the age of the bloody Victorians!' bellowed Shaun.

'It was a long time ago. Attitudes were very different. Especially for a man like Henry Burton. He couldn't publicly admit to being the father of an illegitimate child.'

'So instead he forced you to endure the shame of being an unmarried mother. And he was happy for me to be the village bastard!'

'Please, Shaun, he was a good man. You mustn't blame him.'

'Then why couldn't he have married you if he was such a good man?'

'I was just a girl from the village. Henry was lord of the manor. He needed to find a wife from the right social background.' Josephine softened her voice. 'I've always tried to provide a good home for you, Shaun. And Henry did his best to help too, in his way. I hope you know that I've always put you first, even if I couldn't tell you the truth.'

Her words had the effect of calming him down.

'I know, Mum,' he said, laying his big work-roughened hands on her bony shoulders. 'I know you have.' After giving her a hug, he turned his attention to Bridget. 'Can I see the will?'

She handed the document over to him. He read it with a frown, then passed it to his mother. Josephine put on her reading glasses and picked up the piece of paper with trembling hands. 'It... it's witnessed by Rosemary Carver and Lindsey Symonds,' she said. 'Neither of them said anything about it to me.'

'Henry Burton swore them both to secrecy,' said Bridget, 'although Rosemary told me that she felt bad about keeping it from you.'

'But why has this only come out now?' asked Shaun. 'Henry Burton died over two weeks ago. Where has this will been all that time?'

'It's complicated,' said Bridget, explaining how the will had been concealed and used to blackmail Tobias. 'If it's any consolation,' she concluded, 'this whole business came to light because Rosemary finally found the courage to come forward and admit her involvement.'

Shaun leapt to his feet again. 'Lindsey Symonds, that scheming bitch!' But there was a glint of something that looked like satisfaction in his eyes. 'I always hated that stuck-up cow. Now she's got what was coming to her.' He laughed out loud, then an idea seemed to strike him. 'You know that book I stole from the library? Turns out it was mine all along. I can't be done for stealing my own property, can I?'

'That'll have to be reviewed in light of the changed circumstances,' said Bridget. 'But right now I need to see Tobias Burton.'

'You gonna arrest him?' asked Shaun. 'I want to see this for myself!'

Jake stood up. 'I'm afraid that won't be possible, mate. You'll have to wait here.'

Shaun looked disappointed, but didn't protest. 'All right, then. But I want to see the look on his face when you lead him away.'

'I'll take you to him now,' said Josephine, still looking stunned by the day's events. 'Come this way, please.' She led Bridget along the corridor and knocked on a door. There was no response, but Bridget could hear Tobias's voice from inside. She twisted the handle and pushed open the door.

Tobias Burton was pacing about his office, mobile phone to his ear. 'Yes, what is it?' he said when he saw Bridget and the housekeeper in the doorway. He tossed the phone onto his desk in irritation. 'And where's that bloody estate manager? I've been trying to get hold of her all day. She's not picking up or answering my messages.'

'Ms Symonds is currently being held in police custody,' said Bridget, stepping into the room. 'She's been charged with blackmail and intent to defraud.'

'She's been what?' demanded Tobias, but the look of dismay on his face told Bridget he knew the game was up.

'I think you know exactly what I'm talking about, don't you, Mr Burton? I have your father's new will in my possession and I've already shared the details of it with Josephine and Shaun Daniels. The will names Shaun Daniels as son and sole heir to your father's estate.'

Tobias didn't bat an eyelid at this revelation. 'Does it, indeed? We'll see what my legal team has to say about that.'

'I can assure you that the will is genuine. It has been signed and witnessed in full accordance with the law, as I'm sure you're well aware.'

Tobias said nothing, pressing his thin lips tightly closed.

As if on cue, Shaun Daniels muscled his way into the office. 'Let me see him!' he bawled.

'Sorry, ma'am,' said Jake, unable to stop him from pushing his way inside.

'What do you think you're doing?' said Tobias indignantly. 'You can't just barge in here–'

'Oh, but I can, can't I?' said Shaun. 'You see, all this' – he gestured at the wood-panelled walls, the mahogany furniture, the stained-glass of the windows – 'belongs to me now. Every last brick of this house. So I've got every right. You, brother' – he jabbed a finger at Tobias – 'are the one who has no rights around here anymore. In fact, I want you out of my house by the end of the day.'

'What utter nonsense!' said Tobias. 'I'll have you know that I intend to challenge the contents of this so-called will.'

'Really? You must have believed it was genuine, otherwise you'd never have paid Lindsey Symonds to keep her mouth shut about it.' Shaun shot Tobias a nasty grin. 'She might be a scheming bitch, but credit where it's due – she had you wrapped around her little finger, didn't she? So, how does it feel to be the idiot? The one your own father turned his back on and rejected? Get used to it, brother. When everyone finds out about this, you'll be the laughing stock of the village!'

Tobias's features contracted in fury and he lunged at Shaun, grabbing the collar of his shirt. But the gardener was the stronger of the two. All those years spent in manual labour out of doors paid off now. He shoved his half-brother away, sending him reeling across the floor.

'That's enough!' shouted Bridget, as Jake moved between the two men to prevent any further violence. 'Tobias Burton, I am arresting you on suspicion of intent to defraud.'

CHAPTER 24

That evening, bellringing practice was cancelled. After all the extra sessions they'd put in practising for the funeral and the wedding, and with Jamie away on his honeymoon, Bill had told the remaining six ringers to take the evening off and enjoy the fine weather. They all deserved a rest, he'd said.

Under normal circumstances, Amy would have used her unexpected evening off to see Jake, but tonight she had other plans. Instead of telling him about the cancelled practice, she hoped to surprise him with her own detective work.

She hadn't quite been able to believe her luck when Jake – a tall, good-looking detective! – had become her boyfriend. It had been chance that had brought them together – neither had expected much from a dating app – but they'd been together for over two months, and were having a fantastic time. They had a shared sense of humour, and enjoyed the same films, the same food, and even the same beer.

But sometimes she worried it was all too good to be true.

People tended to only see the bubbly, confident version of her. It was a facet of her personality that she'd cultivated, in part, because she'd never been one of the "cool" girls at school. She wasn't glamorous, but she could be funny; she wasn't super-brainy, but she did her best to be kind. But the doubts still lingered. Did Jake want more from a woman?

Her job in the library was boring compared to his. Did that make her a boring person? She knew that he didn't read much, perhaps didn't even like books.

She knew that he had once had a relationship with a female detective at work. Amy had never met Ffion, but one of Jake's colleagues, a guy called Ryan, had mentioned the Welsh detective when Amy had joined Jake and a few of the other detectives in his team for a drink at their local, the King's Head in Kidlington. According to Ryan, Ffion was "fit" and dressed in skin-tight motorcycle leathers and rode a neon green Kawasaki Ninja H2, whatever that was. She was a long-distance runner and a Taekwondo expert who had been known to take down violent criminals with a well-aimed kick.

Amy knew that she was no great beauty, that she wore a high-vis vest that made her look like a council workman, rode an old bicycle with a basket on the front and a pannier on the back, and that apart from cycling to and from work, her exercise consisted of climbing belltowers and pulling bell ropes. She wasn't remotely in Ffion's league.

But the murder of Harriet Stevenson in Amy's home village presented her with a unique opportunity. She might not be able to compete with Ffion in the fashion or fitness stakes, but there was definitely something she could do to prove to Jake that she wasn't just a boring old librarian.

'Doing anything interesting tonight?' asked Evan, as she packed her bag before leaving work. She'd spent the whole day working through the titles from Henry Burton's library, adding them to the library database to make them available to search in the online catalogue.

'Not a lot,' said Amy, keeping her head down. She wasn't about to tell Evan what she had in mind. 'Just a quiet night in.'

She rolled up the map of Hambledon and inserted it carefully into her backpack, the top sticking out of one corner. 'See you tomorrow,' she called as she headed for the door.

She hurried down the library steps and out into the quadrangle where the statue of the Earl of Pembroke in full body armour struck a slightly camp pose, his left hand on his hip, his right holding a scroll away from his body.

Donning her high-vis vest and cycling helmet, she retrieved her bicycle from the railings surrounding the Radcliffe Camera and set off down Brasenose Lane, expertly weaving her way around tourists and students. The quickest way home was to brave the traffic on the Abingdon

Road and then pick up the Thames Path south of Iffley. At this time of year, it was a pleasant ride and she liked to take her time, enjoying the abundance of wildflowers that grew in the hedgerows and along the water's edge, but today she pedalled hard until she reached the village.

She dropped her bicycle off in the shed around the back of the pub where crates of beer and soft drinks were kept, and went upstairs to change out of her work clothes into something more suitable for what she had in mind – cropped jeans and a T-shirt. Her dad was busy in the bar and she knew that her mum would be hard at work in the kitchen. As it was a bellringing evening, they wouldn't be expecting to see her until later, so she didn't bother to disturb them. Taking the map with her, she slipped unnoticed out of the side door.

The pub garden was thronged with people making the most of the warm weather. Amy passed them unnoticed and made her way through the village to the church. It was a perfect evening for taking a stroll along the river and then sitting with a cool glass of homemade lemonade, but she didn't see anyone she knew. As she passed the gates of the manor house, the air became heavy with the scent of freshly cut grass from the village green. Bees buzzed lazily in the warm summer's evening, sated with pollen.

She made her way beneath the old lychgate of the church, passing along the well-worn path that led to the north porch. Pushing open the heavy oak door, she stepped inside. The sudden drop in temperature caused her to rub her bare arms. She was relieved to find that the church was empty.

She walked quickly down the central aisle, pausing as she passed the north transept to remind herself of where she had found the body of Harriet Stevenson. It wasn't difficult to pinpoint the exact location. The flagstones there had been scrubbed so hard they were now cleaner and paler than in the rest of the building. Nearby, the effigies of Lord and Lady Burton lay in peaceful repose, the only witnesses to what had taken place here last Wednesday.

She carried on and opened the door to the vestry. She knew that the keys were kept in the wall cupboard here, because she often came to fetch the key to the belltower. This time, it wasn't the belltower key she wanted, but the key to the crypt. She hesitated a moment before removing it from its hook, but told herself not to be such a goose. She was only going to take a look.

Before she could change her mind, she slipped the key off its hook and made her way to the south transept and to the small arched doorway located there. She had never been inside the crypt, and wondered if it was wise to be going down alone. What if she slipped on a stone step and hit her head? Nobody knew she was here. But then she imagined what Ffion would do in the same circumstances, and pushed the key into the lock.

She'd expected it to be stiff, but it turned easily, as if it had recently been in use. The door creaked open, revealing a narrow flight of stone steps reaching into darkness.

Descend into my chamber cold and darke. Therein thou shalt thy reward come to marke.

Using the light on her mobile phone to guide her, Amy slipped through the stone archway, closing the door behind her.

CHAPTER 25

The time on Bridget's phone said half past five but it was already light outside. Beside her, Jonathan lay peacefully, his deep, regular breathing evidence that he was still enjoying a restful slumber. How she envied him.

Last night they'd enjoyed takeaway pizzas and ice-cream with Chloe to celebrate the end of her exams. Alfie had called around too, and they had talked late into the night, with Bridget and Jonathan managing to polish off a bottle of chilled rosé between them. The end of GCSEs had felt like a special occasion and, whether as a result of the wine, or the palpable relief that the exams were over, Bridget had fallen asleep almost as soon as her head hit the pillow.

But her hours of blissful oblivion had been short-lived.

It wasn't just the bright sunlight streaming through the curtains that had woken her, nor the piercingly loud birdsong coming from the trees behind her house. It was the fact that, despite uncovering a great number of tangled relationships in the village of Hambledon-on-

Thames, not to mention arresting and charging several of its residents for various crimes, she was no nearer to solving the murder case, and her subconscious simply wouldn't let her take time off.

She pushed back the duvet, scooped up her phone, and crept downstairs. Maybe a coffee would clear her head and get her brain fully in gear. She really shouldn't have drunk so much wine the night before.

She made the drink strong, heaping an extra spoonful of sugar into the mug for good luck, and took it outside to the small wooden table by the back door. Pulling up a chair, she stared in amazement at the jungle that had taken hold of much of her garden and was now threatening to engulf the last surviving bastion. Blackberries, roses and other climbing plants snaked across flagstones, encroaching on the patio and working hard to reclaim it for Nature. Perhaps now that Chloe had finished at school, Bridget could employ her to clear some space. With a little work – or perhaps quite a lot – it could be quite pleasant out here.

She turned her face to the sun – already warm, but not yet too hot to burn – and closed her eyes. The church of St Michael and All Angels came unbidden to mind, presenting her with an image of the churchwarden's body, lying dead in a pool of her own blood at the foot of the Elizabethan tomb in the north transept. Harriet Stevenson had been a highly respected resident of

Hambledon, untiring in her devotion to the place where she had been born, and where she had once been engaged to the lord of the manor before leaving to pursue a career as an academic. Harriet had returned to her childhood home after retiring, and thrown herself wholeheartedly into village affairs, as churchwarden, as chair of the parish council, and as school governor. What set of circumstances had led to this elderly lady being brutally struck on the head with a candlestick and being left to die in the church she had loved and served?

Bridget allowed her mind's eye the freedom to roam about the old building, exploring the tall space of the nave with its timbered roof, the chancel – Norman in origin, according to the Reverend Martin Armistead – where light filtering through the stained-glass image of St Michael defeating the Devil illuminated the altar in red, blue and green. She remembered the elaborate floral display that had decorated the altar on the day of the funeral, taking in the heady perfume of roses, freesias and peonies. Her mind rested for a moment in the vestry, picturing the wooden key cupboard fixed to the wall, with its carefully-labelled handwritten signs above each hook: *north door, south door, belltower, organ vestry, crypt.* Sweeping onwards through the main body of the church, she recalled the south transept – built by the industrious monks of Abingdon Abbey – and the small wooden door that led down to the crypt, where the murder weapon had been hastily tossed aside. On past the south porch to the embattled tower with its ring of bells hidden behind louvred windows, and out to the churchyard, the final resting place of Hambledon residents for a thousand years or more, not to mention generations of Burtons. Over the centuries, all the important rites of passage had been enacted in that church: baptisms, weddings, funerals. And now a murder. Although not the first, if Maurice Fairweather was to be believed, with his story of religious persecution in the time of Bloody Mary.

But who in the village could be believed?

Tobias Burton, falsely claiming to be the sole heir of Hambledon Manor, had wanted to turn the old house into a hotel, a move opposed by Harriet Stevenson who, despite whatever people thought of her, had sought to preserve the historic nature of the house, not see it turned into a commercial venture. Tobias was clearly a businessman of considerable means. In Bridget's experience, those who already had a lot of money were usually keenest to make more. They thrived on the pursuit of wealth, seeing the world in terms of profit and loss, and forever calculating their return on investment. Tobias had been willing to make blackmail payments to keep his father's final will out of the public domain, not only defrauding his half-brother out of his rightful inheritance, but also keeping from him the knowledge that he was Henry's son. Had the churchwarden's loudly-expressed opposition to

Tobias's plans driven him to commit an act of murder? He had admitted re-entering the church after the burial ceremony but had given no convincing reason for doing so. He had even owned up to finding the body but failing to report it, knowing how it would look.

Then there was the estate manager, Lindsey Symonds. Bridget hadn't warmed to her at their first meeting at the restaurant in Oxford, and now she had good reason for her instinctive dislike. The woman was clearly capable of scheming and deceit. She had lied at the restaurant in order to give Tobias a false alibi for the time of the murder. And by concealing Henry Burton's last will and using it to blackmail Tobias, she had demonstrated once again that she wasn't above breaking the law in the pursuit and preservation of her own interests. Did that make her capable of murder? She was ruthless enough, but given her capacity for plotting, might it not be the case that she would drive someone else to do the dirty work for her? Someone known for having a short fuse... like Shaun Daniels.

Shaun was an odd character. He had obviously grown up with a very large chip on his shoulder, resentful of the fact that his father had supposedly abandoned him and his mother before he was even born, and constantly comparing himself to the Burtons in the "big house". With a history of petty crime – some proven, some, like the theft of lead from the church roof, merely suspected – he was just the sort of person to fall foul of Harriet Stevenson with her interfering nature and strict moral code. And he had a temper, as he had amply demonstrated, first by throwing a glass when drunk in the pub, and again when he had shoved Tobias to the floor. Could a chance encounter between Shaun and Harriet in the church have led to a spur-of-the-moment act of brutality? It was easy to believe that Shaun had grabbed a nearby candlestick in a moment of rage, then taken the key from the vestry and tossed the candlestick into the crypt. But had Shaun even known about the location of the keys?

Reluctantly, Bridget was forced to acknowledge that one person who definitely knew where to find the key to the crypt was Emma Armistead, the vicar's wife. Emma was clearly a disturbed young woman who had suffered a great trauma. She had come to Hambledon in the hope of finding healing, but in the person of Harriet Stevenson – a woman who held great sway in the life of the church and the village, and who as vicar's wife, Emma would have been unable to avoid – had found a callous lack of sympathy that must have driven her even further into her own despair. She had told her husband that she hated Harriet and was glad she was dead. She had admitted to blanks in her memory and disturbing dreams. Was it possible that in a fit of madness brought on by her depression she had lashed out at the person who was causing her even more pain? If the evidence pointed to Emma Armistead, Bridget would try to persuade the Crown Prosecution Service to push for a charge of manslaughter on the grounds of diminished responsibility. Emma needed help, not punishment.

But was there something significant about the location of the body? The north transept; the tomb of Sir Edmund and Lady Ellen; the mysterious inscriptions on the bells that seemed to hint at buried treasure. Bridget was inclined to dismiss the idea as fanciful nonsense, but Maurice Fairweather with his deep interest in local history had clearly believed there was more to it. He'd clashed with the churchwarden over his desire to have the tomb opened. The tomb next to which Harriet had been killed. And a silk thread had been discovered on the candlestick. It was still unidentified, but if it could be matched to one of Maurice's silk cravats… Could Harriet have been murdered because of a legend? The idea seemed far-fetched, but the village historian had clearly been fixated on his theory, and people had committed far greater atrocities for the sake of their beliefs, as Maurice, with his tales of medieval martyrs must surely be well aware.

Bridget's phone rang, startling her out of her musings. The sun had moved higher in the sky and was beginning to prick at the scalp on top of her head. She answered her phone, noting that it was now a quarter past six.

'Hello?'

'Ma'am? Sorry to wake you so early.' Jake's northern vowels were immediately recognisable on the other end of the line. He sounded upset, an emotion she didn't normally associate with her cool-headed sergeant.

She sat up straighter. 'No problem. I was already up. What's the matter?'

'It's Amy. She's gone missing. Her mum phoned me as soon as they realised. I'm on my way to Hambledon now.' The roar of the Subaru's engine came over the line and Bridget guessed that Jake was putting his foot down.

She felt a chill of fear sweep through her, despite the growing warmth of the sun. From what she knew of Jake's girlfriend, Amy Bagot wasn't the sort of person likely to do something stupid; nor would Jake have raised the alarm unless he had legitimate concerns for her welfare. And for a young woman to go missing in a place where another woman had been attacked and killed precisely a week earlier was obviously of grave concern. Bridget was already on her feet and heading back indoors. She tossed the remains of her coffee down the sink.

'Tell me what you know,' she said.

'I didn't see her last night because she always has bellringing practice on Tuesdays, although her parents, Robert and Sue, say they didn't hear the bells being rung last night. They were busy working in the pub until late, so they didn't notice Amy wasn't home. But her bicycle is in its usual place in the shed behind the pub, so she must have cycled back after work last night. Sue only noticed Amy's room was empty this morning.' The car's engine fell silent and Bridget heard the sound of the door opening and slamming shut. 'I'm at the pub now, I've got to go.'

'All right, Jake, listen, we'll do everything we can to find her. I promise.'

'Thank you.'

Bridget didn't waste any time, but dialled Ffion's number straightaway. It was still only six thirty but Ffion answered on the second ring, sounding bright and refreshed. Bridget pictured her in sportswear, perhaps engaged in a morning yoga and meditation practice, or eating a light breakfast of muesli and soya milk. She briefly explained the situation and Ffion promised to meet her at Hambledon in the next half hour.

It took significantly more than two rings to rouse Ryan from his slumber.

He eventually answered sounding as if he had a mouthful of cotton wool. 'Yeah?' He obviously hadn't bothered to look at the caller ID.

'Ryan, it's Bridget.'

She heard the sound of a crash followed by a stream of expletives 'Oh, sorry, ma'am,' said Ryan groggily. 'What can I do for you?'

She summarised Jake's call as quickly as she could. 'I've already spoken to Ffion. She's on her way to the village. I'm leaving now. Can you call Andy and Harry and tell them what's happening?'

'Will do.' Ryan now sounded bright and alert. 'I'll arrange for some uniforms from Abingdon to come and help us search too.'

'Excellent.' Bridget ended the call just as Jonathan appeared in the kitchen.

'Trouble?'

'A missing person. It might be connected to the murder investigation.' As soon as Bridget voiced the words, she felt convinced that the two incidents were linked. It was just too much of a coincidence. She had only met Amy once, but had immediately warmed to her cheerful and bubbly personality. The idea that she might have suffered the same fate as Harriet Stevenson was unthinkable. Few people in the village had shed tears over the demise of the churchwarden, but if something happened to Amy Bagot, the consequences were too awful to contemplate.

She threw on some clothes, then dashed downstairs again, giving Jonathan a quick kiss on the lips before leaving the house.

CHAPTER 26

Ffion roared into the sleepy village on her Kawasaki, not caring how many people she woke up in the process.

Jake's orange Subaru was parked outside the pub, so she pulled up behind it and went inside. She found him there with an older man and woman who she took to be Amy's parents. All three were busy on their mobile phones; the mother on the brink of tears, asking the person at the other end of the line if they'd seen Amy, the father and Jake working through a list of names, asking each person they called if they would be able to help with a search. They were ticking the names off one by one, and Ffion could see that so far the response had been one hundred percent positive.

Ffion had never met Amy, although she'd heard a lot about her. She hadn't joined Jake and the team at the King's Head the other evening, knowing that Amy would be there. No one had been surprised when she'd declined the invitation – it was what her colleagues had come to expect of her. She rarely, if ever, joined the guys for a drink after work, having no desire to spend her free time enduring Ryan's smartarse comments. So she'd simply said she was busy. To be fair, she usually was busy in the evenings, either attending Taekwondo practice or going for a solo run across Port Meadow. But not this time. She could easily have gone that night. In fact, she was even finding Ryan's company less irksome these days. So why hadn't she joined them?

The truth was, she'd been afraid. Afraid of meeting a bellringing librarian. It sounded ridiculous when she put it like that, but there it was. She ought to have been happy for Jake, and no doubt she would have been if he was nothing more to her than a friend and colleague. But Jake meant more than that. After their brief but intense relationship, Ffion had found happiness with Marion. But Marion had moved to Edinburgh, and ironically, just as they had gone their separate ways, Jake had met Amy.

Anyone could see that Amy made Jake happy. He was more cheerful at work, more confident in meetings. Amy had wrought a transformation that neither Ffion nor Jake's previous girlfriend, Brittany, had managed. This bellringing librarian clearly had something about her, and Ffion, to her shame, had avoided meeting her, scared to find out what that special quality was.

But now Amy was missing and the worry etched on Jake's face was plain for all to see. Ffion pushed her personal feelings aside. She was here as a police officer, and she would do her job to the best of her ability, just as she would for any person who had gone missing in suspicious circumstances.

Jake ended the call he was making, adding a tick to another name on the list, and came to greet her. 'Let me introduce you to Amy's parents. Robert, Sue, this is DC Ffion Hughes. She's the best we have.'

Ffion was touched by the unexpected and obviously heartfelt compliment, but there was no time to bask in it. 'Tell me everything,' she said. 'Where are we so far?'

'I've phoned round all her friends,' said Sue, trying to hold back the tears, 'but no one has seen her. Not since the day before yesterday.'

Robert put an arm around his wife. 'Jake and I have been rounding up a search team. All the bellringers have volunteered to help. They're a tight-knit bunch and they want to do everything they can. They'll be here any minute.'

The door swung open and Ryan came in, unshaven, his tie askew. But he looked like he meant business. He acknowledged Amy's parents with a nod. 'Robert, Sue, I know this must be difficult for you. I can't imagine what you're going through. But I want you to know we've set up a missing person's enquiry and we're treating this very seriously indeed.' To Jake he said, 'Don't worry, mate, we'll find her. Harry and Andy are on their way, and I've put in a request for more manpower from Abingdon.'

'Thanks,' said Jake.

The door opened again and a group of six men and women entered, looking dressed for a hike in walking boots. The oldest, a man of about seventy, shook Robert's hand gravely.

'Hello, Bill,' said Robert.

'This is Bill Harris, the belltower captain,' Jake explained to Ffion, 'and these are the other ringers.'

Apart from Ffion, everyone seemed to know each other, and the gathering radiated a sense of purpose.

'Right then,' said Ryan, 'let's put a plan together and get this show on the road.'

★

After calling in at the Eight Bells, which had become the unofficial HQ for the search operation, with Sue Bagot serving up soft drinks and offering sandwiches to everyone who lingered there for longer than a minute, Bridget decided to head back into Oxford. Amy had gone into work as usual on Tuesday morning, so perhaps she had said something to one of her work colleagues that would provide a clue to what she had done after cycling home that evening.

Bridget was at the Bodleian Library the minute it opened. The surprised security guard took one look at her warrant card and immediately arranged for her to see the Librarian.

Professor Patrick Danvers listened intently to what she had to say, clearly taking her concerns seriously. 'Amy has just started working on a project to transfer a book collection from Hambledon Manor to the Bodleian,' said Danvers. 'Is it possible that she went to the manor house to tie up some loose ends?'

Bridget was well aware of Henry Burton's legacy and of Amy's involvement in moving the book collection. 'Detective Sergeant Jake Derwent – that's Amy's boyfriend – already phoned the manor house and she's not there,' she told the professor. 'She lives with her parents at the Eight Bells pub in Hambledon and they say that her bed wasn't slept in last night.'

At this Danvers's face fell. 'Oh dear, that doesn't sound good. How can I help?'

'I'd like to get a better understanding of Amy's movements yesterday. We know that she set off for work in the morning, and her bicycle was found in its usual place, indicating that she returned to the village, but can you confirm that she was definitely at work yesterday?'

'I believe so, yes, but I don't see all the staff every day. I'm in my office a lot of the time, or in meetings with other Oxford librarians. Yesterday I spent most of the day in a meeting with the Vice-Chancellor to discuss funding.' He thought for a moment. 'You'd be better off speaking to one of Amy's colleagues.'

He made a phone call and asked for Evan Jones to come to his office right away. Two minutes later there was a knock at the door and in walked a gawky-looking young man in his mid-twenties. He was all arms and legs and didn't seem to know where to put himself in the Librarian's office.

'Take a seat, Evan,' said Danvers kindly. 'This is Detective Inspector Bridget Hart and she would like to ask you a few questions about Amy Bagot.'

'Is Amy okay?' asked Evan, sitting on the edge of a chair as if afraid to leave a mark on it. His Adam's apple bobbed up and down as he spoke. 'Only she hasn't shown up this morning and that's not like her. I wondered if her bike had a puncture or if she was ill.' He glanced at Danvers and back to Bridget, his eyes wide and earnest behind his thick glasses. Bridget could see that the young man cared for Amy, that she was more to him than just a colleague.

'Amy is currently missing,' said Bridget. 'Was she at work yesterday?'

'Yes,' said Evan, nodding his head vigorously. 'We work in the same office together. She was there all day, adding the new book collection to the computer system. She left work at five as usual. I asked if she was doing anything and she said, no, she didn't have any particular plans. But she took a map with her.'

'A map?' queried Danvers, his brow furrowing. 'What map was this?'

'Not an original, sir,' said Evan hurriedly. 'Just a copy she'd downloaded and printed. It was a map by Ralph Agas.'

'Sorry,' said Bridget. 'Who is Ralph Agas?'

Evan seemed delighted to offer her an explanation. 'He was a famous sixteenth-century surveyor and cartographer.'

'Famous in his field,' remarked Danvers. 'But perhaps not to a wider audience. Could you explain to us what this map showed?'

'Oh, yes,' said Evan. 'It was a map showing the village where Amy lives. Hambledon-on-Thames. The date was 1585.'

'Is it possible to see a copy of this map?' asked Bridget.

'Of course,' said Evan. 'I'll print one off for you.'

CHAPTER 27

Ryan checked his phone, hoping for a missed call or a text, but there was nothing. He slipped the phone back inside his pocket, and returned to the job in hand.

The search was well underway, and in Bridget's absence, he had taken on the role of coordinating the various teams. There was certainly no shortage of volunteers, with not only the bellringers but half the village turning out to join in. The Bagot family were universally known in Hambledon, and Amy was a popular girl. Everyone, it seemed, wanted to help.

Ryan had assigned Harry the job of organising the uniformed officers, going door to door to find out if anyone had seen the missing woman or had any information that might help them locate her. If they received any tip-offs, Harry would relay the news back to Ryan, but so far there had been nothing.

The search had begun in the vicinity of the Eight Bells, scouring every corner of the pub, garden and outbuildings, and had moved steadily out into the village. Bill Harris had taken three of the ringers to the church. Other groups had begun searching the area around the village green and the school. That left Ryan with the remaining bellringers.

'All right,' he said to them now. 'It's time we started looking along the river.'

'The lock would be the best place to start,' said Jill, a short woman with grey hair who hardly looked strong enough to ring a bell weighing a hundredweight or more. 'Just in case...'

She didn't need to finish the sentence. Ryan could tell from the look on their faces that they all feared the worst.

He nodded. 'Good idea. We'll start at the lock and work our way along the river bank. We're looking for anything that might give us a clue to where Amy might have gone. A phone, a key, an item of clothing, whatever. But there's absolutely no reason to believe that she's come to any harm. Chances are, she'll turn up, right as rain, wondering why everyone's out looking for her.' He smiled, trying to persuade the others that Amy was just fine, but he could tell that his warm reassurances were having little effect. Hell, he couldn't even convince himself.

★

'Thank you, Mrs Carver,' said DS Andy Cartwright. 'And if you do remember anything...'

'I'll be sure to call you straight away, don't you

worry,' said Rosemary Carver over the phone. 'That poor, poor girl. I do hope nothing terrible has happened to her. You hear of such awful things on the news these days, don't you? And her poor parents. What must they be thinking? I was saying to Simon just the other day –'

'Thanks once again for your help, Mrs Carver,' said Andy, cutting the nurse off before she could launch into another of her tangential and longwinded anecdotes. 'Just call me if you think of anything.' He ended the call and consulted his list of names.

He was working his way through the list, tracking down and interviewing the various people connected with the murder inquiry, to find out whether they knew anything about Amy's disappearance.

His first stop had been the manor house, where he'd spoken to the housekeeper, Josephine Daniels, and the gardener... he corrected himself, the *lord of the manor*, Shaun Daniels. Both had been at home the previous evening, and no, they hadn't seen Amy. 'I'll have a good look around the grounds,' Shaun had assured him, worry writ large on his face. 'Amy's a good girl. And she's plucky. I'm sure no harm has come to her.'

'Just let me know if you find anything,' said Andy, 'no matter what.'

The former lord of the manor, Tobias Burton, was staying at the Randolph Hotel in Oxford. He'd been charged the previous day with intent to defraud his half-brother out of his rightful inheritance, but had been released on bail. Andy had interviewed him in person in the downstairs lounge of the hotel, where he was taking breakfast.

Tobias had appeared unperturbed by news of Amy's disappearance. 'The Bagot girl? Yes, I know her. Red-haired, freckled, rather dumpy and plain.'

Andy bristled at the unflattering description of Jake's girlfriend. Andy had met Amy on a couple of occasions and found her to be a very pleasant young woman. After Jake's recent romantic disasters, he deserved some happiness at last, and Amy was good for him. Andy hoped that the pair might settle down. Jake was the marrying sort, he reckoned, just like himself. Not flighty, like Ryan who went through girlfriends like Andy went through clean socks. It was exhausting just watching him. But even a guy like Ryan might mellow one day. Everyone did.

'Please can you account for your movements yesterday evening?' he said to Tobias.

'After you released me from custody, you mean?' said Tobias with a sneer.

'Yes, after that, sir. If it's not too much trouble.'

Tobias leisurely spread a pat of butter over his toast. 'You sure I can't get you a coffee?'

'If you could just answer the question, sir?'

'Very well. I left Kidlington at around five and took a taxi here. You can check with the front desk. I booked a room for the night, as I'd had rather an eventful day and didn't fancy going straight back to London.'

'And what did you do after checking in?'

'I had a quiet evening in my suite, watching some rather trashy TV.'

'You didn't see anyone?'

'I had the contents of my mini-bar for company.'

'So no one can verify your whereabouts?'

'No. So it looks like you'll have to do some running around, looking at CCTV and speaking to witnesses, doesn't it, Sergeant?'

'Yes, sir. It does.'

The last name on Andy's list was Lindsey Symonds, the estate manager at the manor. *Former* estate manager, since one of Shaun Daniels's first actions on taking over had been to fire her. Like Tobias, she had also been charged and released the previous day. Andy tracked her down to her house in Hambledon.

The house was a small one, forming an end of terrace on the road leading to Clifton Hampden. The curtains were drawn, but some vigorous knocking eventually brought her to the front door. She was still in her nightwear, a dressing gown pulled around her.

'Yes?' she asked warily on seeing Andy.

'I'd like to ask you if you know anything about the whereabouts of Miss Amy Bagot.'

'The publican's daughter? Why would I know anything about her?'

'She's been reported missing. She was last seen yesterday at work in Oxford.'

'I haven't seen her,' said Lindsey. 'Why are you asking me this? You know that I was held in custody yesterday.'

'But you were released on bail, ma'am.'

'Yes, I was.'

'Can you tell me what you did after being released?'

'Well, one of your cars brought me home.'

'What time was that?'

'Late afternoon.'

Andy made a note. 'And after that?'

'I stayed in my house.' Lindsey glanced up and down the road. 'I didn't fancy meeting anyone from the village. You wouldn't believe how people gossip in a place like this.'

'Can anyone confirm your whereabouts?'

'I don't think so. You can't seriously think I had anything to do with the disappearance of this girl?'

'We like to keep an open mind, ma'am. So if you do think of anything that might be relevant...'

He gave her his contact details, and crossed the last name off his list. He checked his phone, but there was nothing there to see. He just hoped that the rest of the team was having more luck than he was.

★

All around him people were in a state of great activity, coming in and going out of the pub, reporting results or a lack of them, engaging in hurried conversations, nodding, shaking heads. Robert Bagot had a phone permanently glued to the side of his head. Even Sue had pulled herself together, and was dashing about, making tea and bringing food from the kitchen to feed the search parties and anyone else she could find.

And yet amongst it all, Jake stood motionless, his mind a boiling cauldron of conflicting thoughts and emotions.

He couldn't begin to express how much Amy meant to him and what a vital component of his life she now was. In two short months, she had become the bedrock that everything else rested on. He vividly recalled the first time they had met, in a rainy pub off the Cowley Road, not expecting much from his latest date, but within the space of a few minutes being enchanted by her open nature and quiet, unassuming charm.

A vision of her round freckled face skimmed before him, her warm smile lighting up the darkness. 'Amy,' he muttered.

This was all his fault.

She'd told him on their very first date about her love of detective books, and mysteries, and had quizzed him eagerly about his police work.

'It's not all like that,' he'd told her, trying to downplay her enthusiasm, but he had been unable to dampen her infectious curiosity. Even when he'd poured cold water on her crazy idea about the buried treasure, she'd gone away undeterred. He could tell that she was determined to investigate further. And now, she'd gone missing...

If it turned out that she'd come to harm while trying to prove him wrong, he'd never be able to live with the guilt.

'Hey.'

He looked up and saw Ffion's almond-shaped eyes on him, studying him with concern. Everyone else he'd spoken to had given him warm but empty reassurances, that everything would be okay, that Amy would turn up soon, that she had come to no harm. Ffion offered no false hopes.

'You must be worried sick,' she said.

'I am.'

'That's understandable. Everyone says Amy's a sensible girl. This is out of character.'

'It is,' he said. 'Something must have happened to her. She wouldn't have just disappeared.'

Ffion nodded. 'But you know that we'll find her. One way or another. With so many people scouring such a small village, she can't stay hidden for long.'

Ffion was right, as usual. They would find her. One way or another.

'Come here,' she said. 'You need a hug.'

She wrapped her arms around him, and pulled him to her, so that he could feel her warmth against him. Her touch seemed to reanimate him, driving away the stupor that had briefly swallowed him.

'Right,' she said, releasing him from her grip. 'What Amy needs now is every hand on deck. You know her better than any of us. So get out there, and get looking.'

He smiled at her, grateful for lifting him out of his despair. 'Yes, boss.'

But where to begin? Search teams were scouring every corner of the village, and officers were knocking on doors. No stone would be left unturned.

'Amy had this idea about the buried treasure,' he told Ffion.

'That old legend? Do you think she went looking for it?'

'I do.'

'But where?'

He shrugged. 'I don't know. If I'd only listened to her, and let her tell me about her theories. But I know that one idea was that it was buried in the church, in the Burton tomb.'

'A search team has already been into the church,' said Ffion. 'If Amy was there, they would have found her.'

Jake felt his hope begin to ebb away once more. 'Then –'

The door of the pub burst open and in came Bridget, clutching a rolled-up tube. Seeing Jake and Ffion, she bustled over to them and showed them what she was carrying. 'This is what Amy was studying at work yesterday.'

'What is it, ma'am?' Jake asked.

'A map. Now clear some space and let's have a proper look at it.'

CHAPTER 28

At a table in the back lounge of the Eight Bells, Bridget, Jake and Ffion clustered around the map of Hambledon, their bent heads almost touching.

Bridget had driven straight from Oxford as soon as Evan had printed her a copy of the map. A casual appraisal had revealed nothing new, but if Amy had brought a copy with her when she cycled back to the village after finishing work, then there must have been something in it that had caught her eye. Bridget spread it out on the circular surface of the table, explaining its significance to Ffion and Jake.

'I don't see anything,' said Jake in frustration after they had pored over the map for several minutes. 'There's nothing shown on this map that we don't already know about.'

Bridget was inclined to agree. Jake had told her about his hunch that Amy had gone off searching for buried treasure. Yet the map, while exquisitely detailed, revealed nothing as obvious as an X marking the spot. While some of the buildings drawn on the map differed a little from their modern-day counterparts, Bridget was unable to see anything that might have inspired Amy to embark on some kind of quest.

'According to Maurice Fairweather,' said Ffion, 'the inscriptions on the bells point to the church.'

'Beneath the tomb of Lord Edmund and Lady Ellen Burton,' said Jake.

Bridget nodded silently. She was in no doubt that they were all thinking the same thought – that the tomb was where the body of Harriet Stevenson had been discovered.

'But a search team has already been inside the church,' said Ffion. 'If anyone had disturbed the tomb, they would have noticed.'

'There couldn't be a secret door or something, could there?' said Bridget. But she knew she was clutching at ever flimsier straws.

'No secret door is marked on the map,' said Ffion. 'But the map does show the whole of the church.'

'What do you mean, the *whole* church?' asked Jake. 'Of course it shows the whole church.'

'I mean that because the map is drawn from a bird's eye view, it shows the whole church, both above and below ground.'

What Ffion said was true. Although no bird had ever seen the crypt of St Michael and All Angels while flying overhead, the map nevertheless showed the underground space as a kind of ghostly shadow beneath the building. 'The crypt was where the candlestick was found,' said Bridget.

'You're saying that the treasure is buried in the crypt?' said Jake.

'What I'm saying,' said Ffion, 'is that Amy might have looked at the map and decided it was worth taking a look in the crypt.'

'But how would she have got in there, with the key missing?' asked Jake.

'Hold on,' said Bridget. 'Let's see if I can find out.' She took her phone from her jacket and dialled a number. It was answered after a single ring.

'Martin Armistead here?'

'It's DI Hart. Can you tell me what happened to the spare key to the crypt after the SOCO team finished down there?'

'The key?' said the vicar. 'Why, I hung it on the hook in the vestry cupboard. Since the other one was still missing… did I do the wrong thing?'

'No,' Bridget reassured him. 'I just wanted to check. Thank you.'

She ended the call. 'The vicar put the spare key back in the vestry.'

'So Amy could have taken it and used it to get into the crypt,' said Jake, with obvious excitement.

'Then she could be down there now,' said Ffion. 'Come on.'

★

Jake and Ffion sprinted off in the direction of the

331

church and Bridget lumbered after them, knowing that she really did need to work at her fitness regime. It just wasn't good enough, being the slowest and least agile member of her team. Ffion and Harry were keen runners, and even Andy with his middle-aged spread and Ryan with his beer belly could outpace her by miles.

When all this is over, she promised herself. *No more pasta; no more chocolate; no more wine. Workouts instead.* For a while, at least.

Her face was hot and she was all out of puff when she arrived at the church and descended the stone steps into the welcome coolness of the crypt.

Jake and Ffion were already down there, the white beams of their torches doing little to penetrate the thick darkness that filled the underground chamber.

'Amy!' shouted Jake. 'Amy! Where are you?'

His voice echoed off the vaulted stone ceiling of the sepulchre, but there was no response to his calls.

'The key was missing from the vestry cupboard,' Ffion explained to Bridget. 'The door to the crypt was closed but unlocked. So Amy must have come down here.'

'Then where is she?' asked Bridget. The lights from the torches were narrow and weak, but surely if Amy were here, they would have found her by now. Her glance drifted involuntarily towards the stone coffins in the centre of the room. She shivered, and not just because of the chill damp air.

'How does the verse go?' she asked.

Jake seemed to know the lines by heart. '*Bee it knowne unto all men far and wyde, That in this place a secret doth reside. Where mortal bones are set to rest within, And blind wormes creep and lay their eggs hidd'n, 'Gainst northern wall in wynter's chill embrace...*' He stopped, playing the beam of his torch across the stone walls. 'Which wall is north?'

'That one.' Bridget pointed to the wall furthest from the steps. She might not be an athlete, but she knew her religious architecture well enough. Every church in the Western tradition was orientated on an east-west axis, with the altar and sanctuary facing east.

'*To iron girde and stone then turn to face,*' continued Jake. 'Everyone look for an iron girde!'

'It must be on one of the coffins,' said Bridget, moving closer to the stone sarcophagi that dominated the centre of the crypt. The others joined her, and together they began to inspect the huge stone slabs. But there was no hint of iron, or any kind of metal.

'What about the south wall?' said Ffion. 'If you turn from the north wall to face stone, you're looking in the direction of the south wall, aren't you?' She advanced carefully across the uneven floor of the crypt until the light from her torch was faint and distant.

'Can you see anything?' called Bridget.

There was no reply, only the shifting beam of

light as Ffion examined the ancient stonework of the southern wall. The torchlight came to a halt, angling down. 'I've found something!'

Bridget and Jake quickly made their way over to a place in the middle of the south wall, a little way from the steps. There, at ground level, an iron grating was set into the blocks of stone. It looked like a ventilation or drainage shaft.

'*Descend into my chamber cold and darke,*' recited Jake, '*Therein thou shalt thy reward come to marke.*'

★

The grating was about three foot square, made of heavy iron, and hinged on one side.

'Can you open it?' Bridget asked Jake.

He took hold of the grate with both hands, pulling it with all his strength, but it refused to budge. 'It must be fixed into the stone.'

'Then how did Amy open it?' asked Bridget.

'We're only assuming that she did,' said Jake. He sounded close to despair.

'Wait,' said Ffion. 'Can you lift it?'

'Lift it?' Jake frowned. But he tried, and to Bridget's amazement the iron grid rose up an inch and then swung forwards into the room, ancient hinges squeaking in protest. A dark opening was revealed in the wall. Even with three torches trained on it, it seemed to swallow all light.

'We should go and get help,' said Bridget. 'We

334

have no idea what's in there. It could be dangerous.'

'Call for help if you like, ma'am,' said Jake. 'But I'm not waiting.' He pushed his head and shoulders into the hole in the wall, shining his torch ahead.

'What can you see?' called Bridget.

Jake's voice came back muffled. 'I'm not sure.' He slid even further forwards, until his entire body was enclosed by the space behind the grating. 'I think it's a tunnel!'

Bridget exchanged glances with Ffion. It was obvious from the Welsh detective's face that she was as surprised as Bridget by the discovery. Then a flash seemed to pass over Ffion's features. 'I think I know where this tunnel goes.'

'Where?' asked Bridget.

But Ffion was already running back up the steps, taking them two at a time. 'See you on the other side!'

Feeling helpless, Bridget watched her go. When she turned back to the tunnel, she was even more alarmed to find that Jake had completely vanished. Even the light from his torch had passed beyond sight. 'Jake!' she called, but there was no reply.

'Dammit!' she said to herself. Ffion oughtn't to have run off without saying where she was going. And Jake shouldn't have gone into the tunnel alone. But Bridget knew she had no choice about what to do next. She would have to go in after him.

CHAPTER 29

With a sigh, Bridget bent her knees to the cold earth of the crypt and cautiously poked her head inside the hole in the wall. It was pitch black, and the light from her phone reached only a few feet ahead. The air inside smelled of mildew and mould, and her every instinct was to draw back. But that wasn't an option. Crawling on her hands and knees, her phone held awkwardly in one hand, she set off into the gloomy hollow.

She knew that she was probably breaking about a hundred rules relating to the regulations for handling a potential crime scene, not to mention health and safety guidelines, and she dreaded to think what Chief Superintendent Grayson would have to say if something went wrong. But she had made her decision, and to hell with matters of protocol and procedure.

The tunnel was narrow, and as she crawled along it, the walls and ceiling seemed to close in on her. Never mind being unable to fit into a dress, at this rate she was going to end up stuck fast underground. She had a vision of having to be dragged out backwards by her ankles. But there was far more at stake here than her dignity, and although she had lost her faith a long time ago, she prayed that wherever this tunnel may lead, she was not about to find Amy's body at the end of it.

As she made her way further underground, she was reminded of a visit she'd once made to the catacombs located beneath the streets of Paris, where skeletons of the city's dead had been relocated during the eighteenth century from the cemetery of *Saints-Innocents* to a tunnel network left over from ancient stone quarrying. There, she had walked through eerie subterranean passageways whose walls were made from bones and skulls. She feared reaching out and touching bones now, but instead her hands grasped only earth and stone.

She had long since lost sight of Jake, and the only light was from her own phone. She hoped the battery would hold out. The thought of being stuck here, alone and in total darkness, was terrifying. Her mind turned involuntarily to the stone coffins standing in the crypt behind her. And as she crawled, her imagination preyed on her, presenting her with images of stone lids lifting up, and skeletal creatures emerging, and following her into the tunnel.

The idea took hold, and she found herself quickening her pace, stumbling forwards into the endless dark, wishing desperately for fresh air and sunlight, and the feeling of summer breeze against her face once more.

★

On hands and knees, Jake made his way carefully along the tunnel, lighting the way with his mobile phone, feeling the rough wall with his other hand. It was cold and dark down here, the air stale, the ground uneven.

A tunnel was the last thing he'd been expecting to find when he'd pulled open the iron grate. The inscription on the bells had hinted at buried treasure, and even in his wildest dreams he'd imagined discovering nothing more than a small hollow space, perhaps with a chest of gold inside. He'd dreaded seeing Amy's body sprawled out before him. A tunnel was unexpected, but at least it offered hope that Amy was still alive. And that was worth more than any treasure hoard.

He couldn't imagine who had made this tunnel, or why, but they had clearly invested a lot of effort into it. The walls and ceiling were lined with stone, although in places this had collapsed, revealing bare earth behind. In those places, white tangles of roots thrust their way inside, seeking water, but clutching only at air.

Now and again the burrowing of moles, or perhaps even rabbits, intersected with the tunnel. There was certainly no shortage of blind worms down here, not to mention insects and spiders. Fortunately, Jake wasn't afraid of spiders, even when their webs brushed his arms or stuck to his face. What did worry him was that the tunnel was heading directly for the river. He pressed his palms to the earthen walls, afraid to feel water seeping through them and flooding the confined space. But the soil beneath his hands was parchment-dry.

One thought kept him moving forwards. Amy. It was only the hope of finding her alive that gave him the strength he needed now. He wouldn't have willingly entered a tunnel like this for anyone else.

And there it was. The truth as plain as day. He loved her, and the thought of any harm coming to her was more than he could bear.

His previous relationships, first with Brittany and then with Ffion, had been based on a strong physical attraction. Both women were the sort who made heads turn when they entered a room. Amy was different. In her cycling gear of waterproof trousers, high-vis vest and safety helmet, all traces of femininity were lost. But when she smiled, it was as if the sun shone out of her eyes. She radiated warmth and humour and an inner beauty that he had never known before in a woman. In her, he had finally found his soulmate, and he would do anything to keep her safe.

He pressed on through the darkness, with no idea where he was going. He was surprised at how long the tunnel was, although it was hard to gauge distances underground with no points of reference. With every step he dreaded stumbling across Amy's body, but the path remained clear, the tunnel following a line as straight as a dart.

Eventually the ground beneath him started to rise upwards. He must be nearing the end of his journey, though what he might find there he couldn't begin to imagine. Suddenly he found himself in front of a wooden door. Panting from his exertion, he paused and listened.

The heavy door muffled sounds from beyond, but even over his own heavy breathing, he could hear something. A voice. And another. He tensed, then reached out to grasp an iron ring set into the door. Turning it slowly, he pushed open the door, blinking in astonishment as light spilled into his eyes and he took in the scene before him.

★

Ffion ran back up the stone steps of the crypt and left the church by the north door. She made her way around the other side of the building to the tall arched window of the south transept, where she judged the entrance to the tunnel to be. Then, facing directly south, she began to cross the churchyard.

She picked a path between the graves, doing her best to keep in a straight line. The headstones were leaning over in places, and as she proceeded further into the graveyard, the ground grew rougher, the grass less closely cropped. In places, trees and shrubs appeared before her, and graves clustered together around plantings of flowers. She dodged around the various obstacles in her path, glancing back occasionally at the church to check her bearings. But there was no doubt where the tunnel was heading. Towards the manor house.

She reached the edge of the churchyard and eyed the wall that bounded it. It was about six feet tall and built from crumbling dry stones. Carefully, her hands reaching up to the top, and her feet seeking out hollows where she could find support, she clambered up and over, dropping down silently on the other side.

Now she was in the grounds of the manor. There were no headstones here; only trees and shrubs. She could no longer see the church behind her, but she had a good grasp of her direction now, fixing her attention on a willow rising up at the distant riverside. The tunnel surely couldn't pass beneath the river, so it must emerge before that. But the manor house stood some way off to her left, and there was no building in her line of sight.

She began to move forwards, pushing through the long grass and nettles next to the wall. Before long, these gave way to a wildflower meadow, and then to more closely-tended grass, with roses and topiary to either side.

All the while she kept her gaze fixed to the distant willow, retaining a picture of the map in her mind's eye. She felt sure that if a sixteenth-century villager had been transported into the twenty-first century, they would find the layout of the manor house and the adjacent churchyard virtually unchanged.

She thought of Jake, making his way through the tunnel beneath her. She had no way of knowing how far he might have progressed by now, or whether the tunnel was blocked, preventing him from going any further. She didn't envy him going into that confined place.

Ffion had always suffered from a mild claustrophobia, and much preferred the freedom of open spaces to being indoors. Out running across the wide grassy expanse of Port Meadow, or eating up the miles on her motorbike was how she liked to be, not stuck in a narrow tunnel underground. It was perhaps because of her upbringing in the Welsh valleys, where pitheads were still to be found marking the entrances to deep coalmines. Her own grandfather had been working in the Cambrian Colliery near Clydach Vale when an underground explosion claimed the lives of sixty-four men. He had been lucky to escape with his life, and his descriptions of mineshafts and pits had left her with a fear of enclosed spaces, especially underground. Better by far to be up in the open air with the sky above, instead of a stone vault.

The fact that Jake had so willingly entered that dark, cramped space before anyone could stop him told Ffion all she needed to know about his feelings for Amy. But right now, there wasn't time to analyse how that made her feel. She carried on, following the route she believed the tunnel took.

Up ahead, a low rise in the land came into view. It was clearly an artificial mound, and as she approached it, she recognised it as the ice house where she and Bridget had encountered Shaun Daniels, emerging with his gardening tools. If she had judged the direction correctly, it was precisely in the tunnel's path.

Running round to the other side of the grassy mound, she saw that a short flight of steps led down to a half-opened door set into the front of the ice house.

She heard voices. First a man's, then a woman's.

She tiptoed down the steps and peered around the edge of the door.

★

Just when she thought the tunnel was never going to end, Bridget glimpsed a pale light ahead. She crept along the last few yards as the light grew steadily stronger and the sounds of voices became audible. She reached an open wooden door at the tunnel's end, and stopped to take in the scene beyond.

The tunnel opened into a circular chamber, its domed roof covered in stone, and its floor made from bare earth. The ice house. Light from the half-opened door opposite illuminated the space. The room wasn't large – perhaps about twenty feet in diameter – and apart from the tunnel entrance, the only exit was the doorway opposite.

There were no windows, and the air in the room was chill – barely any warmer than the tunnel itself. All around the walls were shelves, laden with collections of old gardening tools, sacks of feed and weedkiller, seeds, earthenware pots and assorted machinery, a lot of it rusted. To one side sat Amy, propped against the wall, her hands tied behind her back, her mouth gagged, but still mercifully alive.

The housekeeper, Josephine Daniels, was present, and towering over her was her son, Shaun. In his hand he held a knife.

In stark contrast to the rusting old tools ranged along the shelves, the knife was in pristine condition, its blade about ten inches long and wickedly sharp. It caught the light, flashing brightly in Shaun's grip. Vanessa had just such a knife in her kitchen, and Bridget was used to seeing it slicing effortlessly through parsnips, turnips and other tough-skinned vegetables. Bridget had cut herself with it once, much to Vanessa's annoyance. A knife like that could be lethal if used as a weapon.

The fourth person in the room was Jake, standing a few feet in front of where the tunnel emerged into the room, and helping to conceal Bridget's presence from Shaun and his mother. He was turned to face Shaun Daniels. 'Mate, put the knife down,' he said.

Shaun glanced down at the knife in his hand, as if puzzled how it had come to be there. But he made no move to comply with Jake's instructions. Instead, he took a step in Amy's direction.

'Don't you dare harm her,' said Jake, also taking a step forward.

Amy shook her head, her eyes fixed on the knife in Shaun's hands. She made a sound, but the gag in her mouth prevented her from forming intelligible words.

'I'm not going to,' said Shaun. He raised his arm, lifting the knife higher.

'I'm warning you,' said Jake, advancing once again. 'Keep away from her.'

Shaun backed away from him. 'Don't come any closer!' He turned the blade towards Jake.

Out of the corner of her eye, Bridget saw a hand appear around the edge of the half-opened door, and Ffion's slender frame crept inside, catching Bridget's eye. Bridget raised her palm, and saw Ffion understand her meaning immediately. She stayed where she was, taking in the scene, unobserved by mother and son whose attention was all on Jake.

Shaun moved away from Jake again, taking another step towards Amy.

'This is your final warning,' said Jake.

Shaun stopped in his tracks. 'I'm not going to hurt her. When you got here, I was just about to cut her free.'

'You expect me to believe that?' said Jake.

'Believe what you want.' Shaun shrugged, and in that instant, Jake sprang at him, making a grab at his wrist.

He nearly made it, but as he lunged, Shaun turned to face him. The distance between the men was too small and the blade too long. It sliced through Jake's shirt, drawing a line of crimson across his belly. Shaun's eyes widened in horror and he released the knife, sending it clattering to the floor.

An agonised moan came from Amy's direction as she watched what happened, and Bridget slid out of the tunnel, making herself visible to all its occupants.

Jake doubled over, clutching his side, blood flowing from the wound between his fingers.

'Shit!' said Shaun, his face pale. 'I'm sorry. I didn't mean that to happen. You shouldn't have rushed at me.'

Bridget's gaze shifted to Josephine Daniels who had remained strangely silent throughout the whole exchange. She was standing beside her son, making no attempt to go to Jake's aid.

The knife lay on the ground, its blade smeared red, equidistant between Bridget and the housekeeper.

Bridget looked again and saw a look of cold calculation on Josephine's face. And then she noticed the silk scarf knotted around her neck.

Before Bridget could stop her, Josephine rushed for the knife. She grabbed it and raised it aloft. 'Nobody move!' she cried. 'Everyone stay back!' Then, moving quickly to Amy's side, she held the blade to the girl's throat, pushing the tip against her skin.

★

When Ffion saw the blood spill out from between Jake's fingers, her instinct was to run to his defence. But with him acting like a hothead, the last thing the situation needed was another person rushing in.

Jake had been an idiot trying to disarm a man with a knife. It was obviously a sign of how much he cared for Amy, and how far he was willing to go to prevent her from coming to harm. But all it had got him was a nasty stab wound.

Ffion made a quick assessment of the situation and decided to hold back. She knew enough about knife injuries to tell that so long as Jake remained conscious and kept his hands pressed to the wound, his injury wasn't immediately life threatening. Better for her to stay cool, and keep her presence unknown for the moment.

Shaun had his back to her, and Josephine didn't seem to have seen her, distracted as she was by all the activity. The young woman – who had to be Amy – was sitting against the wall, her hands tied, her mouth gagged, with the housekeeper's knife pressed to her throat. She caught Ffion's eye, but Ffion put her finger to her lips, and the woman stayed still.

Ffion watched to see what would happen next.

CHAPTER 30

'Josephine, please put the knife down.' Bridget's voice sounded surprisingly calm, even to her own ears.

But Josephine Daniels made no move to comply. She stood next to Amy, the knife touching her throat. 'No,' she said simply.

Shaun stood transfixed as if unable to believe what he was seeing. 'Mum?' His voice sounded almost childlike. 'What are you doing?'

But Josephine's only response was to press the knife more firmly against Amy's throat.

A red pearl of blood formed at the tip of the blade and trickled down Amy's pale skin. Her eyes opened wider with terror, and a strangled whimper emerged from her gagged mouth.

'Put the knife down,' repeated Bridget. 'It's over.'

'Do what she says, Mum!' pleaded Shaun. 'Put the knife down. Let Amy go!'

'No!' Josephine's voice was high and shrill, reverberating off the hard walls of the ice house. The knife trembled in her hand. 'All of you, stay back.'

'This is madness!' said Shaun. 'What are you doing?'

'I know that you killed Harriet Stevenson,' said Bridget to the housekeeper. 'This is only making matters worse.'

Josephine shook her head. 'That horrible woman! When I found out what she'd done…'

'What did she do?' asked Bridget. Her best chance now was to get Josephine talking. If she could calm her down, there was a good chance of talking her into surrendering the knife. She glanced at Jake, who was lying on the floor, his hands to his wound. His eyes remained open, fixed on Amy's. He was in need of urgent medical attention, but until the hostage situation was resolved, he would have to look after himself.

'Mum, what are you talking about?' Shaun Daniels was staring at his mother in disbelief.

Josephine turned to her son. 'Oh, Shaun! That woman ruined our lives! Henry would have married me, if it hadn't been for that interfering busybody. He loved me. I always knew he did. And he wanted to do the right thing, I could tell. But something held him back.'

'I don't understand,' said Shaun. 'What do you mean?'

'I was only a girl when I came to work in the house. Sixteen years old. Henry was twelve years older, a grown man, and lord of the manor. I was terribly shy around him. At first, I could barely summon up the courage to look at him. But he was kind. He spoke to me, not as a master to a servant, but as one person to another. Slowly, I grew to admire him, and then' – she tailed off, before resuming, a light kindled in her eyes – 'I fell in love with him.'

She gazed at Shaun and at Bridget, as if daring them to contradict her, but neither did.

'He loved me too, or so I thought, and one thing led to another. After a while I fell pregnant. I wasn't sure if I ought to tell Henry. I didn't know if he'd be angry with me. I didn't know what he'd think about becoming a father. But eventually it was impossible to hide the truth any longer. When he found out, he wasn't angry at all, but he became very thoughtful. He wouldn't tell me what he was thinking. I asked if I should leave the village and go away, but he said that was the last thing he wanted. He told me that he had a big decision to make, and that he would seek advice from a friend.'

The light in Josephine's eyes turned dark. 'When I saw him next, a change had come over him. He called me into his study, and made me sit down in the chair while he stood behind his desk. He wasn't my Henry anymore, he was lord of the manor again, and I was a servant girl. Worse, a foolish girl, who had given away her virtue. He told me that he had taken sound advice from a trusted person, someone of the highest integrity, who knew what was for the best, and they had told him that it was impossible for a man in his position to contemplate marrying a girl with no education, no money and no prospects. He said that I could keep my job as housekeeper and continue to live in the house, and that my child could also live with me. He assured me that he would provide for both of us, but that I must never tell anyone who the child's father was.'

Josephine turned to her son, her eyes now shining with tears. 'Not even you, Shaun. I promised the old squire that I would keep his secret, and in return he promised to take care of us. I kept my word, and Henry kept his. I remained as housekeeper, and when you became a man and it was time for you to find work, he took you on as his gardener, and gave you the cottage to live in. He did the best he could for us, you mustn't hate him for what he did.'

'I don't, Mum,' said Shaun. 'I never hated the old squire. But I still don't understand. How was Harriet Stevenson involved in all of this?'

But Bridget had already guessed the truth. 'Harriet was the trusted friend that Henry spoke to. Is that right, Josephine?'

She nodded. 'Harriet was once engaged to Henry. This was just before I started work at the house. Harriet came from a wealthy family in the village. She was well-educated and respectable; a suitable match for a lord of the manor. They planned to marry, but Harriet had ambitions. She wanted to study at Oxford and become an academic. In those days, it wasn't easy for a woman to do that. Women couldn't go to the men's colleges; they were only allowed to join the women's colleges. Henry wasn't happy about her going off to study. He wanted a wife who would stay and be lady of the manor, and do what was expected. And so Harriet broke off the engagement, and went to study at Lady Margaret Hall. But she remained in touch with Henry, and he trusted her judgement. I know now that she was the one he turned to for advice.'

Josephine's hold on the knife had grown loose as she recounted the story of the past, but now she tightened her grip once more, holding the blade to Amy's neck. Out of the corner of her eye, Bridget spotted Ffion begin to move, sliding feline-like and silent around the curved wall of the ice house.

Josephine began to speak again, her gaze turned back to her son. 'For nearly half a century, I didn't know what Harriet had done. I kept Henry's secret, and he stuck to his half of the bargain. He married soon after you were born, Shaun. A proper lady, who was more than happy to do what was expected of her. Not like me. Not like Harriet. Even after his wife died, I didn't tell anyone what had happened. Not even when Henry himself died – I had kept the secret too long, and it seemed impossible to ever reveal it. But then' – her knuckles turned white and the blade slid against Amy's neck, drawing fresh blood – 'at Henry's funeral, when I was making the last arrangements for the flowers, Harriet came up to me, and she whispered in my ear,

"He's gone now, and you can't hurt him." I turned to her in astonishment. "Whatever can you mean?" I asked, and she said, "I know all about you and your bastard son. Henry came to me when he found out how you tricked him. He was thinking of marrying you! I told him in no uncertain terms that he must put such foolish thoughts aside. He could never marry a servant girl. The shame it would bring on him!" I told her that I never tried to trick Henry, but she wouldn't have it. She called me all kinds of names. I can't even repeat them now. And that was when I decided.'

Shaun was standing transfixed by his mother's story. 'Decided?'

'To kill her. I went into the vestry and took the key to the crypt. You see, Henry had shown me the tunnel when he and I were first together. He brought me to the ice house one day, and lit a candle. I had no idea what he was going to show me. Then he led me through the tunnel, all the way to the crypt, and showed me how to open and close the iron grate so that no one would know. "It's a secret," he told me. "A Burton family secret."'

'But I knew about the tunnel,' said Shaun. 'You told me it was built by Edmund Burton as an escape route during the times when Protestants were being persecuted for their beliefs.'

'I told you because you were a Burton,' said Josephine. 'Even though you didn't know it.'

'And so,' said Bridget, 'after the funeral, you returned to the manor house, but instead of going inside, you came here, to the ice house.'

Ffion was now crouching beside Jake, checking his pulse. Josephine seemed not to see her, or not to care. She was too lost in her own memories.

'Yes,' she said. 'I crawled through the tunnel, came up through the crypt, and there was Harriet, fussing about like she always did after church. I grabbed the candlestick and crept up behind her. She was standing by the tomb of Sir Edmund and Lady Ellen with her back to me, but I didn't want to do it like that. I wanted her to know. So I waited until she turned around, and then I hit her. I struck her as hard as I could. I wanted to be certain she would die. She'd destroyed my entire life, it was only right to destroy what was left of hers.'

She fell silent.

'All right, Mum,' said Shaun. 'I understand why you did what you did. But Amy has nothing to do with this. You've got to let her go.' He turned to Bridget. 'When I found Amy here, I thought this was Tobias's work. I thought he had done it to discredit me. A policeman came to the door this morning and told us that Amy had gone missing, so I decided to search the grounds and the outbuildings. I found her here, all tied up and gagged. I thought it was Tobias's way of getting back at me for throwing him out of the house. I told Mum to fetch a sharp knife so I could cut her free.'

Josephine nodded, but she didn't move the knife from Amy's throat. 'This girl is the reason I got caught,' she said. 'First, she came poking around the house, asking me all kinds of nosey questions when she was supposed to be in the library. She ought to have known better, but she was just like Harriet, sticking her nose into other people's business. And then she found the tunnel. I caught her, coming out of the ice house. She ought to have known better!'

A mad gleam entered Josephine's eye and she tugged hard at Amy's hair, jerking her head back to reveal the white flesh of her throat. Amy screamed, the sound emerging as a muted wail.

Then everything seemed to happen at once.

Shaun rushed towards his mother, making a grab for the knife, but she twisted it towards him. The blade bit deep into his arm, drawing a fountain of blood, and he sprang away with a howl.

Then Ffion came at her, sprinting from her crouched position at Jake's side. She grabbed Josephine's knife arm, twisting it behind her back. The housekeeper cried out and dropped the knife to the ground. Ffion pushed her down, pinning her arms behind her back, before snapping on a pair of handcuffs.

When it was safe, Bridget went to Amy and pulled the gag from her mouth.

'Jake!' cried Amy. 'Quickly! Someone call for help!'

'Help's already on its way,' said Ffion. 'I

messaged Ryan while Josephine was talking. An ambulance will be here any minute.'

Josephine Daniels lay on the floor, her eyes filled with tears, her anger leaking steadily away. She turned her face in her son's direction. 'I'm sorry, Shaun. I've let you down so badly. I've been a terrible mother.'

Bridget waited to see if he had anything to say, but he turned away from her, holding his arm, which was running with blood from his wound.

'Josephine Daniels,' said Bridget, 'I am arresting you for the murder of Harriet Stevenson and the false imprisonment of Amy Bagot. You do not have to say anything. But, it may harm your defence if you do not mention when questioned something which you later rely on in court. Anything you do say may be given in evidence.'

As she finished, she could hear the distant wail of an ambulance approaching.

CHAPTER 31

'DI Hart,' said Grayson from behind his desk, 'it seems that on this occasion you managed to break just about every rule in the book.'

It was the day after the arrest, and Bridget had spent the night torn between a sense of relief that the investigation was over and the perpetrator behind bars, and fear of what the Chief Super might have to say about the way she had handled the case.

'Sir, I –'

Grayson tapped his pen on the desk. 'First, you entered a crime scene without any attempt to preserve evidence.'

'Sir, if I could just –'

A second, more forceful tap followed. 'Second, you allowed a junior officer to go into a confined and potentially dangerous space without undertaking any kind of risk assessment.'

'Sir, with all due respect –'

Tap. 'And then, instead of calling in and awaiting backup, you actually followed him in!'

Bridget remained silent, awaiting any further additions to her list of misdemeanours.

'Your actions resulted in the officer in question sustaining a knife injury and being taken to hospital.'

Jake had been rushed to the John Radcliffe, along with Shaun and Amy. Ffion had gone with them, following the ambulance on her bike, and had reported that all three had been treated for their wounds, and that none of them had sustained a serious injury. Shaun and Amy had been discharged quickly, while Jake, after being stitched and bandaged, had been kept in overnight for observation. The knife had missed all vital organs, and although he had lost blood, he was expected to make a full and rapid recovery.

Grayson seemed to have finished listing his complaints, and Bridget was about to begin fighting her corner, but he waved her into silence. 'Well, good job,' he said. 'I understand that DS Derwent's injuries are not serious. Both he and DC Hughes acted bravely and showed good initiative, enabling you to apprehend the murderer and free a young woman who had been detained against her will. A good outcome, in my opinion.'

Bridget peered at him suspiciously. 'So there won't be an enquiry into my conduct?'

'Well now,' said Grayson, 'I didn't say that. You know how it is. Procedures have to be followed. But I wouldn't worry about it. Instead, take some time off. You deserve it.'

'Time off? Are you suspending me from duty,

sir?'

Grayson seemed irritated by the question. 'Of course not. How long have you been a detective inspector, now?'

Bridget thought back to the first murder investigation she had led after her promotion to DI. It had been the murder of a student at Christ Church, and Grayson had – reluctantly – appointed her as Senior Investigating Officer on the day of Chloe's fifteenth birthday. Her daughter would turn sixteen this Sunday.

'It's been just over a year, sir.'

'Exactly,' said Grayson. 'And how many days off have you taken during that time?'

'A few.' It hadn't been easy for Bridget to take much of her annual leave during that year. There had always been another case, and she had felt under constant pressure to prove herself. Grayson's continuous demands hadn't helped.

'It's about time you took it easy,' he said. 'Book yourself a holiday. It's well deserved.'

'And this enquiry, sir?'

'Just routine. Nothing to worry about. It'll all be gone by the time you get back.'

'All right, sir. Thank you, sir.'

'Good. Now clear off and have some fun,' he said, a tiny grin spreading briefly over his stern features. 'I don't want to see you for another two weeks at least.'

★

Shaun Daniels put the phone down. That call hadn't been too difficult to make after all.

Rosemary Carver had been surprised to hear from him and had been deeply shocked to learn that her friend had been charged with the murder of Harriet Stevenson. But she'd been extremely grateful when he offered to pay for her husband to receive treatment at a private clinic that was known to work wonders with spinal injuries.

'I don't know what to say,' said a tearful Rosemary, who was normally never lost for words. Shaun had always avoided going into the manor house kitchen when she was there with his mother because the pair of them could talk for Britain and the constant prattle did his head in.

The thought of his mother caused his heart to contract painfully. 'You don't have to say anything,' he said to Rosemary. 'It's my pleasure.'

It felt strange giving away money. All his life he'd had to scrimp and save – and yes, sometimes steal – to make ends meet. But those days were over. He'd already called around at the Eight Bells to make his sheepish apologies to Robert and pay for the damage he'd caused. And on the way back from the pub he'd popped in at the vicarage to speak to the vicar about paying for the church roof to be repaired. After all, he had been the one who had stripped it of lead, so it was only right he should pay for it to be replaced. Handing out money was easy when you had plenty to spare.

He had spoken to the man at the Bodleian Library too, Professor Danvers, and told him that he could keep his father's collection of books, including the one about bellringing that had got him into so much trouble. What did he need with a pile of dusty books?

Now he had a much more difficult call to make. First, he took a walk around the garden, inspecting the roses, noting that the grass needed cutting, pulling up a couple of weeds from the gravel drive. It was astonishing how quickly a garden reverted to a wild state if left unattended. He would have to get someone in to look at it. The thought made him chuckle. Why pay someone to do the work when he could do it himself? Perhaps he would go back to being a gardener, but with some help this time. A youngster from the village, looking to learn a trade. He could help them get started in life, just like the old squire – it was still hard to think of Henry Burton as his father – had helped him.

Taking one last look, he went inside and made himself a cup of coffee. He knew that he was just playing for time. *Enough,* he told himself. *Just get on with it. What's the worst that can happen?*

He took the coffee through to the office, picked up the phone and dialled Tobias's number.

His brother's haughty voice – Shaun supposed he'd picked that up at his posh boarding school, so it wasn't entirely his fault – came down the line loud and clear. 'Hello? Tobias Burton speaking. Who is this?'

'Tobias, it's me, Shaun.'

There was silence at the other end of the line, then: 'What do you want?'

Shaun pressed on before he lost his nerve. 'Listen, I know we've had our differences, and that I kicked you out when I found out about the will, but... after all that's happened, we are brothers and I thought... well, maybe your idea about doing something with the house wasn't so bad after all. I mean, what am I going to do rattling around this old place? It's far too big. And there are too many memories. Too many ghosts. Maybe we could chat about it... come to some sort of arrangement. I don't know... a business partnership or something. Between us I reckon we've got the skills to make a go of it. What do you say?'

He held his breath, the thumb and forefinger of his left hand pressed into his closed eyelids.

When Tobias finally spoke the haughtiness had gone from his voice to be replaced with a guarded warmth. 'Yeah, let's talk about it. I'm not doing anything this weekend. I could drop by. How does that sound?'

'That'd be great,' said Shaun. 'I'll see you Saturday.' He put down the phone and let out his breath with a great sigh.

For the first time since the old squire had died, he felt at peace. The old man's death had filled him with dread at the prospect of change, and he hadn't been wrong about that. Change had come faster and harder than he'd imagined, and much of it had been even worse than he'd feared. But now things were moving in the right direction. It felt like a miracle, that he'd been given this chance to start his life all over again, avoiding the mistakes he had made before. His father had taken a long time acknowledging him, but once he'd made up his mind, he had done it in spectacular style, and Shaun owed it to him to make the most of the opportunity he'd been given.

Yes, things were going to change for the better around here, and it would start with mending bridges that should never have been destroyed in the first place.

★

Ffion arrived at the Eight Bells bearing a bunch of yellow and white flowers and a box of chocolates.

It was the evening after the day of the arrest and Jake was now on sick leave recuperating from his injuries. After being discharged from hospital that morning, Amy and her parents had arrived to pick him up and take him back to the pub for some serious convalescing. Ffion imagined that Sue Bagot would likely be feeding him up and attending to his every desire. She hoped that Amy might treat him a little less indulgently. The last thing Jake needed was to lie around all day stuffing his face with comfort food. He'd already put on a few pounds in the year she'd known him.

When Ryan had found out that she planned to visit Jake, he'd been all in favour of bringing Andy and Harry along and making a night of it, but Ffion had persuaded him that Jake probably wasn't ready for a big drinking session just yet. So she had come on her own, feeling unaccountably nervous, but knowing that this was something she had to do.

At the hospital the previous evening, she had witnessed at first hand Amy's devotion to Jake. Despite Amy's own knife wound, she had stayed at Jake's side throughout, refusing to leave until the hospital staff had finally insisted that she go home to rest. And she had been so full of praise and gratitude for Ffion's rescue efforts, it had been almost embarrassing.

Ffion had returned to the house she shared in Jericho with a couple of graduate students, feeling strangely deflated despite her heroics in the ice house. For the first time in months, she hadn't felt like studying for her sergeant's exams. Instead she'd gone for a long run and tried to drown her feelings listening to one of her classic trance mixes on her headphones.

Today she'd been busy preparing a statement that would help build the case against Josephine Daniels for the Crown Prosecution Service and there had been no time to dwell on Jake and Amy and what their relationship meant for her.

Taking a deep breath, she pushed open the door of the pub and went inside.

Robert was behind the bar, pulling a pint and chatting to Maurice Fairweather. He acknowledged her with a big smile and a nod. 'This is the young woman who rescued Amy,' he said to Maurice.

Maurice Fairweather gave Ffion an appraising look. 'I can quite believe it. She has the look of a modern-day Hippolyta about her.'

Robert laughed. 'Who on earth would that be, Maurice?'

Ffion answered him. 'Queen of the Amazons. Daughter of Ares, the Greek god of courage. I'll take that as a compliment.'

Maurice raised his glass to her appreciatively. 'That's how it was intended. Robert, we could use this woman in the next pub quiz.'

'I'll think about it,' said Ffion.

Sue appeared then from the kitchen carrying two plates of pie and chips. She greeted Ffion like a dear friend. 'I expect you're here to see Jake and Amy,' she said. 'You'll find them in the garden. What can I bring you? On the house, of course.'

Ffion scanned the pub's range of teas and coffees and asked for a peppermint tea.

'Coming right up.'

Outside, she spotted Jake and Amy sitting at a table in the shade of an oak tree. They were deep in conversation and Jake was laughing at something that Amy had said. Ffion stopped in her tracks. The two lovers were so engrossed in each other that she almost turned around and left, but Jake spotted her and waved her over.

As she neared the table, Amy jumped to her feet, embracing her in a hug that took her by surprise. 'I'll never be able to thank you enough for what you did yesterday,' she said. 'Oh, what pretty flowers, you shouldn't have! And chocolates too! Thank you. But it should be me buying you chocolates after what you did.'

'I was just doing my job,' said Ffion, sitting down at the table.

'And in the future, I'll stick to doing mine,' said Amy. 'No more playing Miss Marple for me. I think I've learned my lesson.'

'But don't forget it was the map you found at the Bodleian that helped to solve the case,' said Ffion. 'If it hadn't been for you, we might never have found out about the tunnel.'

'I suppose so,' said Amy with a grin. 'I don't think Maurice is ever going to forgive me for that. He was convinced about his theory of treasure in the tomb.'

Sue came across the grass, bringing a pot of peppermint tea to the table. 'What lovely flowers,' she said. 'Shall I put them in water?'

'Thanks, Mum' said Amy, handing them over. When Sue had disappeared again with the flowers, she said, 'Mum's decided to stand for the parish council. They've got a casual vacancy now that Harriet's gone.'

'They'll be lucky to have her,' said Jake. 'She's just what the village needs. Lots of positive energy.'

'She certainly is that,' said Amy.

As Jake and Amy chatted about how the village was healing itself after the death of Harriet Stevenson, Ffion reflected how Jake had found contentment, not just with Amy, but by being accepted into the bosom of her family, and into the wider village. She could easily picture him leaving his tiny flat on the Cowley Road and moving into a rose-covered cottage in the heart of Hambledon, perhaps even raising a family of ginger-haired, freckled children. In Amy, he had found his perfect match. But where did that leave Ffion?

'Anyway, enough of the parish council,' said Amy, tearing the wrapping from the chocolates. 'Who wants one of these?' She offered the box to Ffion.

'Actually,' said Ffion, rising to her feet, 'I need to get going. I've got my sergeant's exam tomorrow, and there's just time to do some last-minute revision. The chocolates are for you two to share. Enjoy them.'

She left quickly, before Amy had a chance to embrace her again.

'Good luck with the exam,' called Jake. 'Not that you'll need it.'

Ffion waved a hand, but didn't look back.

CHAPTER 32

'Try this one, Mum.'

'I couldn't possibly wear that! Look at the neckline.'

'Just try it, Mum.'

Reluctantly Bridget took the dress from Chloe and disappeared into the changing room, the sales assistant giving her an encouraging smile. The sooner she got this over with, the better. And Chloe might be right – maybe this dress would miraculously fit, despite every other dress in Oxford being the wrong size or shape.

She didn't really have much choice. She'd left it until the day before the wedding, and if she didn't find an outfit today, then she didn't know what she would wear. Perhaps her subconscious was secretly trying to sabotage the whole affair. But she knew that Chloe and Jonathan wouldn't permit her to avoid going to the wedding just because she hadn't bought a new dress. She would have to go, one way or another. Better to keep trying on clothes. After all, Grayson had sent her home and it wasn't like she had anything better to do.

Chloe had brought her to a place she'd never been to before, a designer boutique in the Westgate shopping centre, and Bridget was doing her best not to look at the price tags.

She shrugged off her clothes – black trousers, white shirt, sensible shoes – and stepped into the dress, zipping it up at the side. Well, the zip went all the way up and she could still breathe, so that was a promising start. She straightened up and looked at herself in the full-length mirror.

She almost didn't recognise herself.

The midnight blue silk dress, although figure hugging, was ruched in all the right places, masking a multitude of sins and making her look pounds lighter. The neckline showed off her collar bone and seemed to have the effect of miraculously elongating her neck and making her appear taller. The length was neither too short – which would have revealed her stubby knees – nor too long – which would have shortened her legs still further. It was perfect.

'Let's have a look, Mum,' called Chloe from outside the changing room.

Bridget opened the door and stepped out.

'Wow,' said Chloe.

'It looks amazing on you,' said the shop assistant.

'I'll take it,' said Bridget.

★

Ffion had woken early and started the day with a

quick run across Port Meadow, filling her lungs with the fresh morning air. She had followed this with an invigorating cold shower and a breakfast consisting of homemade muesli and a mug of ginseng tea to boost her concentration.

Now, as she entered the examination hall, she felt rested, energised and focused. She had put in the long hours of preparation necessary to succeed, and her mind was calm and collected.

Jake had found happiness with Amy, and Ffion was glad for them both. As far as her own life was concerned, the only thing that mattered now was passing this exam and moving up the career ladder. There were no limits to her ambition. She would take her career as far as she could and she would have no regrets. No looking back. Only forwards.

She found her allocated seat, took everything out of her pencil case, and readied herself for battle.

A woman of about her own age entered the room and took a seat just across the aisle from her. She was slim, with long auburn hair tied back in a neat ponytail, and was dressed casually in a crop top and faded jeans that showed off her long, tanned limbs. Her face was familiar, and Ffion recognised her as a new DC who had recently transferred from Bracknell. The newcomer opened up her pencil case, sending pens and pencils rolling out. They spilled onto the floor with a clatter.

A pencil rolled over to Ffion's desk, and she

reached down to pick it up. As she handed it back to its owner, their fingers touched, their eyes met, and for a second their gazes locked. Time seemed to stop, the moment stretching out forever. A warm smile broke out on the other woman's face, lighting up the whole room like the sun. She accepted the pencil gratefully.

Ffion smiled to herself. Who knew? Perhaps there would be more than just work for her to look forward to. Whatever came her way, she was more than ready to embrace it. Move forwards, never back. That was Ffion's motto.

'Please turn over your papers,' said the invigilator from the front of the examination hall.

Tucking the thought away for later, Ffion turned over her exam paper, unscrewed the lid of her fountain pen, and prepared to knock the spots off the other candidates.

★

'Time off?' said Vanessa scornfully. 'You don't know what time off means.'

'Well, I have two whole weeks of it,' said Bridget, 'so I'm about to find out.'

She had already made tentative plans for her holiday. The day after the wedding, she was going to throw a birthday party for Chloe's sixteenth, inviting all her friends around, including Olivia and Alfie. And this time, unlike Chloe's fifteenth, there would definitely be a chocolate cake. She had already bought one from the Italian patisserie in North Oxford.

'Well, anyway,' said Vanessa, 'the reason I'm calling is because I have news.'

'Good news?'

'I think so. I spoke to Mum and Dad and suggested they could move in with me and James. You know, the more I thought about it, the more I realised that it would be the perfect solution. The facilities at the retirement village would probably have been wasted on them anyway. I can't imagine them going to morning yoga classes, can you? And as for the restaurant, well you know how timid Mum is when it comes to food.'

Bridget could already tell the way this was going. Vanessa had claimed the idea as her own, and would shortly be demanding that Bridget congratulate her over her creative solution to an intractable problem.

'So what did they say?'

'Well, they wanted a few days to think it over, but I called them back this morning and they said yes.'

'That's brilliant.'

'Isn't it?' said Vanessa. 'So I'm going down next week to speak to the estate agent about selling their house, and then we'll make arrangements for them to move in here straightaway.'

'And they definitely agreed?' said Bridget. 'You didn't railroad them into it?'

'Well, of course I didn't. Honestly, Bridget,

you know that all I ever want to do is help.'

'I know, Vanessa. I know.

CHAPTER 33

Bridget sat between Jonathan and Alfie in the plush surroundings of the Savoy hotel, wishing she could be anywhere else. The dentist's waiting room perhaps. Even the dentist's chair itself would be preferable to the very comfortable seat she now found herself in.

They had driven up to London that morning and checked into the hotel – a double room for Bridget and Jonathan and two singles for Chloe and Alfie. Bridget wasn't prepared to let her daughter share a room with her boyfriend. She was still only fifteen, even though her sixteenth birthday was the following day. Bridget would cross that particular bridge when she had to, but for now she was glad of an excuse to insist on separate sleeping arrangements.

As chief bridesmaid, Chloe had gone off to help Tamsin prepare for her big occasion. Soon, when Chloe walked down the aisle in Tamsin's wake, Bridget would see her daughter for the first time wearing her much talked-about bare-backed red dress. She would also catch her first glimpse of Tamsin, another hurdle that she was dreading. In her imagination, Tamsin had acquired goddess-like attributes – youthful, beautiful, impossibly slim and glamorous. Even if she was just half as stunning as Bridget pictured, she would make Bridget feel a dreadful frump, despite her new dress, which both Chloe and Jonathan agreed was a triumph.

Jonathan squeezed her hand and gave her one of his most reassuring smiles, obviously sensing her nerves. As she had changed into her outfit in the hotel room, he had said all the right things about her appearance and that had gone a long way to calming her down. But now, as she waited for the ceremony to begin, fresh butterflies began to flutter in Bridget's stomach. And when Ben, her ex- appeared, decked out in his finery, a broad grin plastered across his face, the butterflies turned into angry bees and Bridget began to feel sick.

But Ben was at his most charming, going out of his way to compliment her. 'Bridget, you look fabulous!' He kissed her on the cheek. 'And good to see you too, Jonathan.' He shook Jonathan's hand with a bonhomie that suggested they were best of pals, never mind the fact that Ben had once arrested Jonathan on ridiculous trumped-up suspicions of drug dealing. 'And, Alfie, so glad you could come.' He slapped Chloe's boyfriend jovially on the shoulder, making the lanky young man sway briefly before recovering his natural elan.

Bridget exchanged a few polite words with

him, but her heart wasn't in it. She just wanted this to be over.

'Anyway,' concluded Ben after a few minutes, 'so glad you could all make it. It means a lot to me.'

'We're pleased to be here,' said Jonathan, and Bridget did her best to smile.

Ben's eyes were already fixed on his next guest. 'Must be getting on now. Great to see you all. Catch up later.'

Bridget gripped Jonathan's hand tightly. 'I'm going to close my eyes. Tell me when it's all over.'

'Don't be silly,' he whispered. 'Just relax and enjoy it.'

They were sitting in the flower-bedecked room used for weddings, while a pianist in white tie and tails played Chopin on a gleaming white grand piano. Ben had always been fond of grand gestures, but even he, on a DCI's salary must be finding this ruinously expensive. The thought gave Bridget a little consolation.

She wondered again what the etiquette was for attending the wedding of your ex-husband. Should she be acting like the wicked fairy, throwing curses at bride and groom, or was she expected to be gracious in defeat, giving everyone sickly smiles? She fancied that the eyes of all the other guests were fixed on her, watching her every facial movement for signs of an impending meltdown. But in fact, no one seemed to be paying her the slightest attention.

A sudden hush in the assembled throng told her that proceedings were about to start. The pianist flexed his fingers and launched into a rousing rendition of Mendelssohn's Wedding March from a *A Midsummer Night's Dream*. Bridget rose automatically to her feet, clutching the order of service in both hands.

This was the moment she had been dreading most. She hardly dared look as the bride entered and made her way towards the dais at the front of the room. Bridget had lived for so long with a mental image of Tamsin being at least six inches taller than her and two dress sizes slimmer, that at first, she wondered who this strange woman walking down the aisle might be.

Tamsin was nothing like Bridget had imagined. For one thing, she was older. Why had Bridget assumed that Ben would marry someone in her twenties? And while it would have been uncharitable to describe his bride as fat, Tamsin was at least the same dress size as Bridget, so clearly nothing to gloat about there. The difference between the two of them, Bridget had to acknowledge, was that Tamsin looked radiant in her body, while Bridget always worried that she looked a fright.

She was so focused on Tamsin that she forgot to look at Chloe until her daughter stepped forwards to take the bouquet from Tamsin's hands. The red dress wasn't half as revealing as Bridget had feared and suited Chloe's girlish figure to perfection. Bridget was suddenly overcome with emotion and reached for a tissue from the clutch bag that Chloe had chosen for her while she'd been trying on the dress.

'Are you all right?' whispered Jonathan.

'Yes,' said Bridget in a small voice.

Afterwards, when they were lining up to congratulate the bride and groom, Jonathan took her hand in his. 'That wasn't so bad, was it?'

'No,' admitted Bridget. 'In fact' – the line shuffled forwards – 'I rather enjoyed it.'

The experience had been curiously cathartic, and Bridget felt a lightness of spirit that she hadn't felt for a long time. It was as if the ghost of Ben had finally been exorcised, and she was free of him at last. There was no reason why she shouldn't remain friends with Chloe's father, like a grown-up, civilised person, instead of feeling bitter and resentful all the time. And as for Tamsin, it was clear that Chloe thought a lot of her, and it had been silly for Bridget to harbour secret feelings of jealousy towards her.

When it was their turn to greet the bride and groom, Tamsin seemed nervous in Bridget's presence. She extended a hand, which Bridget gladly accepted, and they embraced tentatively.

'Congratulations!' said Bridget.

'Thank you,' said Tamsin. 'I'm so glad you could come. It's so nice to meet you at last. Chloe has told me so much about you.'

'Has she?' asked Bridget.

'Oh yes! She thinks the world of you.' Tamsin blushed. 'You know I've been a little in awe of you all this time. You have such a high-profile career and a busy life, and I hear you've just solved another murder case.' She leaned in and said earnestly, 'The world needs more women like you, Bridget. And that daughter of yours is simply wonderful. Honestly, I don't know how you do it all.'

Bridget was momentarily lost for words. 'I have good people around me,' she said at last. 'I couldn't do it without them.' She reached out again, and this time the two women embraced each other warmly.

★

It had been a simply lovely day. The food had been delicious, the company genial, and the speeches entertaining without dragging on too long. Tamsin, as a modern woman with a voice of her own, had made a short, amusing speech in her own right. Bridget could see why Chloe liked her so much. She was an intelligent, confident and warm-hearted woman, not the bad influence that Bridget had feared for her teenage daughter. Maybe she and Bridget might even become friends.

The happy couple eventually departed for their honeymoon – a fortnight in Barbados – amid much cheering and waving, and the evening's entertainments continued with live music.

Chloe and Alfie were happy in each other's company, and were one of the first couples to take to the dance floor. Bridget would have been willing to attempt a dance too, but Jonathan had other ideas. 'Let's go for a walk,' he said, taking her hand.

The night was warm and balmy as they strolled down the Strand, past cafés, bars and restaurants full of happy, chattering people. They cut down Duncannon Street, past St Martin-in-the-Fields where the strains of a chamber music concert – Vivaldi's *Spring Concerto* – drifted on the night air.

At the top of Trafalgar Square, by the steps leading to the National Gallery, Jonathan stopped and turned to face her. The floodlit fountains sparkled and tinkled, whilst Nelson's Column stood tall and majestic against the indigo sky.

Jonathan gazed into her eyes, his own eyes twinkling like diamonds.

'What is it?' asked Bridget.

He took both her hands in his, then bent to one knee. 'Bridget Hart,' he said, as passing tourists turned to point and gawp. 'Will you marry me?'

Her breath caught in her throat. Whatever she'd thought he was about to say, she hadn't expected this.

Then suddenly she was throwing her arms around him. 'Yes,' she said. 'Yes, of course I'll marry you.'

A cheer went up from the small crowd of onlookers.

The Landscape of Death (Tom Raven #1)

A Murder. A Homecoming. A Day of Reckoning.

A man's body washes up on a beach on the North Yorkshire coast with a single gunshot wound to the chest. The only clue to the victim's identity is a ring engraved with two names.

DCI Tom Raven is back in his hometown of Scarborough for the first time in over thirty years. When offered the chance to lead the murder investigation, he takes it.

Raven quickly discovers that the prime suspect is his once teenage friend, now a wealthy but shady businessman. He finds an ally in Detective Sergeant Becca Shawcross, but not everyone in the team is on his side.

As Raven delves into the case, he is forced to confront the events that drove him away from Scarborough so many years ago. Given a chance to undo past mistakes, he must make the biggest decision of his life. But first he must learn who he can trust. Because lies can kill.

Set on the North Yorkshire coast, the Tom Raven series is perfect for fans of LJ Ross, JD Kirk, Simon McCleave, and British crime fiction.

The Bridget Hart series
Aspire to Die (Bridget Hart #1)
Killing by Numbers (Bridget Hart #2)
Do No Evil (Bridget Hart #3)
In Love and Murder (Bridget Hart #4)
A Darkly Shining Star (Bridget Hart #5)
Preface to Murder (Bridget Hart #6)
Toll for the Dead (Bridget Hart #7)

The Tom Raven series
The Landscape of Death (Tom Raven #1)

Psychological thrillers
The Red Room

About the author

M S Morris is the pseudonym for the writing partnership of Margarita and Steve Morris. Together they write the Bridget Hart series of crime novels set in Oxford. The couple are married and live in Oxfordshire. They have two sons.

Thank you for reading

We hope you enjoyed this book. If you did, then we would be very grateful if you would please take a moment to leave a review online. Thank you.

Find out more at **msmorrisbooks.com** where you can join our mailing list.

Printed in Great Britain
by Amazon

18298802R00226